THE OMEGA CORPS III

The Way of Power

I0685363

KEITH HUNTSMAN

TREATY OAK PUBLISHERS

PUBLISHER'S NOTE

**Printed and published in
the United States of America**

TREATY OAK PUBLISHERS

ISBN 978-1-943658-74-9

also by Keith Huntsman

OMEGA CORPS I: *Into the Breach*
OMEGA CORPS II: *The Giant and The Ghost*

Available in print and digital on Amazon

CAST OF CHARACTERS

SENIOR COMMAND OF THE OMEGA CORPS

- **Jackson Alexander (Jander) Steele**, Lord Orion of the Omega Corps, Captain and Commander of the *Angel*; force projection and analysis, eidetics, second-level telepathy; husband of Vickie
- **Victoria Cunningham (Vickie) Steele**, Lady Alpha of the Omega Corps, First Officer and Chief of Staff of the *Angel*; telepathy, telekinesis, telehypnosis; wife of Jander
- **Jacob (Jake) Anson**, Lord Commander Binary of the Omega Corps, Director of Gaean Operations; telepathy, radiopathy; Arden's brother
- **Arden Anson**, Senior Commander Mercury of the Omega Corps, Master Engineer; teleportation; Jake's brother
- **Denver (Denny) Connors**, Senior Commander Kodiak of the Omega Corps, Chief Engineer of the *Angel*; titanism, Chelsea's husband
- **Theresa (Terry) Kirkland**, Senior Commander Chloe of the Omega Corps, Chief Science Officer and Chief Medical Officer of the *Angel*; transmutation-microvoyance
- **Pavel Kalanev**, Senior Commander Cobra of the Omega Corps, Chief of Security, telepathy; Jander's most trusted advisor
- **Richard Ford**, Corpsman Hermes, teleportation; Jander's adjutant
- **Gabriel Vargas**, Corpsman Kinkajou, teleportation; Richard's apprentice

Bridge Crew of the *Angel*

- **Nwoye Lam**, Corpsman Scatter, Helmsman, telekinesis
- **Alexiy Pashkov**, Corpsman Seshat, Navigator, computopathy
- **Tsin Li-san**, Corpsman Jinwu, Communications Officer, telepathy
- **Kurino Yukio**, Corpsman Kitsune, Sensors Officer, spectrality
- **Geraldo (Aldo) Belocci**, Corpsman Portunes, Analytics Officer, computopathy
- **Mealla O'Hearne**, Corpsman Neamhain, Armaments Officer, clairvoyance-clairaudience, twin sister of Quinn

Crew of the *Angel*

- **Harold (Hal) Summers**, Commander Surrey of the Omega Corps, Second Engineer of the *Angel*, telekinesis
- **Chelsea Connors**, Corpsman Nebula, med tech, spectrality; Denny's wife
- **Wade Gayland**, Corpsman Mimic, special ops, multimorphism
- **Sharon Gibson**, Corpsman Harmonia, zoologist, zootelepathy
- **Mark Norwich**, Corpsman Janus, special ops, dyadics
- **Gustav Kamerun**, Corpsman Mentor, special ops/psychologist, telepathy
- **Saburo Retana**, Corpsman Toucan, psychologist, telepathy
- **Maeda Hideki**, Corpsman Ryōken, astronomer/sensors tech, telepathy

- **Hortensia (Tensia) Gutiérrez**, Corpsman Fantasma, horticulturist, spectrality
- **Janet Flowers**, Corpsman Wildflower, beam gunner, spectrality
- **Medina Hussein**, Corpsman Bella, geologist/lab tech, spectrality
- **Cielo Kiaga**, Corpsman Raankhak, special ops/pulse gunner, metamorphism
- **Ann Whitney**, Corpsman Sabrina, lab tech, transmutation/microvoyance
- **Arai Osamu**, Corpsman Tenome, teleport engineer, clairvoyance/clairaudience
- **Anton Gastogne**, Corpsman Ouvrier, teleport engineer, telekinesis
- **David Malloye**, Corpsman Clarion, special ops/beam gunner, teleportation
- **Panomar Singh**, Corpsman Panda, special ops/pulse gunner; telekinesis
- **Vanessa Lozano**, Corpsman Guardiana, special ops/ pulse gunner, telepathy
- **Quinn O'Hearne**, Corpsman Seabhac, metallurgist, clairvoyance-clairaudience; twin brother of Mealla

The Arcadian Defense Force

- **De'angela (Dani) Phillips**, Commander Dragonfly of the Omega Corps, commander of the freighter *Phasmida*; levitation
- **Yan Kun-Li**, Commander Pi-Fang of the Omega Corps, Administrator of Arcadia, telepathy
- **Feliks Radschck,** Commander Rarog of the Omega Corps, Chief Hardware Engineer, telepathy; developer of the tablicy disk
- **Maximilian (Max) Elser**, Corpsman Cadmus, computer engineer, computopathy; a developer of the

quantum plasma computer

- **Jonathan (Jonny) Cobb**, Commander Ajax of the Omega Corps, Banshee pilot/group leader, telepathy
- **Marama Tahiwi**, Corpsman Kohai, Jonny's gunner/navigator; clairvoyance-clairaudience
- **Nasim Badami**, Corpsman Garud, Banshee pilot/squadron leader, teleportation
- **Roksana Sayanova**, Corpsman Tasha, Nasim's gunner/navigator; radiopathy
- **Liam MacBrewster**, Corpsman Dáire, Banshee pilot; telekinesis
- **Domingo (Domo) Gomez**, Corpsman Asper, Liam's gunner/navigator; teleportation
- **Montrell Loiseau**, Corpsman Cheval, chief mechanic; telepathy

THE STELLAR CONFEDERATION

- **Nil Spart**, of Sabar, Admiral of the Confederation Fleet
- **Tondo Lim**, of Sabar, Director of the Confederation
- **Ghgundh**, of Hasgonde, Captain of a merchant ship
- **Kleš**, of Fthlon, Spart's chief of security
- **Arani Arac-honi-ché**, of Dwat, Spart's chief researcher
- **Me'Ephyrrzzz**, of Leosa, astronomer
- **Niskili (Niki) Galen**, of Sabar, Medical Lieutenant of the Confederation Fleet

THE TWIN PLANETS

- **The Head of Ertain**, the absolute despot of the Twin Planets
- **Rando Hamar**, of Liev, former bodyguard, now prize

fighter; name assumed from a Sabarian
- **Hanash,** of Ertain, Captain, the Head's chief aide
- **Slicken,** of Ertain, General, Commander of the Elite Guard

ÆZANT

- **En'Tal,** Captain of an Æzant exploration ship

THE OMEGA CORPS III

The Way of Power

CHAPTER 1

Even clean, as were all the streets of Dephlet, this particular lane was dreary. It was not a matter of disorder or neglect or even low rent, but an aura of long and slow activity, an average old man in a city of brilliant youth. The pervading color of the multistory structures was the gray stone of the veneers, counterbalanced by the homey possessions visible in windows above the brightly painted if time-worn doors that led to the residences within. The few people in sight, mostly the hominin Sabarians but with a mix of other species who could live in the architecture, blended with the scene as if they had been birthed from the aging walls.

The man who turned wide around the corner was an exception. He strode the duracrete sidewalk with an easy grace, seeming far less at home in this place than he would have been in an atmosphere of caution and intrigue. Even though his mind seemed fully occupied his ice-gray eyes quested everywhere, noting and dismissing the ordinary, retaining the few things that might be out of place. The long sleeves of his Sabarian tunic hid the single-jointed wrists that would attest he was not of that species. He was

Pavel Kalanev, the telepath known as Cobra, one of the deadliest men with a handgun ever born on any planet.

The man who followed him was a mild-looking gentleman, whose youthful features appeared full of quiet peace. Not even glancing at his smaller friend, he crossed the street and strolled down the other side. One had to look closely to see how carefully he walked, how he unconsciously avoided anything that might prove breakable. And well he might; he was gigantic, over seven feet tall, and his strapping proportions masked the fact that he weighed more than a third of a ton. He was Denny Connors, called Kodiak, and his strength was more than proverbial.

A solar-powered monorail bus whooshed by on the cross street behind them. The mix of passengers stared vacantly out the windows or stayed busy with something in their hands. Neither man paid them any heed. The two strode to the end of the block and turned, looking back. Kalanev, in rapport with his colleague and seeing what he saw, narrowed his eyes and sent a mental message back the way they had come. He and the titan started retracing their steps, taking in every detail of the seemingly innocent multifamily residences. No video device, no sensor instrument, no idle resident escaped their notice.

Around the far corner came another pair, and the street was instantly transformed. One was a woman of stunning beauty, whose face and form were of such perfection that no one of any species could help but know she was the acme of her kind. Then the observer would glance at the man at her side, and immediately forget any hope of forwardness. For here was a man who was clearly her match, a man of dynamic presence, one who radiated power with every confident stride. His eagle eyes missed nothing and dominated all. He was without question the leader of the group; indeed, he was the only man possible for the job. Even though the pair were dressed like their colleagues in casual clothing of Sabarian style, the man and woman together presented a picture of awesome majesty, of boundless might under perfect control. They were Jander and Vickie Steele, Lord Orion and Lady Alpha of the Omega Corps.

Pavel and Vickie shared a glance and paced toward each other, each telepathically scouting the area in a wide scan while also searching for one particular mind. Vickie and Jander stopped a third of the way down the street at a broad semicircle of steps leading up to an emerald green door. The Ukrainian moved to meet them, with Denny keeping watch from across the street.

Vickie climbed the steps and stared at the electronic keypad on the doorframe. There was a double click as her telekinesis bypassed the lock, and she pressed the door latch and pushed it open. The others followed her inside, with the titan sweeping their back trail with habitual caution as he crossed the street. The door clicked shut behind them.

A moment later a bluish-furred Dwatan slipped

out a third story window of the building opposite, prehensile tail waving from side to side in mild agitation. His hands, feet and tail allowed him to hop swiftly from ledge to pipe to rail as he made his way down to the street. No one gave the common sight more than a glance.

The wiry form glided across the street and let himself through the portico the Corpsmen had just used. He re-emerged shortly, tail high and flicking, staring perplexed in all directions. He parted the thick fur of his wrist to reveal a small communicator. He spoke rapidly in his chittering, lisping native tongue, listened, spoke again, then dashed back through the door.

His eyes were wide with alarm. The best security framework on the planet had just been breached with ridiculous ease.

"GOOD MORNING, ADMIRAL."

Nil Spart successfully controlled his physical reaction, although his brain thrilled with shock. He had been training himself for this moment for weeks; he was determined not to give Orion the satisfaction of seeing him jump. He swiveled his contoured desk chair with studied casualness, then saw Alpha and growled crossly. He could tell from the twinkle in her wide-set hazel eyes that all his preparations were wasted. He gave Steele a baleful look and said in his acquired London accent, "I'll get you yet, you despicable savage!" His scowl turned into a welcoming smile as he rose to his feet.

Steele grinned and reached over the desk as the Admiral offered his hand in the Gaean manner of greeting. "You've hidden your operation beautifully, Nil. Took us the better part of an hour to find you."

Spart snorted. "Not bad, since no more than ten people on the entire planet know our real purpose – and all but one of them are here." He took in the rest of the group, his eyes resting with frank admiration on the ash-blonde goddess at Orion's side.

"You remember Alpha, of course," Steele said, and the woman smiled meltingly and nodded.

"Of course. You're bewitching even when you're not trying to be." He stepped around the desk and bowed low over her hand.

"Your deducer is working as usual, Admiral," she chuckled, and he thrilled anew to the lilting music of her voice. So, he had been right; during their first meeting on Gaea, she had used some sort of hypnotic ability to make him trip over his feet like a teenager.

"And Chief Engineer Kodiak, whom you met over the communicator." Taking the big man's hand was like gripping a cement block. "And may I present Cobra, my Chief of Security."

Pavel's eyebrows twitched a millimeter in surprise. In the casual, informal way of the Omega Corps, he had just been promoted. In recognition of the honor, he bowed a bit lower than he ordinarily would have in greeting. He wondered fleetingly if

Steele had timed the announcement to gain just that effect.

Steele, who could read second-level minds unnoticed, caught the notion and smiled a bit wider. It was just such analytical thinking that made the Ukrainian so valuable. "Pardon us for dropping in without warning, but we thought you'd like to know how we're doing on that piracy problem."

"Very much. Find yourselves some chairs. It will take a couple of you to drag over that, what is your apt expression, white elephant." He indicated a massive, ornately carved and cushioned wooden throne in a corner with a sweeping gesture made elaborate by the double-jointed wrists of his species. "A gift from the Director, I'm afraid. It must weigh at least…" His voice trailed away as he watched Kodiak grip the back of the chair with one hand and lift it easily off the hardwood, then swing it in a gentle arc to set it light as a feather closer to the desk. "… Uh, half a ton," he finished weakly.

The titan chuckled and thumped himself down. The solid wood creaked under his weight. "Chair fit for a man," he rumbled in his deep bass.

Steele pulled a small Confederation-style data stick from his pocket and tossed it onto the desk. "That's what we've done so far. Not much progress, as you'll see." He and Vickie took two standard chairs in front of the desk. Pavel, preferring to remain mobile, leaned his shoulder against the paneled wall between the frames of two three-dimensional landscape images he guessed were of Spart's native Sabar.

"Well, let's take a look." The admiral snapped the stick into his desktop data processor, found a file named Summary and speedballed through it, muttering under his breath as he read. "Six hundred ships destroyed in two battles, thirty thousand enemy dead... ground action, eight Corpsmen defeated ten thousand... new nitrogen-oxygen-carbon planet discovered, heavy metals... complete cessation of pirate activity..." He leaned back with a wry smile. "Whatever would you do should you choose to bear down?"

Steele waved it aside. "I say 'little progress' because we have yet to discover the location of the Ertainian home system. Except for the incidental damage mentioned there, which is less than a fifth of the Ertainian space navy, we've barely started. I'd like your permission to tap the Confederation computers to see if our demographic information amounts to anything."

Spart waved his hands in mock resignation. "Of course. Whatever you need, I'm authorized to provide. What kind of data do you have?"

"Well, we have the name of the planet itself, which we suspect is either an ancient language or one from another society since it clashes with our linguistic information. And we've got medical and morphological details on the natives, scientific applications unknown to the Confederation, the existence of a subspecies, things like that. We need help because we failed to get hold of a master navigation computer – these guys are secretive to the point of paranoia. But we'll finish the job ourselves. A Confederation fleet attack would be prohibitively costly."

"I'm glad you think so. I had no idea that these pirates... Ertainians worked on such a grand scale. What sort of people are they?"

Vickie took over. "Paranoid, mean and dictatorial," the psychologist said. "Our Chief Surgeon holds the opinion that they're a rodentine species, rather than primate. Their military discipline is rigid, brutal and efficient, and probably extends to the population at large. The Lievan mercenaries are of the same stock, big, bestial dullards descended from the colonists of a very heavy planet. Chances are good that the two planets are in the same system, with Liev closer to their G2 star."

"Unusual. Larger NOC planets are normally found orbiting brighter stars." Spart was looking into his reader again. "Laser weapons, eh? Can we have a few?"

"No reason why not, considering all they've been stealing from you," Steele said. "We've already adapted their laser gunsights to our small arms – they're outstanding. Kodiak... the ships?"

The heavy throne groaned as the titan shifted. "Their fleet ships, now, are nearly identical to your Confederation cruisers, just a little smaller because they're smaller people. About five percent of the blockaders Alpha demolished were way too much like those big, slow battleships you use. Transports and cargo ships are akin to your merchant marine. It's pretty clear there's been some kind of contact in the past." He squinted impishly. "Speaking of contact, do you know your office is bugged?"

"What?" Spart snapped erect in near panic; they had been talking in English. His one great fear was that someone would discover that the Omega Corps hailed from Gaea; that knowledge would be his ruin.

Steele held up his hands. "Relax. Alpha disconnected the wired stuff, and I have a leak-proof mental screen around the whole complex." He grinned crookedly. "Sorry, didn't mean to scare you."

Connors rose from his throne and ambled to the wall to his right. A rap of his thick knuckles and the bamboo-like paneling explosively caved in. He dug into the insulation and his hand re-emerged with a tiny microphone pinched between two sausage-like fingers. "There are half a dozen of these things in here. I'd take a look at your renovation crew if I were you."

Spart stared at the tack-sized instrument and slapped his desktop in fast-mounting anger. "This is supposed to be the bloody most secret facility in the city. Someone will swing for this!"

Denny moved behind Spart's desk, shifted a framed certificate aside and made another hole in the wall. He palmed the tiny transmitter and displayed it for the Admiral. "Squn-built electronics, the best that estels can buy. Nice stuff. This little baby can be actuated either by direct current, sound or remote excitation, sensitive enough to hear a quadwing fly blinking half a klick away."

Spart growled and again slapped the edge of his palm on the desk.

Steele cleared his throat. "I can have a crew come in and clean the place up for you —"

The door burst open with a crash and a gray pelted Fthlonian dashed in. His quick eyes saw five people where one should be, holes in the wall, and a very alarmed and angry Admiral behind the desk. Crouching, he flashed his hand for the weapon on his hip.

CHAPTER 2

Kalanev had a pistol in his hand so fast it could have been teleported there. "Gently, my friend," he gritted in Sabarian.

The Fthlonian gasped, then spread his four-fingered hands, his eyes leaping from the heavy weapon to the mocking smile on the Ukrainian's face. "Nobody's that fast," he muttered.

"*Kleš!*" The Fthlonian jumped at the furious volume of Spart's voice. "What the hell are you doing in here?!"

Kleš gaped at him, then stammered, "Uh, sir, these people... I heard the noise, sir, and I-I – "

"*Silence!* Come to attention. You're in the presence of the top command of the Omega Corps!"

Kleš whined in shock and slapped against the wall as if struck. His feet almost blurred as his coarse-haired shoulders scraped upward to attention. "A-Admi– "

"*Shut up!*" Spart came around the desk, slammed the door shut and shoved his face almost into the button nose of the Fthlonian. "You call yourself a security chief, *hah!*" Orion's been in here for fifteen minutes, my office is bugged to the ceiling, you can't even get your gun out of your holster — that's security? I'd be better off having my great-aunt in here — and she's been dead for thirty years! I said *attention!* I told you never, *ever* to come into this office unannounced, even if a volcano erupted through the floor! What the bloody *hell* are you *doing* in here, Kleš?"

He spun on his heel. "Do me a favor, Orion? Strip this place. I want this snot-nosed idiot to see the kind of security he's providing!"

Steele, who like Vickie had not moved from his seat, raised an amused eyebrow, then swept a hand to Connors. The titan grinned and strode to the desk, hooked a finger under the massive structure and flipped it over on its side, spewing papers, electronics, styluses, everything everywhere.

Vickie telekinetically snared the data processor and held it aloft, out of harm's way. Kleš trembled as he gaped at the computer hovering unsupported near the ceiling.

Denny wrenched a leg off the desk with a bone-chilling crunch and shoved the hollowed upper end into the Fthlonian's face. Kleš swallowed convulsively at that feat of strength and stared at the tiny mechanism within. Denny snapped the thick hardwood leg over his knee like a dead stick, grinned again, then reached for one of the metal-framed chairs.

"That's quite enough." Spart immediately regretted his request — the giant could tear the building down around his ankles and enjoy every minute of it. He turned back to the Fthlonian. "I trust you get the point," he said with studied viciousness. "Now that you know how inept you are, do you think you can possibly find the door?" Mesmerized by shock, Kleš nodded. "How very splendid. I also trust that you'll forget where it is when it comes time for work tomorrow, *right?*" His voice rose to a snarl. "Now suppose you employ those fabulous Fthlonian reflexes? Get *out* of here, you son of a...."

He bit it off; Kleš was long gone, barely clearing the door as he wrenched it open. Spart growled under his breath and stalked after him. His staff in the outer office was remarkably busy. He growled again and slammed the door nearly off its hinges. "Security," he spat.

Vickie could stand it no longer. Her bright, melodious laughter filled the room, soon offset by the bear-like chortle of the titan as he thumped back into his sturdy seat. Spart glared at them, then slowly relaxed, finally breaking into a hoarse chuckle of his own. Sighing, he ambled to his chair and sagged into it, shaking his head.

"Look at my desk." He threw back his head and laughed aloud, then stretched and locked his hands behind his head. "I was long overdue for a blowup."

"Did you by chance begin your career as a petty officer?" Pavel grinned. The gun had vanished as magically as it appeared. Crisis over, he at last took a seat – one with its back to the wall, of course.

"Weren't you a little rough on him?" Vickie, ever compassionate, asked between chuckles. "He's scared green under that impressive pelt of his."

Spart shrugged. "If he's any kind of security specialist he knows I have a habit of exploding occasionally. He'll be here in the morning."

"I'd better suggest it to him; he's not so sure." Her disconcertingly clear eyes took on a faraway look,

"You mean, tamper with his mind?" Spart frowned.

"No, just make him inclined to review what he knows about you. He'll reach his own conclusions. If he does come back, you'll know he made the decision himself." She thought for a moment, then nodded once to indicate that the job was finished. "Besides, he's not as inept as you think. His lookout across the street saw us and reported to him. I suppressed the memory in both of them so we'd be undisturbed."

Spart sucked in his cheeks. "Hmph. Still, there was no reason for him to come barging in here like that."

"With the walls caving in? Come on."

"I suppose." He sighed and shook his head. "Would someone kindly put my desk back together?"

Denny made to rise, but the desk lifted by itself, floated back to horizontal and eased down to stand tottering on its three remaining legs. A whirl of miscellany spun from the floor and alighted with the ultimate woman's touch around the newly resettled data processor. The leg was too damaged to hold together without her help, so she left it in splinters. "Don't lean," she warned.

Steele broke into the Admiral's wide-eyed distraction. "I'll have an engineer come down tonight to repair the leg – and get rid of the rest of the bugs."

"I'd appreciate it." Spart's eyes glittered again. "When I find whoever's responsible for that...."

"Several entities, I presume," Jander told him. "There's one in the arm carving of the throne – you said the Director gave it to you?"

"Blast." There was no longer rancor in the word. "Yes, but he didn't build it personally. And it sat in his home for years."

"You might ask him if he'd like a periodic house-cleaning. I have people who can talk to those things like you talk to your staff."

"Mockery noted. Yes, I'll ask him. That reminds me. Wasn't there a theory about pi – er, Ertainian spies on Dephlet?"

"Your theory, and though we agree we haven't had the time to check it out. That's one of the things on the docket for the next week or so."

Spart leaned on his desk, then quickly lifted his elbow as it rocked under the weight. "I find it hard to believe there's a whole planetary species of these people."

"Fact; and they're so fanatic they make the Sforans look vacillating." A few months earlier, a fleet from the planet Sfor had attacked Spart's cruiser for no other reason than that he had a hairless face, chasing him for parsecs before the *Angel* had intervened. "The Ertainians of whatever rank we came into contact with didn't know the true reason for the piracy, they were just following orders – with élan."

Vickie put in, "From the psychological profile we've reconstructed from Cobra's telepathic data, it's pretty clear they're a warrior race. I'd suspect that they sought out their primitive natural enemies rather than defending against them."

"In other words, they're instinctively hostile."

"Much like the Eleakans in their psychological development," she agreed. Eleak was a major error of Sabarian interstellar expansion, and the reason for the adoption of the First Law. They were warm-blooded reptiliads similar to velociraptors and were much given to ferocity; their emotional evolution had been retarded in favor of the ruthless intelligence required to ensure their survival on their harsh home world.

The people of Sabar, Spart's species, discovered the Eleakans' home planet early in their spaceflight days and aided them in reaching the stars; the result had been a war that lasted for decades. They had matured somewhat in the following centuries, but they were still valued by the Confederation more for their military might rather than for any intellectual accomplishment.

"One of the reasons for the distinction between Ertainians and Lievans, according to our chief surgeon, could well be radiation-induced mutation," Vickie finished.

Spart raised his eyebrows, then nodded respectfully. "If he can distinguish that, he's quite a morphologist."

"She," Vickie corrected. "She's a transmutator, and microvoyant. If anyone knows about molecular structure, she does."

"Transmutator," Spart shook his head. "You people never cease to amaze me,"

"Which reminds me," Steele changed the subject. "How much publicity did that Sforan business get?"

"Too much," the Admiral said. "That's why I'm hidden away in a ghetto – and why I've had to dream up a report for the Council. Like to see it?"

He opened a drawer in his teetering desk and pulled out a data tablet. Steele took it and adjusted the Sabarian font to his liking.

Spart continued, "Exhibit A for that is the data disk you left me when you visited my old office. You gave me enough to write the report without making it look like I had inside information, for which I'm very grateful."

Jander nodded once. "There's more on the stick I just gave you than that old disk. We got that format from your *Kaltim*, and we learned later that it's an old style."

"Yes, the *Kaltim* was an old ship even before I commanded her. She's already slated for decommission, sadly. She was my second home for decades."

"I'm sorry you lost her." He quickly speedballed through the report. After a short minute he handed the tablet to Vickie and sat back to review his eidetic photocopy more thoroughly.

Vickie took her time, feeding a steady stream of thought to Pavel and Denny, and even reading parts of it aloud. "...'Origin of members is unknown. Those learned in the history of underdeveloped planets may recognize the term "Omega Corps" to be of Gaean origin; this must not be taken as a clue to the origin of the people...' Very nicely put. 'In coloration variety and some customs, the Omega Corps personnel do bear a passing resemblance to the dominant species of Gaea; this, however, can be assumed to be an example of parallel evolution, as is their distinct resemblance to Sabarians. In truth, the people of the Omega Corps have mental and scientific attributes far in advance if the Confederation, not to mention Gaea...'

"'The leader of the Corps has chosen descriptive code names for his operatives from the uniquely rich mythology of that planet, of which I am a leading authority and therefore apparently his source...'" She met Spart's eyes and nodded, "'... and he has taken the name of Orion, a mythical Gaean master of the hunt, as his own. Even the adopted name of their gigantic starship, *Angel*, is taken from Gaea; the word equates to "guardian spirit". I can personally attest that it is appropriate; in rescuing my cruiser from the misguided Sforan fleet, eighty strong, the *Angel* not only sustained no damage but was never seriously threatened...' Wait'll they hear what we've done since!"

She fell silent and skimmed through the rest. It went on a glowing terms, describing the mental and mechanical prowess of the Corps from an apparently unenlightened point of view. There were also affidavits from the crew of the *Kaltim* and some Sforan officers whose ships had survived the battle, and a report from the Hasgondi ambassador sent as the Confederation's first contact, with his interview with the Sforan Sovereign. "An excellent piece of work, Admiral. You must have stayed up all night."

"Are you joking? It took me three weeks. I had to say as little as possible that might give the veracitor the shivers and still be thorough. I expect I'll have to take a veracitor test; most of that lot is rather fantastic."

"Especially this." Denny had the tablet now. "'Orion descended to the planet Sfor alone and brought peace to that warlike race in a few hours with no additional loss of life.' Diplomacy, my size nineteen – he scared the livin' crap out of 'em."

"Why should they be different?" Spart remarked, and was surprised to see Cobra nodding vigorously. He wondered how a man who could outdraw a Fthlonian could be afraid of anything.

"Very well done, Nil." Jander broke into his thoughts. "I was worried about our being 'mistaken' for Gaeans. Now we can run around freely, including those of us of darker coloration."

"Hold on a minute, friend. I'll thank you not to turn Operation Messiah into a circus booking agency."

He bit his tongue; he had promised to change that name. But to his relief, Orion did not bat an eyelash; of course, he already knew.

"That's the last thing you have to worry about. But we would like to pick up some provisions from your markets. We have this kind of fondness for ethnic foods."

Spart chuckled. "I'm certain we can give you our share of variety."

"Dead certain. Oh, and I'd also like to give my people shore leave – you can be assured as to their conduct."

"I'm not the least bit worried about that. May I suggest, the Playground? It's a combination amusement park and exposition along the way to the spaceport. You can learn a lot about the Confederation there."

"I'm sure they'll appreciate that. Especially Kodiak; he's on his honeymoon."

The Admiral grinned in surprise and genuine pleasure. "Congratulations. Don't tell me there are women your size."

"Nope," The titan wriggled in embarrassment. "My wife's a ghost."

Spart pounced. "What was she before the wedding night?"

CHAPTER 3

Chelsea Winschell Connors was very much alive, and as she clung to her husband's cabled forearm she stared around her in amazed delight. She already had the galactic equivalent of a baby doll, a replica of a blue-furred Dwatan infant that Denny had won by almost destroying an arcade throwing game. They were now strolling around the enormous Playground, disguised as Sabarians by their clothing, taking in the sights and soaking up an atmosphere found nowhere else in all of space.

People of every species and shape jostled each other as they moved through the crowds:

Kanitaks, with multicolored faces changing hue to the force of their emotions and voluntary sex changes, rubbed shoulders with the virtually human Sabarian majority.

Porcine Leosans with their sinuous speaking noses and the thick ring of stiff pink bristles around their necks were dodged by the hirsute and agile Fthlonians that vaguely resembled flat-faced raccoons.

Glowering, stub-tailed and heavy-snouted Eleakan reptiliads glared sullenly at anyone who dared to meet their gaze, while the slender Dwatans, with prehensile tails and rich fur in shades of blue, openly sought out anything that would engage their intense curiosity.

Lumbering, bear-like Hasgondi, taller even than Denny and clad only in their thick natural coats, very carefully avoided tripping over the bonobo-sized, tall-eared and huge-eyed Karani or the even smaller, half-meter tall batlike people of Squn who, born to half of Dephlet's gravity, rode tall-wheeled solar-powered carts to give their fragile bodies some height and heft.

Coal-black Nokilonians, their pentagonal heads, long bodies and short legs swathed in heavy winter clothing, found themselves isolated from those who tried to avoid their tremendously high body heat.

There were even a few of the normally reclusive, four-legged and two-armed people of Ygun, small centaurs with foxlike bodies beneath startlingly human faces save for the two pairs of eyes. Adapted to Ygun's eccentric orbit, the upper eyes were used for infrared and bright light while the lower, larger set captured ultraviolet and darkness.

Also scattered about were several non-Confederation species, some of them wildly bizarre to human eyes or encased anonymously in elaborate environmental suits. They in turn were watched unobtrusively by security agents to ensure their curiosity was properly limited.

The midway was akin to Gaean fairs or carnivals,

but with a diversity that was well beyond compare. All around them they discovered cultural entertainment, thrill rides, games of dubious chance, exotic foods and bizarre trinkets for sale, and audience participation shows and contests, all promoted in raucous competition by proprietors of all species hoping to relieve the crowds of their treasure.

Their ears picked up the calls of the hucksters from the hubbub around her: "*... just tenth estel, five little grams of platinum, one tiny piece of silver metal...*" "*... and climb the fabulous Dwatan funhouse...*" "*... one minute in the ring and win five estels...*" "*...the strangest, most dangerous creatures in the yoo-niverse...*" "*Show your skills and win a great prize...*" "*Git yur rush fruit, fresh and hearty...*" "*... hey, big guy, show your lady you're strong enough to ring the chimes...*" The last was directed at Denny, and she grinned conspiratorially. Her man could flick his finger and ring the chimes.

Connors was astonished by the almost casual display of technology in the exhibition halls surrounding the midway, technology that the average Gaean would have to wait hundreds of years to see. He had dragged Chelsea from one exposition to another, using her clairvoyance to learn the latest in Confederation popular engineering, until the woman was ready to mutiny. She threatened to turn transparent and blow something up if he kept her from having some fun.

"*... See how fat he is! Anybody can beat him! Just*

half estel...."

Chelsea poked her man in the ribs. "There's one for you," she grinned.

"The hustler would sue me for destruction of property." He craned his neck in that direction. There was a family group of Hasgondi in front of him, the adults side by side facing opposite directions as they instinctively kept close track of their three excited cubs. "Tell me what he looks like," he said. Anything to please his bride.

Chelsea glanced around, then turned spectral to activate her clairvoyance. She extended it toward the wrestling ring, peering through the crowd to ringside. Denny saw her freeze in shock. Suddenly she solidified and clutched at him, eyes like saucers. She was so agitated she could barely squeak. "De-Denny... Denny!"

He had seen her in the most hazardous of situations with every hair in place; her attitude now frankly scared him. "What is it, honey?"

She struggled physically to find her voice. "Denny, it's a Lievan!"

He stared at her wide-eyed, then cleared a space around him with a side-stepping sweep of his arm and leaped straight up. With his head fourteen feet above the ground, he could see the ring clearly. There was no mistaking the elephantine body, five feet tall and nearly as broad, with long arms and short legs, the piggish eyes glowering at possible marks in the crowd. Denny landed flat-footed, unmindful of the stares of the people around them. "I don't believe it," he muttered through clenched teeth.

Chelsea was squirming. "What shall we do?" She had seen that look in his eyes before and had watched a Lievan die horribly. She had yearned never to see it again. "We can't cause a scene here!"

Connors glared unseeing in the direction of the ring, his facile mind working at full speed. Then he crouched, bringing himself down to Chelsea's level. "Find Orion – he's with Spart. Tell him we've found our clue to Ertain!"

"What are you going to do?" She laid her slender hands on his tremendous breadth of shoulder as if she could hold him back.

"I'm gonna see that that bastard stays here!" He rose and started moving through the crowd, leaving her to stare after him. He rushed until he was in sight of the ring, then slowed his pace to an unconcerned amble, forcing his face into its usual bland mildness.

The Sabarian huckster, always looking for good competition for his boy, saw the unusually large man passing by. "Hey, *you!* You, big guy! Bet you can't take my boy, here." He saw the giant flick his eyes in his direction and locked them in with his own practiced stare. "Yeah, *you!* I bet you ten to one you can't stay in the ring for one minute! You look tough, maybe you can get your half estel back – *ten times!* Come on, how about it?"

He could see he had the big rube's attention, so he threw the big bait. "Nobody's ever beaten him, big guy, but if you can do it, I'll *give* you one *hundred* estels!"

That caught him. The giant took a few steps forward to get a better look, hesitant but hooked. "Yes sir, one *hundred* estels! Pocket money for a month! *Two hundred times* what you stand to lose! Here he is, folks, the last hope for all you puny critters who can't fight for yourselves!" He waved his arms expansively and the crowd took him up, shouting in growing volume for the titan.

The big fellow stared around him with a silly grin, then shrugged and stepped forward. The huckster led a cheer while his boy growled and swung his arms, ready to tear this frail goliath apart. "Here you are, fella, one half estel for some exercise. What more could you want? Place your bets, folks...."

Denny, putting on his best abashed grin, matched his thumb to the lock on his belt pouch and drew out a pencil-thin rod of platinum, the equivalent of cash in the Confederation. The Corpsmen were using cash rather than the traceable electronic estel. The huckster slipped the rod into his micrometer, snipped a chunk from its end, and returned the rest – the merest trifle short of true, of course.

Warming to the crowd, Denny slipped off his loose tunic, showing his rock-hard muscles – and his single-jointed wrists – with a carefully gauged trace of self-consciousness. The huckster was momentarily paused from realizing the rube was not a Sabarian, then shrugged and beckoned him up to enter the ring.

Any stranger's money was as good as anyone else's. His pair of Fthlonian bookmakers hurriedly worked the crowd for side wagers, urging all who would listen to bet on the amateur. There lay the profit.

Chelsea did not wait to see more; she had full confidence in her man. She turned her back and hurried through the crowd, looking like a lost little girl with her Dwatan doll clutched to her breast, searching for a quiet corner from which to disappear. At last she found an empty kiosk off the beaten fairway. Inside, she took a quick look around and then triggered her spectrality.

Her slim form and its clothing became hazy and almost completely transparent, then she flipped end for end and took a shallow dive into the ground, the doll's long tail trailing behind. The Eleakan who had marked and followed her stepped into the deserted booth and glared around him in surprise; he was standing in the only exit.

The Playground was on the edge of the city, strategically set on the long route toward the spaceport many kilometers beyond. Chelsea paused ten meters underground to orient herself. She had never been to Spart's office, but all the variants on shore leave had directions on how to find it. She turned toward the center of the city and searched for a landmark with some difficulty; things looked different from underneath. Unlike a true clairvoyant who could project vision from any direction, her point of reference could not change; she always saw things as if through her organic eyes.

She decided on a soaring office building in the center of the city as her landmark and started in that direction. Since her body was now pure psychic energy, she was unbothered by such trifles as gravity or granite. She flowed through the strata at a cautious speed, flitting through rock, nanosteel, sewer pipes, even power lines with equal ease.

She reached the office building and started after a tall Leosan tower, cut a corner through a cellar full of mechanics working on a Nokilonian residential building, and altered her course lower to avoid any other sublevels. She pulled up beneath her tower and followed the broad avenue toward the older part of town.

She soon spotted the headquarters of Operation Messiah above and to the left, where the admiral was in casual conversation with her lord. She grinned at the damage to the office. Her Denny had done that, her sweet, naïve little titan. Imagine, he was so afraid of hurting her! A wonderful lad, that, did an old pub maid proud. Grinning from her secret memories, she affected a spiraling turn and pushed upward, surfacing through the center of Spart's desk.

The Admiral's reaction was normal. "*YAAAHH!!!*"

She treated him to her best ghostly cackle, then solidified in front of Steele.

He rushed to speak first. "Nebula, what is it?"

Chelsea caught her breath, thanking him for the hint with a flicker of eyelids. She had been about to call him Jandy. "Lord Orion, Kodiak and I found a Lievan!"

Steele snapped out of his chair and placed his hands on her shoulders. "I'm coming in."

She nodded and brought her recent memories to the surface. She knew that Jander could read her clear to the soul and she would never notice, but she also knew he never liked to pry. With the memories directly in front of her she sobered, her mood changing to reflect the gravity of the situation.

Steele stared into her eyes for a few seconds, then spun abruptly and started to pace. It took him all of three steps to formulate a plan, and he turned back to the waiting ghost.

"Find Cobra – he's touring the capitol building. Have him contact Alpha in the Archives, and Hermes somewhere in the Playground. Hermes will bring Alpha here to me, then he will pick up Cobra. You will return to the Playground and find them a quiet place to touch down. The three of you will stay there to support Kodiak and await further orders. Clear?" She nodded, her eyes widening in anticipation of action. "Flit!"

Chelsea did a pike gainer and dove through the floor, leaving a thoughtful Orion and a badly rattled Admiral behind. Spart kept a death grip on the arms of his chair and stared at the place she had been, wondering dazedly if he would ever see it all.

Suddenly Nebula popped back in through a wall, giving his nerves another shock. She grinned and tossed him the stuffed doll, then sank again, followed by her haunting laugh.

CHAPTER 4

With a small part of his mind Steele put a tracer on Chelsea; until he cancelled his mental programming he would always know where she was. He already had one on his wife; he had kept in constant touch as Vickie and her team searched the Confederation Archives for prior Ertainian contacts. He then bent a full third of his protean mentality to the task of finding Denny.

Were the *Angel* nearby the task would be easy; he could have had Angela, the ship's governing mechentity, locate Denny's wristpad from overhead. But Steele had been worried that Dephlet's vigilant security forces might spot the ship's enormous gravity field – or lack of it, thanks to her all-concealing baffle screen – so after a couple of quick penetrations to drop off personnel, she was parked in a position far beyond the planet and out of wristpad or teleport range. He did not expect much trouble finding the titan mentally, though, since he had a map of the Playground in his eidetic memory and plenty of reference points.

So, he started casting, and with the bulk of his mind he set about studying the implications of finding a Lievan playing strongman in a Dephlet circus.

Spart interrupted his thoughts with a quavering voice. "That, I presume, was a ghost."

Steele freed a bit of his mind and grinned. "Yes, Kodiak's bride, Nebula. We used to call her just 'the Ghost', but that was before we had dozens of them."

"Dozens of them," Spart repeated weakly.

"All of them women, and all under five feet tall – a meter and a half, maximum. All teleporters are male, by the way. Alpha tells me there are tremendous psychological implications inherent there, but I haven't had time to study it. It's immaterial, anyway."

Spart stared dazedly, then shook his head hard to clear the cobwebs. "Please, I'm not in the mood for your puns. May I ask what's going on?"

"Of course – sorry." Steele told him Nebula's news, then went on, "This may be the break we've been looking for. It's dead certain that Lievan didn't come here by himself. They're subservient, almost slaves, of the Ertainians and don't have the wits of a Fthlonian puddle moth, certainly not enough to have starships of their own. Somebody had to bring him here." He drummed his fingers on his chair. "I'd love to know how that huckster got hold of him."

"Well, well, you're not omniscient after all." Spart touched a key on his processor and rapped orders to a member of his staff, then sat back with a smile. "In a few minutes I can have all the records at my fingertips. Names, dates, transactions, housing, number of teeth, you name it. It's nice to be ahead of you for once."

Steele smiled warmly. "I'm amazed you put up with us as much as you do. Thank you." He settled back, his mind still questing outward on his search for Denny.

In the silence that followed, Spart studied the younger man with a critical eye. He remembered their first meeting in a London flat, where a much less accomplished and certainly much smugger Orion had arrogantly manipulated him into doing things so deeply against his conscience that a trace of resentment still lingered. But things had clearly changed.

"You've grown up, Orion."

Steele looked at him curiously, then smiled. "Experience does that to you. I've been trying to take myself with a bigger grain of salt. I've come to realize that even though my abilities have far surpassed my wildest dreams, I'll never be half the man I used to think I was. That goes for all of us."

"I can agree with that. Alpha, for instance, used to be something of a succubus. Now she's positively queenly."

Jander nodded. "Before our activation we were all fully integrated personalities, properly mature even though most of us were pretty young. Our biggest mistake in the beginning was thinking that didn't change, but in fact we reverted to a different form of infancy. Now we're like children with matches. We know how to use them, but we still can't see their full potential – or danger. When you add the fact that no one, absolutely no one, has any experience with what we're capable of, you can imagine the growing pains."

"If you realize that you've come a long way."

"It was forced on me. I've lost five good people because of my naiveté. To be honest, I'd give half of what I've got for a quarter of your experience. Your tolerance of us shows a foresight I can't begin to match."

"Yet," Spart added. He was tremendously flattered. He felt as both mentor and apprentice to Orion, as the accidental teacher surpassed by the precocious student. It filled him with pride to have had some small part in his development. "It will come, with time. And of course, you can always call on me for whatever you need."

"I'm honored. Thank you." The warmth in his smile conveyed much more than the simple words.

Spart returned it, then felt compelled to change the subject. "I'm not clear as to what a Lievan looks like. Could you describe one for me?"

Jander gave him an impish look. "I can do better than that. I'll build one."

"Buil —" Spart started to ask him what he meant, but hesitated at the look of concentration on Steele's face. He caught a movement from the corner of his eye, then his jaw slowly dropped.

In the center of the room a shadow flickered where no shadow had been, then there appeared a whitely transparent, three-dimensional shape of blocky proportions. The shape molded itself slowly, taking on contours, arms and legs, and finally a fully equipped, fur-topped head. Then Steele made the forcefield projection opaque in various places to various wavelengths of light and added a filthy maroon jumpsuit. There stood a Lievan.

Spart's voice was hushed. "Orion, that's... fantastic."

Steele grinned through taut lips, the glint of concentration hard in his eyes as he juggled several entirely unrelated thought processes. "This is a replica of a man Kodiak killed in hand-to-hand combat. Notice the grayish-white skin, the black fur that starts just above the deep-set eyes and covers the spine. The short legs give him a low center of gravity and the long arms compensate for his girth. The bones are very thick with little marrow, and the muscles are developed to hold the body upright under a constant three Dephlet gravities or so. The heart is about eighteen centimeters in diameter."

He narrowed his eyes, and the monstrous creature came alive. The face contorted into an evil grimace of dim-witted hatred as the form stumped over to the desk and planted his six-fingered hands on its top, rocking it dangerously. He shoved his face almost into that of Spart and bellowed, "Fight me, little man!"

Spart automatically recoiled, almost surprised that he felt no hot breath. "I'll pass, thank you." He watched in fascination as the Lievan – he no longer thought of it as a projection – snorted in supercilious disgust and waddled to the wall. A blocky fist punched in, hammering a hole as broad as a dinner plate, and emerged with an electronic bug. He returned to the desk and shoved the instrument under the Admiral's nose. Grinning wolfishly, he crushed it to a sparkling tangle between his fingers. The threat was obvious.

Abruptly he vanished, and the ruined mechanism tinkled to the desk. Steele sighed and wiped the thin sheen of sweat from his brow. "That's work," he grunted. "I've done constructs before, but never one so precise." He added a wry grin, "Anyway, you're now down to two bugs."

Spart tried to find some words and failed miserably. He could only shake his head in wonder.

Steele nodded serenely. "Silence is the highest form of applause. Thank you." He stretched with a deep sigh. "What I just showed you is typical, clear down to the attitude. They are beastly brutes, with low intelligence and tremendous strength. That fact alone shows thousands of years between the time Liev was colonized and the present. The Ertainians are generally of average first-level intelligence, and though they are the same height as the Lievans they are universally slim – at least those we've seen. Their yellow skin tone may be the original, but may also be the result of atomic... poisoning..."

He paused and cocked his head as if listening. Then he smiled and muttered, "Buddy, you're all right."

"Beg pardon?"

"I've found Kodiak. He's engaging the Lieven in

a wrestling match. He's won his five estels twenty times over, but he's still in the ring. He's working hard, doing his best to keep the fight going."

"From what you just showed me it's a wonder he's still alive."

"No, you misunderstand. It's hard because he's trying not to hurt the guy. He's wasting time by fighting to a draw." He grinned. "Kodiak is tougher than he may appear."

"That's one hell of an understatement." Again, he wondered if he would ever see the last of the Corpsmen's prowess. "That's one fight I'd like to – *Gaak!*"

Three people abruptly materialized in the center of the room, Alpha and a darker-skinned couple. The man, a well-muscled specimen he assumed was the teleporter Hermes, asked, "Mind if I leave the lady here, boss?"

The woman was tall and lithe, with a much darker skin tone and a thrillingly husky, exotically accented voice. "I'll just curl up in the corner like a good little pussycat."

Steele nodded his consent, and Richard Ford vanished to transport Pavel to the Playground.

Vickie brought herself up to date by reading the Admiral's mind. Her husband's involuntary mind shield prevented anyone, even her, from reading his. "You've been showing off again," she chided.

"Just something to pass the time." The look the two shared required no telepathy.

Jander blinked himself away from his lovely wife and waved a hand in the direction of Cielo Kiaga. "May I present Raankhak, of the Omega Corps." The woman's nostrils flared with pride at the introduction.

Spart studied her as he stood and took her hand. Even compared to Alpha, as every woman inevitably would be, she was lovely, long-limbed and consummately graceful, with short, tightly curled brown-black hair and intense amber eyes. She was dressed in what appeared to be one continuous wrap of cloth, with little or nothing underneath. "I imagine you're another telepath," he said with a trace of guilt.

"Sorry, honey. Want to see what I can do?" She started to undrape her sari.

Steele came to his rescue. "Later, kitten. I'll need him for a while." Spart breathed again as she tucked herself in.

A tone sounded from his desk, and he reached to signal his response. The door swung open and a Dwatan woman stepped in, staring curiously and more than a bit awed at the visitors. Genetics made her somewhat larger than the males of her species, but she was still petite compared to the stately Gaean women. She wore no clothing other than a pouch belt. Her velvety fur was a lovely celeste blue streaked with cyan.

Spart switched the conversation to Sabarian for the mixed company. "This is my chief researcher, Arani. With your permission I'll ask her to stay."

"Our pleasure, Nil. I'm sure she'll come in handy."

Steele stepped aside, and Spart indicated a chair to his assistant. Arani settled gracefully into it, securing her touch tablet to her slender thighs with a loop of prehensile tail as she eyed the baby doll resting in a tangle on the desk. With a flick of her tail tip she dismissed her curiosity and returned her attention to her work, poising her fingers over the tablet. She failed to notice Raankhak, who glided silently behind her and dipped for a feral sniff at the Dwatan's neck.

Spart resumed his seat and went over the data Arani sent to his monitor. "I'll have to apologize, Orion, there's very little here. The fighter is registered as Rando Hamar, a Sabarian sounding name. Coincidence?"

"Unlikely," Vickie said. "The modern-day Ertainian languages predominate in sibilants."

"Temporary dead end for him, then. The huckster is from Larkant – that makes him Sabarian colonial stock – and was in business for years with a Hasgondi fighter before he found Hamar. Anyone who can get a Hasgondi to fight has to be rather persuasive. Moderate success, I gather, but there's no indication of any windfall income. Probably just a bystander."

Vickie pursed her lips in thought. "How's this? Some Ertainian came here, likely as a spy, and decided his bodyguard was a liability. So, he cut him loose to fend for himself, with an identity change as a precaution, and the poor fool found work as a carnival freak. I can't imagine any Lievan bright enough to be a spy himself."

"May I speak, sir?" Arani asked in her chirpy native language. Her anatomy precluded her speaking Sabarian. It was a common problem in the Confederation, however, so many of its citizens – and the Corpsmen, of course – were educated to comprehend languages they were not equipped to speak.

Spart nodded his consent, and she ducked her head at the encouraging smiles. "What I found for you so quickly is from the Playground records and is only information from the management's accounts. If Rando Hamar is a real name – and it would almost have to be, they're pretty careful – we might be able to find a missing person report from some Sabarian planet." She twitched a few inches of tail to signify a shrug. "That would answer several questions, not the least of which would be what kind of organization might be behind the identity change."

"A good point," Steele said. "It would be interesting to see if we have two people with that identity – the original might not be missing."

Spart leaned on his desk, then jerked back with a grimace as it tipped toward him. "That's not supposed to be possible – tax records and such."

"I know, but we can't discount it on that basis."

He nodded. "See what you can find, Arani." The woman uncurled and slipped through the door. The excited whispers from the outer office had already started as it closed behind her.

Vickie eyed the door and mused, "She'll find something, I'm sure. That's as steel-trap a mind as I've ever seen."

"Indeed," Spart smiled. "The Dwatans have amazing attention to detail. They pretty much have to – their names are thoroughly descriptive. 'Arani', which is as close as I can pronounce it, means 'third daughter'; next for her comes 'Arac-honi-ché' which means her mother was the second daughter of her generation, and that's followed with the tree under which Arani was born in that grove at that bend of the river, et cetera, through as many matriarchal generations as were born there." Spart made swimming gestures with both arms, his double-jointed Sabarian wrists flapping his hands in unhuman directions. "Then it zigzags through geography, following the ancestry through every personal and tribal move and mating, all the way up to the continent, planet and sun, then to the ancestral planet if the home world is itself a colony...." He shook his head. "Her file is the biggest in the personnel records from her name alone."

Steele chuckled. "Ol' Rando doesn't stand a chance."

Vickie cocked her head, then straightened in her chair. "Cobra's telepathic report is coming in."

Alpha and Orion put their heads together, and Spart settled back to wait. Suddenly he frowned as a thought struck him. "Touring the capitol, my astronaut. That bloke has 'spy' written all over him."

Cielo chuckled from the curled-up position she had found on the throne. "I thought you knew by now, we're notoriously sneaky."

He shook his head – he had been doing that a lot lately, he reflected – then noticed the look of irritation on Alpha's face. "What's going on?"

Vickie made a noise of frustration deep in her throat. "This guy's so dumb he's hard to read. His semantic memory is terrible. Would you believe he actually thinks of himself as Rando Hamar?"

"Well, we don't actually know he's an impostor."

"But he does know, that's the point. He just can't remember his real name, or even his real planet. And he *is* a Lievan, I know it!"

Steele was hitchhiking in her brain. "Hypnosis?"

"Or drugs. Either way, if we can't stimulate his episodic memory, he's a lost cause."

"Maybe we can do that," Jander said. "See if you can contact Kodiak."

Vickie nodded and divided her attention. Abruptly she tossed her head in feigned indignation. "Well, I like that!"

"What did he say?" Spart was overhearing only one side of the conversation.

Vickie locked eyes with Jander, who nodded, and she turned to the Admiral. He gasped and jerked away. Strong in his brain he had heard Kodiak's deep, gruff voice. <*"Don't bother me, I'm busy!"*>

"How did you do that?"

"Used my telehypnosis on the conscious level, with no compulsion added, to stimulate the audial region of your mind. You may consider yourself a successful experiment." Her smile had a touch of sympathy for his reaction. "Want to listen in?"

"I'm not sure." The communication itself, amazing as it was, did not shock him nearly as much as what he had sensed behind it. He had seen a depth and breadth of intelligence so tremendously powerful that he felt like an idiot in comparison. Alpha's mind possessed such scope and clarity of perception that the very touch of it, the very hint of it he had received had shaken him to the core. "I'm not sure I'll even survive the day."

Cielo chuckled huskily and stretched in a way that made him stare. "You ain't seen nothin' yet, honey." She made a noise deep in her throat that sounded remarkably like a cat's purr.

The door tone sounded and Arani came in. Spart took a deep breath and nodded his permission to speak.

"There was a Rando Hamar born on Zalen thirty-four standard years ago, who emigrated to Dephlet five years ago. There are no breaks and no missing person reports, but it's definitely not the same man." Her tail tightly spiraled behind her indicated her perplexity.

"That does it," Steele grunted. "Break in on him. Alpha,"

Vickie nodded and rammed her call through.

<*"Ouch! Hey, I thought – "*>

<*"Orders,"*> Vickie sent, simply. <*"And watch yourself, the Admiral is listening in as of... now."*>

Spart felt a sidereal pressure in his mind as he become a part of the conversation, although Alpha was editing it liberally. He noted with relief that her power was toned down considerably as she mastered the new technique.

"What is your progress?" Steele asked aloud, and Vickie passed the question along. Jander could read variant minds, but he could not communicate.

<*"I'm boiling him down to a nugget, but I don't know what I'm gonna do with him."*>

"You're going to make friends with him."

<*"Like yesterday's coffee I am!"*> Spart got an impression of loathing indignation.

"Listen, he has a mental block, possibly drug or hypnotically induced, that Alpha might not be able to break down without doing damage. We have to pump him – which means you have to get on his good side."

<*"This smelly ape doesn't have a good side."*>

"Sure, he does. If you'd let us in once in a while, you'd know that already. Cobra says he's getting to respect you tremendously."

<*"He hellangone ought to. I'm doing my damnedest not to break him in half."*> Spart remembered his look at a Lievan and shivered. <*"I caught that, Admiral. This guy's been out of his element so long he's gotten soft. So, what do I do with him?"*>

Spart felt another mind enter the conversation, precise, razor-sharp thoughts which could only belong to Cobra. <*"Start verbalizing your grunts. Curse, mutter, work up to an ugly compliment or two.*

He will go along.">

"And wear him out faster – we don't have all week," Steele added. "Fight him to a draw, then buy him a beer."

<*"Are you kidding? Have you tasted that piss?">*

"You know what I mean – it's the technique that counts." Jander's eyes twinkled at the tongue-in-cheek exchange. "Try, by the time you both collapse, to have him think about having a buddy to talk to. I hate to say it, but you'll have to bring yourself down to his level."

<*"And lose my wife? No way!">*

"You couldn't lose her with a bomb – and don't change the subject. We've got to get him reminiscing, get his memories of home and hearth to the surface. Alpha thinks it's the only safe way to get anything out of him."

<*"Well, okay, I guess. Can I bust him up afterwards?">* It relieved Spart to perceive the titan's sense of humor.

CHAPTER 5

The skeletal star freighter, long since flipped end for end to reverse her momentum, dropped below light speed just outside the outermost planet of the system of a class G1 yellow star newly called Themis and continued to decelerate inward. The ungainly-looking freighter, named *Phasmida* at the suggestion of her commander, was a turtle-shaped nanosteel framework fifty meters long, forty wide and twelve deep, with drive and retro zero point gravity accelerators, tachyon sensors, defensive and baffle shields, and a latticework nest on the beams to anchor eighteen cargo containers. The freighter was lightly armed with dorsal and ventral single pulse gun turrets to discourage the avaricious.

In the bow were three airtight cargo holds. Behind them in the center of the flattened disk was a two-deck personnel suite with the bridge above and enough room below to keep passengers and crew reasonably comfortable.

De'angela Phillips, a tall, athletically slender levitator code named Dragonfly, was at the controls. She tapped a key on her console, and a pre-set compressed and coded tachyon signal flashed precisely at a receiver installed on the fourth planet, a watery and mineral-rich Gaea-like orb called Arcadia.

"Commander?" Feliks Radschck called to her from a console behind her left shoulder. The Polish telepath was acting as the freighter's engineer and sensor tech on her maiden voyage. "I'm detecting radiation that couldn't be left over from the *Angel*'s battle here. It looks like there's been some very recent action."

"Twiggy, sound amber alert." The computer broadcast a raucous three tone series of whoops.

Phillips snapped off the unanswered com signal. She widened her sensor view to give the vacuum ahead a more thorough scan as Radschck's more sensitive console populated her 3-D monitor with five amber blips.

Max Elser rushed out of the galley near the stern and threw himself into the gunnery station on the starboard bulkhead. The ship's small but powerful quantum plasma computer had already powered up the two turrets in response to the amber alert and was assigning targeting vectors. "I have five – no, six – bogeys...." Another unknown emerged from the shadow of one of Arcadia's seven misshapen moons.

"Check that," Radschck called over to him. "They're our own Banshees, three flights of two. I know the *Angel* left seven here, so there's one unaccounted for."

Phillips checked a side monitor of her console. The Banshee fighter ship she carried as cargo in the starboard hold was coming alive under the hands of its two-person crew, assisted by two other passengers pressed into service as brown shirts. She blinked at an icon in the heads-up hologram display suspended above her line of sight. "Ajax, this is Dragonfly. Download the sit and get yourself some distance as soon as you can launch. We may need your support."

"Hooking ourselves in now, Commander. Three minutes scant."

"Roger that." She raised her eyes and blinked another icon. "Mentor, Dragonfly. I need you and Janus to crew the Sprite asap." The unarmed shuttle was in the port hold.

The telepath known as Mentor responded mind to mind. <*"On our way, Commander. Sorry, but we're not warrior-quick."*> The pair were special operatives bound for the *Angel*.

<*"Understood, Mentor. I know you planned to be passengers this trip, but we may have company out there. I want y'all ready if we need a lifeboat."*>

<*"No argument. We know there's no such thing as a passenger on your ship. I'll come back on com when we're loaded up."*>

<*"Don't bother. Warm her up and we'll keep you posted."*> Mentor flashed a wordless acknowledgement and broke contact.

Phillips spared a glance behind her as the other passengers, four natural scientists headed for support roles on Arcadia, came up the ladder from the cabin deck below wearing emergency suits and carrying additional suits for herself and her crew.

Max Elser, Cadmus of the Corps and one of its first members, took the opportunity to scramble into his suit since the computer he had a large part in designing was doing the targeting scan for him, but Radschck – a.k.a. Rarog – and Dragonfly did not have the time. The passengers, Corpsmen all, left the empty suits next to their owners and strapped themselves into seats anchored in the rear of the cabin between the galley and the head.

Feliks was alternately typing and speedballing at his engineering/sensors console. "I've extracted the known wreckage of the *Angel*'s battle from the debris out there and have twelve recent hot spots left over. Five of them have Ertainian cruiser-sized remains in them. There are no active hostiles I can find."

"That's a good thing." Phillips tweaked her retros to offset the launch of the Banshee under the capable hands of Jonny Cobb. The Arizonan and his Maori gunner-navigator, Marama Tahiwi, slipped their dangerous little craft into position fifty kilometers ahead and to port of the freighter. It was enough of a comfort to have Ajax and Kohai watching over them that Phillips dropped her baffle screen and opened her relatively sizeable ship to detection by the defense force.

"Yikes, those guys are sensitive." Max was suited up and back at his gunnery station. "Two of the Banshees are already headed this way at speed. I don't think they got your IFF signal." The two pressure-suited Corpsmen who had helped Cobb and Tahiwi launch their Banshee came in through the starboard forward airlock from the cargo hold, secured the hatch behind them and rushed past the command team to strap themselves into seats.

"It was tight beamed to Kohana Base," De'angela told the German. "Nobody outside the base there would have noticed it. Rarog, let's aim a signal at those two before they decide to rat-kill us."

"Tak." Radschck determined the range and bearing and fired their identifying burst toward the far-off Banshees.

The response was fast and in real time, thanks to their shared quantum entanglement communications system that virtually teleported a string of photons from transmitter to receiver. *"Banshee 103 to approaching craft. Please confirm your ID."*

Phillips responded in her distinctive Mississippi drawl, "Omega Corps star freighter *Phasmida*, Dragonfly commanding, inbound from Gaea with supplies, technical upgrades and personnel. We also have a Banshee as cargo, now detached."

"Welcome to Arcadia, Dani!" the pilot said cheerfully. *"Corpsman Garud, at your service."*

"Well, hi, Nasim. Thought I recognized that Mysore accent. Is everything okay here?"

"We've had some excitement, but nothing we couldn't handle. We're glad you're here, though. We beat up a scouting party of two Ertainian squadrons with no losses last week, but these pests are nothing

if not persistent. I hope your upgrades will give us a better edge."

"Oh, they might. Montana's come up with a Banshee-sized baffle screen. Would being undetectable constitute an edge?"

"*Yoopah!*" The sheer joy of the high-spirited Indian's response needed no translation. "*We'll be delighted to escort you in.*" He paused. "*What are you driving? It looks a little fuzzy on my screen.*"

"It's the galactic equivalent of a flatbed truck, the first of her kind. Like I said, Montana's been busy. By the way, we never got a response from Kohana Base. Is everything okay there?"

"*We had to move out. We're now on the lovely beaches of Chelsea Pond, enjoying the cool shade and the clear blue waters. We'll fill you in when you get closer. Right now, we'd better announce you.*"

"Please do. We'll be in orbit at about..." She raised a sculpted eyebrow at Feliks and he transferred the data to her heads-up, "...fourteen twenty hours GMT."

"*Roger, Phasmida. I'll let them know you're coming. Banshee 103 out.*" The com went silent, and the two fighters started their turnback in perfect unison.

Dani canceled the amber alert and shared the recorded conversation with her Banshee. "Let's keep our eyes peeled for bogeys," she added. " The neighborhood isn't as safe as we'd want it to be."

"*Copy that,*" Cobb responded. "*We'll drop back*

and watch your six." The former F-16 pilot goosed his retros and zipped behind the freighter to take up station on her flank, settling into a spiraling barrel roll that allowed it a full view. In the gunnery seat behind him, Tahiwi thinned and broadened her sensor sweep to loosely cover a globe that included the inner planets.

Phillips could not help but feel pride at how efficiently the people in her charge were functioning. Her makeshift company, solidly drilled throughout the long trip from Gaea to handle jobs for which they were unaccustomed, had performed flawlessly. She sat back with a contented sigh, locked her hands behind her thick mocha dreadlocks and let her plucky little ship guide herself in.

CHAPTER 6

Denny belched like a volcano and stared blearily at the light from the rising sun reflected through the dingy window. He had managed to keep pace with his corpulent drinking partner, but it had been a struggle.

Without Ann Whitney's help he never would have made it. The biologist and several other Corpsmen, including Vickie, were clustered in a small flat across the grimy alley next to the two-room apartment. Ann was busy transmuting Denny's alcohol to water and gas – a lot of gas – but the drinking pace had been so rapid she had fallen well behind.

Rando Hamar sprawled his bulk across the table and answered the titan's gastronomic opinion in kind. "Aaaah, yeah, that was a fight!" he grunted, for at least the hundredth time. His Sabarian, always low-grade, was by this time almost unrecognizable. "I can't 'member better compershitshun, shunnn...."

"Comp'tishun," Denny corrected him.

"Yeah, Aheh. Good fight." Hamar rocked back and belched again. "'N' good beer you got."

"A matter o'pinion. Yotta taste the good stuff where I come from." He waved his bioplastic cannister in a wild sweep that sloshed beer on the already raunchy floor. Hamar was not the best of housekeepers.

"Wherezat?" The Lievan huffed himself into a reasonable facsimile of attention.

"Zalen. Good planet. Ever been there?" Arani's research had found that planet to be the original Hamar's birthplace.

It was lost on the Lievan. "Don' 'member. Braaauup. Don' 'member much, anyhow." Hamar stared into space as he searched his mind. "Too many fights, lotta lumps." He spilled beer, some of it into his narrow mouth.

Denny rocked on the crate he was using as a stool. "Why you do it, man?"

"Aaah, can't do nuthin' else. Been fightin' all my life, seems like."

Denny grunted in understanding. "Train fer it?"

"Kinda. Know how to shoot, too. Useta be pretty good."

"You oughta be a soldier, mebbe a bodyguard." He took a hefty chug, crumpled the empty cannister in one hand and flipped it toward the sink across the room. It bounced off the rim and clattered into the pile. "Good eshtel in it, hear, see the galaxy 'n' stuff."

"Naaah." Hamar hauled himself off the heavy banana seat stool that served as a chair for one of his elephantine race and stumped to the primitive refrigerator, came back with two more cannisters. The deep sink was overflowing with foul-smelling empties. "You one o' them?"

"Nah. Eng'neer. Scrounge around inna ship alla time, get dirty an' no money in it." Denny rapped a finger through the top of his cannister and slurped at the opening. "Get to see a lot, though. Like the stars."

Hamar's blunt finger failed to duplicate Denny's can-opening trick and he settled for tearing off the entire top. "Yeah, stars look nice." The lower half of the face under the scraggly fur on his forehead contorted into a sentimental smile.

Denny's eyes flickered, then returned to bleary indifference. "Useta sit on a hill at home, just lookin' up at the stars at night. Useta know 'em all."

"Yeah, 'member my first look at 'em. Home's got clouds alla time, had to get off to see the stars." He patted his belly reflectively. "Lousy planet."

"That why you got off?"

The Lievan wiped his mouth with the back of his hand, stared at it, then licked at the trace of blood from the teeth Denny had loosened for him. "Don't 'member. Went to 'nother planet, looked at the stars, nice, don' 'member why." He was fading fast.

"Funny how they look sometimes, like animals an' people an' stuff. Conshtellashuns, they call 'em."

"Yeah, nice. 'Member one like a big, round..." He looked blearily perplexed. "Some kinda woman. Urrrrph. Don' 'member what kind." He swayed on his seat and would have toppled but for his low center of gravity. "Don' matter much."

"How'd you pick 'er out?" Denny prodded. "There's so many stars in the sky. How'd you figger out the woman?"

"Alla good points... right there." He spread his fingers and waved them in in front of his eyes as if fondling his fantasy. "Right there, an' there. No. Yeah. Yeah."

<*"Ease off the girlfriend track, Denny. He's struggling. He'll get mean."*> Vickie was laboring to probe the dimwitted sot's mind.

" 'Kay. One thing on a ship, one big happy fambly. Captain's nice guy." He belched. "Nice guy. Don' push you around like some do."

"Yeah? 'Member not likin' my master. Guy I work for now is nice, lets me go when I wanna." He grinned, but it was no longer genial. "Good fight."

<*"Don't push it, Denny, the block's too strong. He's really getting jiggy."*>

"Yeah. Three hours, good fight. Nice guy, gave me fifty for the draw."

"Gimme the day orf. Nice guy. Nice...." He gave up on keeping his balance, pitched backward and hit the duracrete floor with a jolt, dead out cold.

Denny sighed and swayed to his feet, then very carefully poured the last of his beer over Hamar's head.

THE *ANGEL* WAS BROUGHT IN CLOSER to the planet so that the Corpsmen could come and go as they pleased. The big ship orbited at twenty thousand kilometers, hidden by her baffle screen and a camouflaging radiation field that stayed in place thanks to her gravity-producing mass. Spart contributed by surrounding her with a web of hazard satellites to warn away the countless vessels that swarmed the vicinity of Dephlet. The illusion was of a dirty wreck awaiting cleanup. Spart called in a favor to mark the "wreck" as under investigation to delay the arrival of any salvage enterprise.

The search for Ertain took place in a large conference room on the top floor of a newer building in the hub of the city. The group of specialists was small, but it represented the best astronomers and systems analysts the Confederation and the Omega Corps had to offer. All the Corpsmen were clad in silver-blue utilities, with their crest proudly on display. Most of the Confederation people were dressed as civilians – or undressed, for the furred species.

Steele, after double-checking that his command was safe, used the ship's teleporter to pop himself into the room. He paused a moment to admire the many styles of architecture outside the windows, then joined the cluster at the center table.

"Everyone's episodic memory is fairly complete," Vickie was saying. She was one of several heads bent over a rough but complex star map rendered by Angela from Hamar's memory. "Unlike semantic memory, which stores factual knowledge such as names and dates, episodic memory relates to temporal experiences.

"In Hamar's case, the semantic information such

as his real name or planet of origin were artificially blocked and could not be brought to the surface. However, by stimulating associations to notable experiences in his life, we were able to induce the recollection of events that piqued his imagination. Unfortunately, the poor guy is mentally deficient and inexperienced as an observer, so even his best memories are myopic. This two-dimensional rendition of Ertain's night sky is the best we can do."

"And you think this map is accurate?" The speaker was a Leosan named Me'Ephyrrzzz, whose corpulent body housed one of the best brains of his near-eidetic race. His language was a clarinet mixture of bleats, gronks and hoots from his flexible four-nostriled nose; the Leosan eating and breathing processes were entirely separate. "If the Lievan's mind was so thoroughly clouded I'd think it odd that the eraser would miss something as basic as constellations."

"Not really," supplied Saburo Retana, whose telepathy had done much to make the map possible. The Costa Rican was a top-drawer psychologist. "The eraser did not realize that his exposure to a starscape would be so unique to the Lievan – his home planet has ten-tenths cloud cover nearly every minute of every year. The experience triggered several pathways to recall."

"No colors," Maeda Hideki mused. "That will certainly make it difficult." He was a second cousin to Kurino Yukio and backed her up on the *Angel*'s sensors station. Both practiced the Asian custom of surname first.

"You underestimate our Nav Central computer," the Leosan told him. "The positions and relative magnitudes of the stars will be enough." He was mildly surprised that Orion's leading astronomer would have such doubts.

The telepath caught his thoughts. "I don't doubt it. But you can't ignore the fact that atmospheric diffusion can throw off the apparent magnitude of low-spectrum stars."

"Not so much that the computer can't compensate for it."

"The computer needs a reference – "

Steele broke into an argument that might have raged for hours. "There's one way to find out. Let's put it through."

The Leosan carefully picked up the map and moseyed toward the complex computer bank built into the wall. With the help of Geraldo Belocci, the *Angel*'s first-team analytics officer, Me'Ephyrrzzz fed the map into the scanner, then tapped the console keys. Under the Leosan's three-fingered touch the link was made to the Nav Central computer deep in the bowels of the planet.

Aldo's computopathic mind traced the connection, Vickie shot the trace through a team of telepaths to the *Angel*, and chief navigator Alexiy Pashkov teleported down with a quantum entanglement transceiver to read Nav Central's memory. In a few moments, and with Spart's agreement, the entire database was being copied to Angela's quantum plasma mind.

Meanwhile Aldo was "listening" intently to the impulses of the mainframe in front of him. "It appears the data is sufficient, but the search engine will require quite a while to arrive at a solution."

The Leosan started to ask him how he knew, but drooped his nostrils as he recalled Spart's admonishment. The Admiral had promised total ruin for anyone who even considered asking questions. In any case, a few seconds after the Corpsman had spoken a message flashed in confirmation. He scratched his neck-ring of pink bristles in puzzlement.

Steele strode over to Pavel, who was instructing the awed Kleš in the art of the cross draw. "Anything on our manhunt?"

"No, my lord." Kalanev slapped his pulse pistol into the holster under his left arm. "I have telepaths all over the city, but so far there has been no sign of any Ertainian thought patterns."

Kleš nervously shifted his eyes, then decided it was safe to speak. His vocal apparatus allowed him to speak Sabarian, but he stayed with his native tongue. "My sources indicate that the original Rando Hamar was a loner, very overweight, and pretty much a social failure. No one has missed him."

Steele pondered that information. "And the rest of the ship?"

"No irregularities so far, sir, although it's pretty difficult trying to track down every passenger after such a length of time. It was a mid-class commuter flight and was near capacity. But the ship line's records tell us that there were no meetings in space, no stops between Zalen and Dephlet, no passengers or crew involved in any altercations, no live cargo."

"Oh, brother." Steele's mind went into high gear. "See if there was anyone of any species who was unusually obese – try the medical records. If the original was as down with the universe as you say he was, he might have been willing to switch identities – starting fresh, as it were." He heard Spart calling him and turned away.

Kleš and Cobra exchanged glances. "That," Pavel said, "we should have seen. Let us pursue it." The two men left the room.

Spart was standing with Arani. "One thing unusual about that linguistic information we've processed: the archaic Sforan word for 'invader' is..."

He pointed to Arani, whose Dwatan vocal structure was more suited to the pronunciation, and she paused a moment before spitting out, "Khrrātānýōcpkh." Spart raised an eyebrow significantly.

Steele whistled, low and long. "Co – no, he's gone. Alpha!" She strolled over, utterly self-contained as always. "Get all the information we have on those people who nearly wiped out the Sforans thousands of years ago. They may have been Ertainians."

Her eyes darkened. "On it." She tapped her wristpad, and there was a soft scent of fresh breeze as she mechanically exchanged herself for a Vickie-sized volume of air from the *Angel*.

Steele called Retana over. "Do you recall any phobias the Lievan may have had?"

The Costa Rican frowned in thought. "Well, he can't stand Dwatans – begging the lady's pardon. They remind him of cats."

"Bravo!" He slapped the telepath on the shoulder, staggering him. "Cats and rats – Sforans and Ertainians. Natural enemies!"

Retana blinked, then read Arani's mind to catch himself up. "Oversimplified and culture-centric, but quite possible."

"But that would mean the Ertainians have had interstellar flight for thousands of years!" Spart protested.

"They may have lost it in between – there is evidence of atomic war, remember, in Ertainian physiology." He cut off as Vickie teleported back in. "What did you find?"

"The attackers were two meters tall, bare-faced with black-furred heads and white skin. The only thing that matches is the face and the hair."

Steele scratched his chin. "Thin down a Lievan, lengthen his legs to proportion, and what have you got?"

Vickie grinned and snapped her fingers. "Two meters tall, black fur and light gray skin. The natural progenitors of the Lievan colonials – pre-war Ertainians!"

"And now that I think of it, the giant cats we sent against the Ertainians on Arcadia terrified them. I thought that was perfectly normal – no one likes a ton of tiger – but it might be indicative of an instinctive fear."

Retana was still skeptical, but wavering. "There's no way of telling now. It might be worthy of experiment."

Spart felt a little left out, as usual. "Don't tell me you're going to scare Hamar with a cat."

"No, we'll wait until we find Ertain," Jander said.

Vickie nodded. "The Lievans may have lost the phobia. The Ertainians were scared to death of the cats, but the Lievans stood strong against them."

"We have one tiger on board left over from the Arcadian campaign," Jander added. "The zootelepath that controlled them during the battle nursed her back to health and they bonded."

Vickie flashed a mental video stream of the behemoth into Spart's mind. Tawny with gray stripes and a long tail, plenty of teeth including doubled eight-inch canines, a flattened brain case, and almost two meters tall at the brawny shoulder. "I see what you mean. Running into one of those things could well leave me lacking in courage." It surprised him that the mental contact left him undisturbed. Lock me away, he thought, I'm getting used to it.

Another person materialized, and work almost stopped as the Confederation specialists paused to stare. The man was nearly four meters tall and incredibly thin, with bluish skin and no hair whatsoever. He was crouched almost double to avoid the ceiling as he handed a tablet to Orion. "Here's the data you wanted, milord." His voice was high and gurgling, and he swayed as if unused to the gravity of Dephlet.

"Thank you, Reed. Go on back to the ship." The human javelin disappeared, and Steele added conversationally, "He can't stand more than half a gravity for very long."

Spart was thoroughly confused. The he felt Alpha's presence in his mind for one word, <"*Multimorph.*"> That was enough to clue him in; he well knew the strategic value of the red herring. Nobody like "Reed" inhabited the backwater planet called Gaea. "What data is that?"

Vickie answered him, "I had him run a search for more on the Sforans' ancient visitors."

"Very little here," Steele mused. "There was a dark age after the attack, naturally, so the history is scant. But indications are that the weapons used in the destruction were a combination of high-energy blasts and smaller lightning throwers – lasers, one might presume."

"Another link, then. Did you find anything on the Ertainian technology, Arani? Arani?" Spart reached out to ruffle the fur of her arm.

The woman woke up with a start; she had been mesmerized by this string of marvels. "Oh, no, sir. No known race has ever had such a highly-developed light wave science, nor has there ever been contact with any species that did." Her tail was wrapped around her waist.

"Thank you, Arani, you've been a big help," Steele smiled warmly. "If you ever need a job, let me know." The effect was instant; her tail unwound and curled into a hoop, tip touching the base. "Would you please check to see if there were any similar massacres or contacts on any other planets in that time period? Start about six thousand years ago and work forward."

"Of course, my lord," she chirped, and turned to Spart almost as an afterthought. He nodded, and she rushed out.

Spart shook his head. "First Kleš, and now Arani. If you cooperate with the Confederation much more, you'll steal my entire staff!"

SEVERAL HOURS LATER they were back where they started, grouped around the table. The major difference was that, instead of the original rough map sketch, there were now three highly detailed three-dimensional holograms hovering over the table.

"I feel compelled to admit that your astronomer was correct," the Leosan tootled. "Without spectrographic information we can't narrow the possible areas to less than three – and none of these has a calculated probability of more than sixty percent."

"All three regions are beyond the areas properly mapped," Maeda added, "so there is little information about the planets circling these suns. Our only real clue is these configurations here, here and here, resembling a very obese – Lievan – hominoid female." He pointed into each of the holograms in turn. "And those are a reach – no computer has the creative extrapolation a sentient being does."

"I see." Steele raised an eyebrow at Bellocci. The analyst nodded slightly and displayed in his mind that Angela had the same information and had yet to come to any conclusion, much less three of them.

That caught Steele by surprise. Angela was far superior to Nav Central, and in an exercise of pure logic she should have been ahead of the game. But then again, her almost-living quantum plasma matrix might be struggling with the concept of imagination.

Something Jander himself had in abundance.

"Give me space." Everyone backed away from the table. Steele scanned the holograms for long minutes, absorbing them into his eidetic memory, then wandered away, totally immersed. He had Hamar's recollections in his mind and was busy comparing.

Me'Ephyrrzzz raised his nostrils to speak, but Vickie gestured him to silence. She knew than only Jander could solve the mystery, and for that he needed total concentration. With a subtle touch of telehypnosis she led the group away from the table to give her husband plenty of room.

He paced, brow creased and hands deep in his pockets, for minute after interminable minute, his eyes clouded with the effort of using his total brain-power. He was impervious to the eyes watching him, following his every step, consciously willing his success. Five minutes, ten, twenty, he paced. Finally, his steps took him back to the table, ignorant of those who slid quietly out of his way. He stared at one hologram after the other as if to bend them to his will, as if commanding them to give up their secrets.

At last he raised his hand, and his finger reached into the lower right quarter of one hologram and settled on a small G2 star.

"This one."

THE TIME HAD COME for a council of war. With Jander and Vickie in Spart's office were Pavel and Terry Kirkland, code named Chloe, the Chief Surgeon and head of the science department of the *Angel*. Representing the Confederation along with Spart was Mati Ganazan, Admiral in command of a strong battle fleet.

Spart had secretly visited the Director of the Confederation, Tondo Lim, and had come away with much more than he expected. Not only had he been pledged the use of five task forces, over seven hundred capital ships, but he had been promoted to Fleet Admiral so he could command them. It was his second promotion in as many Dephlet months. The promotion had its negative point, however; it was a port rank, and he would not be allowed to risk his neck in outer space as he was wont to do. The highly adventurous director of Operation Messiah was still grumbling about that.

He and Ganazan were very much of a kind. They had graduated from the Kiperam Palladium on Sabar, the most prestigious academy in all of space, a year apart and with nearly the same honors. The greatest difference between them was that while Spart had been most comfortable with a single exploration cruiser, the Sabarian woman born of the independent colonial planet Pognegur had always felt destined to command a fleet. The myriad decorations on the forest green vest of her full-dress uniform attested to her success.

So confidential was this meeting that she had come without her own staff, but she carried in her eyes the authority and responsibility inherent in the powerful mobile force at her command.

Still, there was no question who was in charge of the mission. Jackson Alexander Steele, PhD, sat in front of Spart's reconstituted desk with one foot crossed over a knee, holding forth with a tumbler of Hasgondi grogar juice in one hand and a tablet in the other. His only concession to the officiality of the meeting was that he, like his colleagues, was decked out in the full-dress uniform of the Corps.

In keeping with the concept that all Corpsmen carried control authority in the universe at large, none of them wore insignia of rank or decorations of accomplishment, save for the Omega Corps crest over the left breast. The flat cap that was seldom worn under a roof was secured in a pouch on the otherwise unadorned utility belt.

"I'd advise that you not even leave this system until I give the word," Jander was saying. "Pirate activity may have ceased, but there is no guarantee that all six of the remaining Ertainian fleets are in the system. We have to get them back there before we can institute an effective blockade. We don't want them to have any clue you're waiting to move out."

"Understood," Ganazan nodded. "I can drill my fleet without leaving the system. We'll be ready. My chief worry is that my fleet may not be strong enough. Six Ertainian fleets constitute some thirteen hundred capital ships, you say, and their Home Fleet is likely quite a bit larger than any of them."

"But your tactical discipline is far superior. We've seen them in action twice – they're a mess. And don't forget the *Angel*. Under Alpha's command she wiped out four hundred of them in a few hours. Besides, I expect to have them softened up enough to surrender without a pitched battle."

"From what the Fleet Admiral has told me, I can't be *too* skeptical," the woman said guardedly. "I'll start believing it, however, only if your chosen star is the right one. There were hundreds of stars in the Lievan's memory map that don't correspond to the Nav maps. How can you be so sure? How can you just ignore so many potential errors?"

Jander chose to ignore her belligerence. "Four reasons, actually," he said. "First, Ertain has to be close enough to Sfor that they could have found it early in their exploration period, and we know where Sfor is. That pretty much eliminated one of the three maps entirely.

"Second, the Lievan couldn't tell the difference between fixed stars and moving bodies such as planets, ships and satellites. By following his memory through his hours of stargazing I was able to detect relative motion. Once I had taken those out of the picture, the task boiled down to comparisons."

He paused for a sip of the grogar juice, a smooth green berry drink from Hasgonde with an indescribably satisfying aftertaste. He rolled it over his tongue and promised himself to lay in a supply.

"Third, Hamar's concentration was primarily on a single constellation, his dream girl. I had to compensate for that psychological emphasis, one set of stars burned into his memory, to get a proper image of the remaining starscape.

"And finally, the hard part, I had to take hyperbolic geometry into account. His recollection was static to his time and place. When you focus on a cluster of stars from a fixed position, you see them as if they are on the interior of a dome. I had to consider not only the brightness and location of the stars in his immediate focus, but I also had to compress the relative location and intensity of stars in his peripheral vision to reduce the expanding arc of global perception. That lessened the distortion and allowed a better superimposition to the Nav maps. From there, it just took a little concentration."

Ganazan glared at him in hard-eyed skepticism. "Are you expecting me to believe that you can out-smart a quantum computer? That's absurd. I don't care how good you think you are, young man, but I see no reason to waste the time and expense of committing my fleet on the impossible chance that you might be right."

Spart blanched. Terry Kirkland's jaw sagged open. Both knew what was coming.

Steele returned the Admiral's stare with a neutral expression, then turned to Vickie. He took a deep breath, then uttered, "...*vItuHmoH!*"

Vickie nodded shortly, then froze Ganazan with The Look she knew so well how to use.

The mental probe that followed it was far, far worse.

The Admiral gasped and jerked backward, almost toppling from her chair. Alpha's telehypnotic thrust had been wordless, imageless, formless. It was simply a lesson in sheer, undiluted *power*, intelligence supreme and pure, with the overwhelming clarity and bite of two hundred proof alcohol. Only a brief glimpse was it, but enough to last Ganazan for the rest of her life. She could only stare awe-struck, white-faced and shaken, at Orion's Chief of Staff, the second in command of the Omega Corps. The *second!*

Vickie reinforced the point with a few hard-bitten words. "If I, a subordinate to Lord Orion, have such a powerful mind, what of Orion himself? What of the man who can command such power?" She leaned forward, eyes flashing. "What of the man who is so far above me that not even I have the slightest notion of his power?"

Ganazan shivered and ducked her head, eyes glazed. She, who well knew the meaning and the feeling of power, had now learned relativity.

Spart broke the awkward silence. "How much time will you need?"

"Months, certainly," Steele said quietly. His wife's venom had shaken even him. "First, we have to get there, and then we'll need time to evaluate their home culture. Our approach to the siege will depend on a lot of variables we have no way of knowing yet. But this will be a campaign of terror, a war of nerves. We will attack the Ertainians at their weakest point, their hostile and vainglorious minds. As Kodiak said in reference to the Sforans, we're going to scare the hell out of them."

"Of that," Ganazan said weakly, "there can be no doubt."

CHAPTER 7

C ontrary to Nasim Badami's description of shade and beach, Chelsea Pond's shoreline was a bare circular stretch of scoured rock and trampled forest. The small lake was formed a few months earlier when Chelsea Connors née Winschell had turned an Ertainian laser rifle spectral by touch, shoved it lengthways through a prone Ertainian into the ground beneath him and let it go. The resulting molecular fusion blew a crater nearly half a kilometer wide and twenty meters deep, scrubbed the rugged landscape for another kilometer or so and diverted a small river to fill the gaping wound. The still-gritty river water cascaded over the crater's edge from the northwest and swirled in a swift eddy before rolling past the shores and rejoining its previous channel at the eastern end.

The enthusiastic ecology of Arcadia was already working to heal the blast damage, with sprigs of trees, bushes and sharp-bladed grasses working their roots into the tortured landscape.

De'angela Phillips stepped out of the Sprite she had piloted down from the orbiting *Phasmida*, shouldered her kit and looked around from the small landing pad leveled out of the exposed limestone bedrock. The teal sky was crisp and clear in the late autumn, scented with the conifers higher in the mountains upwind to the north. Her ears captured the stereo gush of rapids where the river entered and exited the opposite ends of the new pond. The lighter gravity and higher oxygen content made her a bit giddy even at this elevation. She drew in a deep breath and allowed herself to feel the thrill of her first new planetfall.

After the Battle for Arcadia cleared the Themis system of Ertainians, the *Angel* left a few dozen personnel behind to claim the planet and facilitate development and exploration. They selected an unforested mesa near Cat Plateau, the main battle site, and constructed Conestoga-style housing, workshops and warehouses. They named the new base after Bill Wize, Corpsman Kohana, who was killed in the crash landing that brought the first Corpsmen to Arcadia.

The base had since moved to Chelsea Pond and its structures scattered about the exposed bedrock of natural terraces rising above the shoreline. The crude buildings were supplemented by a few small cottages built with native wood and stone. Someone had even started a garden next to one of them. The loam there was a darker shade than the dusty khaki dirt that was everywhere else, probably imported from the rich forest below the crater.

The hangar for the expedition's seven Banshees and two Sprites was burrowed into the side of a high limestone ridge a few hundred meters to the planetary northwest. As she watched, Badami and his wingman swooped in, did an exuberant roll in unison, and dropped down to carefully back into berths within the enlarged natural cave. One of the shuttles, sent up by ground control to deliver a pair of caretakers to *Phasmida* and collect some of her passengers, slowly nosed into the cavern and disappeared into its darkness. Cobb and Tahiwi were still beyond the atmosphere, doing some thrilled sightseeing over their first new planet. Only Dani's sense of duty kept her from joining them.

Her passengers disembarked and swept past her to be greeted by a small swarm of residents eager for fresh faces. Among them was Yan Kun-li, the engineer in charge of the station, who greeted each of the newcomers with a quick nod and a few smiling words as he made his way to Dani. His comfortable bearing cued her that he was not one to stand on ceremony, so she allowed herself to relax and greet him with a smile rather than a salute.

The Chinese telepath, a foot shorter but heavier than Dani's wiry six foot three, ducked his head in a quick bow and offered his hand. "Commander Phillips, welcome to Arcadia. Feel free to visit any of our facilities."

"Thank you, Commander Yan. It'll be nice to stretch my legs." Their ranks, in Omega Corps convention, were attached to the job rather than to the person. Neither wore insignia and neither was superior to the other in position, but courtesy prevailed. "I thought y'all were set up at Kohana Base. What brought you here?"

Yan grimaced. "Bugs." He turned and gestured for her to follow him. "After the Ertainian high command sacrificed thousands of their own people trying to trap Lord Orion and his combat team, there was a huge population explosion of multi-legged coroners. Kohana Base was too close to the battlefield and got overrun. We couldn't compete, so we moved here."

"Can't blame you for that. This is more scenic than a mesa, anyway. I like the contours."

He gestured for her to follow him. "You haven't seen the skyline up there. Breathtaking. It's more accessible than this, too, not to mention more elbow room." He led her toward one of the larger Quonsets. "But on the other hand, this is more defensible. And we have plans to replace the greenery for more camouflage. Still, I'm a little worried that springtime melts might flood the river here. If that happens, we could be in trouble."

"Hm. Well, when I bring down the building supplies – and the containers they're shipped in – y'all maybe can move up and back a ways like how you have the hangar, there. Oh, and I brought a couple other goodies. One's a full-scale quantum cybernetic computer that'll extend your sensor range, provide a holographic camouflage dome, and let you keep in touch with both Gaea and the *Angel*. The other is an upgrade for the Banshees' tablicy disks that provides a baffle screen."

He stopped and lightly tapped her arm. "Wonderful! No wonder Garud is so excited."

"For good reason." When the *Angel* had lost Banshee 106 and Sprite 202 to four Ertainian cruisers, Lord Orion had furiously ordered his engineers to come up with better shielding to hide them from the danger their small numbers would always face in combat. They were successful, and Feliks Radschck was here to install the new components in the fighters' sensor arrays.

"Our 110 Banshee was damaged when the Ertainians dropped in on us last week," Yan continued. "The crew was pretty shaken up. Perhaps now, that won't happen."

"That's the idea," Dani said. They walked on in momentary silence. "So. Tell me about that raid. How close was it to succeeding?"

"Too close." Yan ducked his head in silent acceptance of the blame. "We had two Banshees up, and they were the ones who spotted the two squadrons coming in from two different angles. We scrambled the rest, but by the time they were aloft the pirates were already crossing the orbit of the fifth planet. It was a little chaotic, but we accounted for all twelve of them for slight damage to one of ours. The crewmen were bruised a bit, but that's all." He shrugged apologetically.

"Well, that's why Max Elser is here. The big sensor array he's going to install will provide much better warning." She waved away a swarm of mosquito-sized gnats that contributed to Arcadia's reputation as bug heaven.

"Good. Good." Yan ducked his head again as they reached the building, and he opened the door for her.

The small office was the anteroom of the command module, where Yan could keep his eye on the development of the station. Phillips peeked through the interior door and saw two people on duty. One wore a headset at the undersized communications and sensors console Max was here to replace. The other was typing something into a keyboard while wearing the mesh beanie-like input-output cap that allowed direct electromechanical contact with the computer. She guessed that was one of the scientists updating her findings.

A contour map of the continent, an inverted triangle with the tip stretching south southeast, took up most of another, larger 3D monitor. Chelsea Pond was identified by an amber blip on the southern slopes of the mountain range that covered the length of the inverted base of the triangle, west northwest to the ice-capped northern ocean. Scattered bright green pips indicated where other members of the expedition were active.

She saw nothing that displayed the activity outside the atmosphere. "Who's monitoring the military situation?"

"The Banshee flight teams and ground crew take turns in the hangar," was the reply as Yan offered her a chair in front of his neatly arranged desk. "I'm in overall command, but I regret I don't have much aptitude for military things." He shrugged again, which seemed to be his usual response when he was in over his head.

Which he clearly was. "So, they draw up their own duty rosters? Plan their own maintenance? Map their own flight plans?" That explained why all six undamaged fighters had been flying when she arrived during a period of no threat. No fighter pilot worth his salt would pass up flight time unless he was commanded to do so.

Again, he shrugged. "They seem confident with their autonomy, and I'm afraid I couldn't do better." His gaze settled on her shoulder, respectfully avoiding her eyes. "Could you?"

Her stomach churned. Her first instinct was yes, anybody with an ounce of sense could do better. But running a flight group of Banshees was way, way above her job description as a truck driver. She had no more training than Yan did on how to control a posse of three-dimensional cowboys.

Or did she? Before joining the Corps she had been a dancer from the age of four, and through dedication and determination she had become exceptionally good in ballet and modern styles. Unfortunately, there was little call for six foot three ballerinas, so she had turned to teaching. Her students had been eager adolescents with no built-in controls, so much of her studio's teaching had revolved around discipline, discipline, and practice, practice, practice.

Then one day she had been talked into a hang-gliding date, and she was instantly hooked on flight. That led to fixed-wing gliders and on to the greater responsibility of single-engine piloting. Eventually her strong second-level potential was noticed by a passing Corpsman, and Lord Orion offered her a place in the Corps. Her activation and the discovery of her gift of levitation had drawn her to the thrill of controlling anything she could get off the ground, including herself, which led to space flight.

Being among the last of the six hundred Corpsmen activated she was too late to get a coveted berth aboard the *Angel*, but she did get to train Sprite crews in rotating teams and quickly proved herself worthy to command the very first freighter.

And her training crews always got the benefit of that kitten-herding discipline from her teaching days.

All of this flashed through her mind in a few seconds, and the combination of circumstance and sense of duty made the decision easy. "Tell you what. Get the word out that I'm assigned to advise them on operations. Some of them might know me, so they'd know my value well enough for me to get my foot in the door." She smiled grimly. "And drop that foot if they need it. It'll help that I already have Radschck on board, and he'll be the one making them happiest. But you have to back me up, too."

His shoulders dropped from their defensive hunch

at last. "Gladly! While it shames me to admit my weakness, it would be foolish not to. The job is yours – unless, of course, you need to get back to Gaea."

"I'm here as long as it takes the technical crowd to make their changes. Radschck and Elser need to go back with me. But that installation stuff is outside my knowledge, so if I can make myself useful some-place else, I'd be happy to."

"Oh, the technical matters are in my yard. I think it will benefit everybody if we swap jobs, as it were. Let me coordinate the installations while you tighten up our security. Between us, we can make our new home safe, secure and efficient."

"Deal." They rose in unison and gripped each oth-er's hands.

DANI'S FEET FOLLOWED the path upward toward the hangar cave as she studied the personnel files on her tablet. There were currently fifty-two Corpsmen on Arcadia. That included herself, Radschck and Elser, who would be making the round trip in *Phasmida*, and Kamerun and Norwich destined for the *Angel*.

The permanent expedition had forty-one Corpsmen on detached duty from the *Angel* plus the six permanent additions she has brought with her from Gaea. Fourteen were Banshee crew, with eight full-time ground personnel and another six part-timers who seemed to find reasons to stay close. Add Cobb and Tahiwi with the Banshee she had brought with her, and she found herself in direct command of eight fighters and more than half the Corpsmen on Arcadia, very few of whom knew her personally.

Radschck was here to plug in and test the new baffle screens. His expertise would contribute to the redesign of the combat tactics for the fighters. Max Elser, the computopath who was instrumental in developing the Corps' family of quantum plasma computers, was brought along to install and fine-tune the new and more powerful quantum entanglement communications and sensor suite. He would be important in any efforts to improve cohesion and reaction time.

That was her command. Every Corpsman was boot camp trained as a warrior first, of course, but the scientific and exploration staff would not get directly involved in defense unless the enemy hit the ground. That included Kamerun and Norwich, who would be using their talents to test the new sensors.

She reached the broad shelf in front of the cave, turned and slowly scanned the little colony, checking the lay of the land. Yan was right; elbow room was scarce. She could see that there was no room to land her freighter, so she would have to bring the containers down one at a time.

Below her to the southeast was Chelsea Pond, dammed from flooding straight south by the high lip of the crater's downhill rim. To her right, the stepped ridges curved northward to accommodate the inflowing river gorge.

The office, lab and warehouse complex was built on a natural flood plain that dropped to the crater's northwestern shore. The reservoir the new pond created left the area high and dry under most conditions. A few buildings took advantage of the ridges above the main settlement where they would be protected from spring floods, but they might have problems with runoff from the barren slopes behind them.

The landing pad where her Sprite was parked was on the settlement's northeast edge between the buildings and the more elevated hangar. A broad path wove upward past the fighter group's barracks to the escarpment on which she stood. The small plateau was made level with limestone blocks rich with marine fossils that had been extracted to enlarge the cave. High above it was a glittering array of panels angled to capture solar energy for the settlement's power needs. To her left toward the river's babbling exit the ridge tops leveled out into broad, stepped tables that looked to have decent drainage. That might be a good place to safely land most of her cargo.

Loud talk and laughter echoed out from the cavern mouth behind her. It had a thin energy shield that prevented most of the ubiquitous bugs from penetrating the cave. Taking a deep breath, she lowered her tablet to her hip, rolled her shoulders under her nanosteel blue service uniform and spun on her heel to pass through. She strode in with her head high and every sense alert.

Badami's Banshee, along with his wing man's,

sat on their landing skids side by side in two left-hand berths with no one near them. She assumed the crews were in the locker rooms getting out of their flight suits. At a berth next to the right wall, two technicians were nonchalantly working inside an opened panel near the tail of the damaged Banshee 110, while a third ran a buffer over the scorched base of the stubby wing. The station's two Sprites were near the back wall with their hatches open to their dark interiors.

At the wall next to the locker rooms, a woman in a technician's fatigues sat in front of a large sensors monitor but paid scant attention to it. The rest of the ground crew in sight were sitting or standing at a folding table where four of them played cards as two others watched.

Behind them the work benches were cluttered with dirty rags, discarded tools and even leftover snacks. The cavern smelled of lubricants and something she thought was mold, likely emanating from a moist wall, green with algae, that sent a weak stream meandered to a corner where it pooled.

The hangar was a pigsty. It looked like a kindergarten playroom with the teachers on strike. She felt her jaw tighten at the indignity of such an undisciplined mess.

A dark-haired player at the table glanced up from his hand and saw her lean height silhouetted in the doorway. "Bonjour, batonne!" he called cheerfully. "Where did you come from, eh?" The others looked her way and popped grins. One woman gave her an airy wave.

She stepped out of the sunlight and into the glow from the LED ceiling lights, head high and eyes flashing. "I'm De'angela Phillips, Dragonfly of the Corps, commanding the star freighter *Phasmida*. You may call me Commander." The title was a growl.

The grins vanished. No, one, but no one, in the Corps would use rank like that unless they intended to apply it. The woman at the sensors console suddenly took a new and ardent interest in her monitor. The others exchanged looks, dropped their cards, rose and lined up in front of the table in height order and slid into an unpracticed semblance of parade rest.

She stalked toward them, her stage trained body displaying her ire with crystal clarity. She snapped her head to the three who had paused from working on the Banshee. "You! Fall in with the others." They quickly laid down their tools and trotted to join the line, which had read her piercing eyes and stretched to attention. Even the woman at the sensors stiffened in her chair without turning around.

One of the card players, the Frenchman, pushed out a telepathic probe offering respectful mental contact. She responded by envisioning the image of a snarling bobcat, and he hastily backed off.

She stalked up to the first mechanic at the left of the line. He was the only one taller than she, and much heavier, but he deliberately focused on an imaginary spot over her shoulder and stared unblinking at attention. She looked him up and down with obvious distaste for his rumpled and filthy fatigues, then stepped sharply to her right to confront the next.

She examined each of the six men and three women in turn, and gave and got the exact same reaction. It was not hard to deduce the reason for their unified response, so she snapped a left face, marched down to the center of the lineup and snapped right to confront the French telepath.

She stared down at him, eyes hard, and said, too quietly, "We're waiting for the locker rooms to clear." His eyes twitched almost imperceptibly, and she knew the word was passed. Dani turned away and took a longer look at her surroundings, leaving the team at attention. "Com. I want this broadcast to the fighters on patrol, plus the crew of the damaged fighter. Make it so."

"Aye-aye, Commander." The tech snatched her earbud into place, leaned forward into the hush field of the console and spoke rapidly. In a few seconds, one by one, six tiny windows popped up on the right edge of her monitor. One of them represented the *Phasmida*, where the two-man crew of the damaged Banshee 110 had taken caretaker duties. She noted the sensor tech also had the presence of mind to include the newly arrived Banshee 116 in the broadcast. Dani had been prepared to give her storming hell if she had omitted them. "Ready, ma'am".

"Very well." She turned and paced the length of the line, staring at the locker room doors. The wait was not long. First to pop out was a smallish, fair-haired woman in jeans and a loose T-shirt, who she guessed was Badami's gunner. With her was a round-faced, freckled redhead in fatigues who hurried to take her place near the taller end of the line of mechanics. The gunner stood apart a few meters away facing at right angles to the line, clearly wanting to distance herself from whatever was in store for the ground team.

A few seconds later the men's locker room disgorged Badami and the other Banshee team, along with the three who had helped them out of their complicated suits. The flight crews joined the row Badami's gunner anchored while the mechanics elbowed their way into the line in front of Dani.

She let them roast a bit more, then spun to face them, hands fisted at her sides. "How can y'all *live* in this dump?" she snarled. "More to the point, how can you expect your Banshees to live here? They're precision instruments, even if *you're NOT!*"

The thirteen mechanics froze even stiffer.

Dani paced back and forth, eyes darting, jabbing her finger at the offenses one by one. "Rags on the chairs! Grease all over the tools! Oil spilled all over the deck! Dirty dishes on the workbench! Rolling cabinets *abandoned* anywhere you feel like it! And a friggin' green *mud puddle* in the *corner!*" She whirled to face them again, her dark skin flushed by a wrath that was not even close to an act. "How *dare* you do this to the best damned fighting ships in the *galaxy!*"

By now even the flight crews had snapped to. She spun on them next. "When I flew into this system all six of your fighters were up there, and four were within a hundred thousand klicks of the planet. What the *hell* kind of top cover is that? Where are the reserves? When do you get the sleep y'all need to keep your edge? And if the fighters don't need somebody to look after them, why are they in this dark hangar when they should be topping their batteries with sunlight?"

Back to the mechanics, with a stiff arm pointing to the fighter under repair. "Banshee 110 was nudged a week ago and flew home under its own power. Why is it taking so damned long to get it back in the air? Did it interrupt your *card game?*" Her head danced on her neck.

"And where's the damage report?" She strode to a spot where she could be seen by both teams. "Where are *any* of your reports? Flight logs? Duty schedules? Patrol plots? Sensor readings?" She waved her tablet out to the full reach of her long arm. "Why is nothing *documented?* Don't you think Lord Orion might be curious about what the *hell* y'all are doing out here?"

She glared at each of them in turn, then marched in a full circle that included them all, with a brush past the sensor tech. Those who were not pale with anxiety were flushed from embarrassment.

She returned to the spot in front of both groups, hissed in a deep breath and let it go with a deep-throated sigh. Her voice was lower but still angry. "It will take me about two days to unload and distribute my cargo. Use... them... wisely."

She turned to the fighter group and raised her voice a bit to include those listening in through the com. "Flight crews. I want the duty rosters for the last four weeks. I want charts of the patrols, who planned them and who flew them, with time and distance. I want in-flight logs and combat briefs of the raid. I want detailed performance analyses for every ship. And I want self-evaluations from each of you, with a critique of your performance. And I want it done with two ships on patrol at all times, no more, no less. I want you sharp and this planet safe!"

She spun and again confronted the ground team. "I want this place *gleaming*. I want the trash policed, the tools cleaned and racked, and the equipment fully operational. Do *not* forget the locker rooms. I want that Banshee repaired and shining like the sun. I want the off-duty ships fueled, provisioned and ready to scramble. And for God's sake, I want that friggin' wall plugged and the pond scum *dead!*"

She turned her back and strode to the cave mouth, then faced them once more in silhouette. Her voice echoed chillingly throughout the cavern.

"Y'all are members of the Omega Corps, each selected for the talent, responsibility and self-discipline that makes you among Gaea's best. When I see you next, I expect y'all to be worthy of that trust!"

She threw a dancer's bounce into her about face and marched back down the hill.

CHAPTER 8

"*Phasmida*, this is Sprite two one two, pilot Dragonfly, requesting berth in cargo bay three."

"*Sprite two one two, this is Phasmida,*" answered a heavy Scottish brogue. "*Permission granted, Commander. Opening outer hatch to cargo bay three.*"

"Roger, *Phasmida*." Dani, already flying backwards for a reverse entry, watched her screen as the portside nanosteel hatch cracked open and slid up the nose of the freighter, revealing a deep red glow that shimmered through the shadows like a beacon. As Themis was behind the planet only the occlusion of stars revealed the ship's turtle-like profile, but she could see the jagged edges of her exterior cargo framework.

Phasmida had the capacity to carry eighteen standard sized forty-foot freight containers, nine on each side, plus three pressurized compartments in the bow that for this trip had transported the two smaller craft, a solar-powered bulldozer and a backhoe with all attachments, and a separate self-contained habitat stocked with songbirds destined for the *Angel*'s park.

The flattish, oblong bubble of the control and passenger cabin occupied the center mass, and the freighter's drive engines, environmentals and engineering, including the superconductor battery banks that powered it all, filled the stern. Scattered over the ultra-strong nanosteel latticework frame were the retro motivators and screen generators, and the stellar accumulators that charged the batteries.

Berthed outside between the forward compartments and the cabin was the huge antigrav crane needed to load and unload the cargo containers. Dani trusted no one but herself to operate it.

She backed the Sprite through the forcefield that maintained the air pressure in the port side compartment. The shuttle's fields melded with the ship's to maintain the seal and dissipate the hull's temperature extremes picked up in the vacuum. As usual, she preferred to do the piloting herself instead of letting *Phasmida*'s computer take command.

As the Sprite's four landing struts touched down the berth's hatch slid closed, the computer gradually increased the internal gravity of the compartment from zero to Gaea-normal and raised the lighting level. Dani shut down, pushed herself out of the pilot's seat and opened the side cargo hatch.

As soon as the Sprite's hatch opened, the computer sent a carefully crafted quantum pulse called the "scrubber" through the entire hold and everything in it. The scrubber identified and sterilized any microorganism that was not Gaean. A good portion of the freighter's small quantum computer was geared toward identifying, analyzing and eliminating any life that might introduce foreign contaminants, while leaving anything above a minimum size and complexity unmolested. Any alien vermin that might pollute the ship's ecosystem were ruthlessly killed or forcefield trapped for later judgment. That included the inevitable bugs that hitchhiked from the surface.

"COMMANDER *PHASMIDA*, ARRIVING," the computer, called Twiggy, announced as she stepped into view. Dani faced the wall-mounted Omega Corps crest with the image of a walking stick insect painted between its feet and slapped her fist, fingers in, just under her left collarbone in the formal Corps salute. It was a disproportionate gesture, but it gave her humble command a gravitas that filled her with pride. Future ambitions notwithstanding, this was *her* ship.

Ritual complete, she climbed the six steps to the bridge level hatch which popped open as she approached, crossed the airlock and passed through the inner hatch that opened onto the bridge forward of the command station. The two borrowed crewmen of Banshee 110 were already at attention. The man standing next to her control console fisted his shoulder. "Pilot MacBrewster, Commander."

She returned his salute. "I remember. As you were." She automatically scanned the board and saw nothing amiss. She nodded to his gunner, who gave her a tentative smile, returned the nod and resumed his station at the sensors console. "The ship is still yours, Liam. I'll be busy unloading the cargo."

"Thank you, ma'am." The Scottish pilot, still stinging from her broadcast rampage of hours earlier, could not have been more precise. "We'll be taking good care of her – as you most clearly have, ma'am." He waved an arm to take in the entire interior. "As brilliant a command as I've ever seen, milady."

"No less than she deserves. She's the first of her kind." She strolled to the engineering station. "How's the neighborhood look, Gunner?" The question did not keep her from scanning the console. She prided herself in knowing every job on her ship.

"No activity, ma'am." Domingo Gomez still retained a silky Columbian accent. "I must say, this board is a lot better than our ground unit. You can spot any leaf in a hurricane with this."

She smiled and briefly laid a hand on his shoulder to ease his nerves. "I had Max Elser as a passenger. He built the unit the *Angel* uses, so yeah, he tinkered the very best out of this one. Saves us from surprises in deep space. But the big unit I'm about to take down there will make it look stone blind."

She walked astern and peeked into the galley. It was spotless. "I'll be in quarters, updating my log..." she gave them a pointed look, reminding them to do the same, "... and suiting up for the freight transfer. Since you touched on how good the sensors are, Domo, I'd like you to keep an open channel with ground control and coordinate the sweeps. You're our first line of defense, Gunner."

"Yes, ma'am. Gracias por la confianza." He straightened his earbud and spoke in rapid English to his counterpart in the hangar. With a nod to the pilot, Dani dropped down the ladder to her cabin.

TWO HOURS AND a power nap later, Dani climbed into the intimate plumbing of her pressure suit and worked her way through the airlock to the starboard airtight compartment, now mostly vacant since the Banshee had joined its fellows on the surface. From there she left the ship through the personnel airlock that on the planetary surface would have extended a ship's ladder to the ground. Unencumbered by gravity in the vacuum, she floated to the cargo crane in its topside cradle above and behind the three pressurized compartments. She relied on her levitation to move about, impelling against the mass of the ship or even her own mass as need be.

She pulled herself into the nanosteel cockpit through what would have been the deck in a gravity environment and slid into the seat, choosing to remain airless in case she needed to EVA. She connected the seat harness, jammed her feet into the pedal stirrups, and powered up the console. The complex of zero point gravity motivators came to life along with the nine monitors that allowed her a full view of her surroundings. The joystick in her right hand controlled horizontal and vertical flight, the speedball under her left controlled yaw and pitch. That was the standard configuration for all Corps craft, and it took a very special skill set to coordinate it.

"Cargo crane, deploying," she called into her com, and got an acknowledging repeat from MacBrewster. Pressing down slowly with her right foot to feed power to her motive controls, she pushed forward on the stick and rolled the speedball back to ease the sixty-foot contraption out of its berth. Six broad vertical posts, the cargo capture arms that doubled as housing for retro cones, pulled out of their parking slots as the crane separated from the mother ship. Because the parking position of the thick, electronics-filled chassis put it upward in relation to the ship, she was relatively flying it upside down and backwards, which made no difference with no gravity to interfere.

The container in berth four, the forward port dorsal berth closest to the prow, was loaded with most of the sensor unit and the communications systems, plus the new tablicy disks. That would be first down. Second would be bulk of the quantum plasma computer with its memory core and defensive screen generators, carried in berth eleven on the starboard underside of the freighter.

Dani turned the crane parallel to the length of the ship and arced over it and forward to hover over berth four. Eyes darting from screen to screen, hands making minute adjustments with stick and speedball, she carefully eased the six capture posts into the barely larger niches between the container and the frame. The crane's small computer read her commands and followed her intent with millimetric adjustments. The Themis-lit glare from her quartz viewports darkened as the cabin dropped into the narrow space left for that purpose at the forward end of the berth.

When the proximity countdown on her center screen reached zero, her left foot punched down, setting all engines to neutral and sliding the four corner and two side capture posts inward into direct contact with the container. She hit the switch that redirected one gravity generator on each post to orient inward, locking the container in a nigh unbreakable grip.

She sighed and closed her eyes for a moment, feeling the tension ease from her muscles. As practiced as she was – and she drilled herself much harder than any crewman – the capture protocol was nerve-wracking. This was her first solo voyage, after all. She took a sip of water from the tube inside her helmet and allowed her breathing to return to normal.

But capture was not delivery. She shook off the last of the tension and triggered her com. "*Phasmida* command, cargo berth four is captured and ready for separation."

"*Roger, Commander,*" MacBrewster returned. "*Have a bonny trip and a smooth landing.*"

"Roger that. See you on the flip side. Dragonfly out."

On the keyboard at her side, she tapped the commands to release the anchors that held the container in its berth. Crane and container alike were now in freefall relative to the ship. She snapped the switches on her console to redirect her engines for free flight, steadied her speedball, tweaked the joystick and pressed the motive pedal. The crane, container included, slid straight "up" out of the berth, eased through the freighter's protective screens and accelerated out of its orbit toward the dawning horizon.

Now the fun part, Dani thought with a slight smile. Atmospheric flight was an entirely different ball game. A twitch of her stick slowly rotated the crane until its broad flatbed base pocked with superconducting cones was "down" toward Arcadia and she herself was looking downward into the atmosphere.

As the surrounding sky started to brighten with reflected light, she pressurized the cabin, switched on the internal gravity to counteract the G-force and activated the deflector screen that would protect the crane and its cargo from the heat of entry. On her landing approach she would rotate the flatbed one hundred eighty degrees relative to the control cabin. The retros in the capture arms would take the load to the surface and set the container down with the body of the crane above it and out of the way.

Unbidden to her mind came the stories about the Corps' first landing on Arcadia, when Denny Connors and Bill Wize, for whom Kohana Base was named, had piloted their crippled Sprite toward the surface only to have the severely damaged shuttle suddenly lose retro power and violently crash land on the surface. Wize had died from the impact along with the previously injured Elga Mançon, and the badly battered Connors and his soon-to-be bride Chelsea had fled toward the mountains with thousands of Ertainian pirates at their heels.

Chelsea Pond was one result of that escape. Dani's ungainly craft wobbled through the winds of the thickening atmosphere and approached the settlement.

"Arcadia command, this is auxiliary cargo transport detached from Corps freighter *Phasmida*, approaching Chelsea Pond for landing." She called up a schematic of the crater to scout a place to touch down.

"*Roger, Phasmida auxiliary, this is Arcadia command.*" The response was gratifyingly instant. "*We have you on vector one six fiver at angels fiver-four scant. Permission granted to approach. Recommend touchdown on the western shore between the river entrance and exit. That'll place you two hundred meters from the hangar.*"

"Not advised." That would put the container right in Yan's presumed flood plain, and once it landed it would stay there. If it was repurposed as a structure as planned, it could be washed away by the first spring flood. Besides, although the baffle screen plugins were destined for the hangar, the massive com/sensor assembly was not. "This cargo needs elevation. Recommend touchdown on the flat of the ridge three hundred meters northeast of the hangar."

"*Copy. Stand by.*" There was a long pause. She maintained course and speed, gliding like an elongated pie tin downward toward the settlement. As she was approaching the point where she would have to make the decision herself, the com reopened.

"*Commander Phillips, this is Commander Yan.*" The use of rank implied an argument might be coming. "*What is your first load?*"

She told him, and added, "The biggest component by far is the com and sensor array. If you want to keep it safe from environmental hazards, it needs elevation. It'll be less complicated to drop the container where it's high and build the housing for the array close by. Remember, *Phasmida*'s also transporting earth-moving equipment, so leveling the foundation and building a road to reach the site won't be much of a problem."

"*You're right, I'd forgotten that.*" There were murmurings that indicated he was consulting with others close by. "*Can you also drop your loads of building materials on the ridge?*"

She took another look at the map. "Maybe two, and that's besides the rest of the unit – it's coming down in two pieces. I need room twice the size of the crane to safely land and level a container. I can make my third load the dozer and backhoe so y'all can nudge the containers from where I have to drop them, and that will improve our options."

"*I see.*" Another pause. "*Very well, permission*

granted to land at your recommended site. Please find the time to meet with me before you lift again."

She smiled wryly. Okay, to be continued. Truth to tell, the details should have been worked out before she started unloading. Rookie mistake. "Roger that. ETA twelve minutes."

"Thank you, Commander. Safe landing."

"Roger. Switching com to Arcadia flight control." She returned her concentration to her piloting.

CHAPTER 9

It took three days rather than two to get all the cargo down, thanks in large part to continuous disagreements on where to drop each load. Conflicts between Yan's ideas of convenience and Dani's limitations on where she could safely land caused delays for every trip. And delivering container six upside down hardly helped her credibility, though the error was from the loading and not her fault. But eventually all the maiden-voyage hiccups were resolved and everything, including the big bird condo, was safely down.

In short order a foundation was laid on top of the ridge, prefabricated walls of non-conductive nanosteel were erected, and the big com/sensor unit was moved by heavy straps slung from a Sprite, aided by five telekinetics and Dani's levitation, from the containers to its anchored position within the new command center. Once the roof was on Max Elser and Feliks Radschck worked their magic on the unit alongside Yan and the station personnel who would operate it.

At the back of the same ridge, a deep cave was blasted into the cliff to house the computer. Once activated, it surrounded itself with a full range of impact, energy and baffle screens to keep it safe. Only a camouflaged entrance hinted at its presence.

By the time Dani had delivered her last load, the safety of the foundling planet from sneak attack was assured. Their sensor's sensitivity to hyperlight-speed tachyon particles meant their real-time reach was now almost two light years beyond the system's outer planets, far enough that the Banshees no longer needed to fly combat patrol.

The communications functions included two features that enormously improved the station's efficiency. One was the control component that drove the Corps wrist pads that included a global tachyon com network, hologram capability, and considerable memory and processing power. The other gave the station the quantum entanglement transceiver that allowed Arcadia to be in immediate contact with Gaea, the *Angel*, and if necessary, even the Confederation.

Jake Anson in the Corps headquarters on Gaea and Jander Steele in the *Angel* transiting between Dephlet and Arcadia joined in a three-way conference with Yan and Phillips. Both Lord Orion and Lord Commander Binary approved of the decision to let Dragonfly organize the fighter wing on Arcadia, but insisted that the assignment was temporary. Anson wanted his freighter and its pilot back, and a hard-eyed Steele wanted the fighter crews to prove they could do their jobs without a babysitter. Dani had to agree with both.

Thus it was four days instead of two before Dani docked her crane on *Phasmida* and ferried the two Banshee crewmen back down in the Sprite. The freighter was now deserted, but since the new ground station was fully operational her sensors were no longer needed, and she could safely sit in orbit empty of both life and duty.

As she, MacBrewster and Gomez made the hike up to the hangar, Dani was pleased to see that one of the Sprites and five of the eight Banshees, including the now battle-ready 110, were parked on the plateau soaking up the autumn sunlight. Their batteries would be at full capacity if needed.

With her escorts longingly eyeing their fighter but keeping station behind her, she reached the mouth of the cave and gave the hangar a critical inspection. The limestone floor was so spotless as to be almost polished; the work benches were meticulously organized with clean tools racked with military precision; diagnostic and repair equipment was precisely parked in even rows between the berths. Best of all, the groundwater leak was diverted to drain out of sight and the weeping wall was patched watertight and artfully painted to match the stone. She pulled in a deep breath and detected only the normal odors of a busy motor pool. Her eyes gleamed with satisfaction.

In the center berths were the three other Banshees, with Ajax's 116 between the other two and all of them stripped of the maintenance panels behind the cockpit. To her left, in the corner created by the jutting locker rooms, thirty folding chairs held almost as many bodies, flight crews and mechanics both, facing away from her.

Radschck stood next to the network computer terminal that displayed a small disk-shaped array incorporating the collision, energy and baffle shield projectors and the sensors and communications transceivers, all surrounding a short-range warp sphere generator. The new disks, currently stacked near Com Central where Dani had off-loaded them, were to replace the disks without baffle screen projectors that were original equipment on the Banshees.

Each Banshee had two dozen of the disks. She could not make out Feliks' words, but he was holding up the complex chunk of electronics that synchronized the disks and was alternately pointing to it, to the open maintenance panels on 116, and to the monitor. She was sensitive enough to feel the periphery of his thoughts as he augmented his words with a broadcast of telepathy.

Leaning on the wall behind him was Jonathan Cobb. Ajax, an impressively muscled Arizonan, spotted her and started to stiffen. She hastily held up a staying hand and shook her head, and he relaxed back to the wall. Dani pointed to her temple to invite contact. Cobb, a telepath, mentally reached out to her.

She opened her Corps-trained mind shield to shared thought. <*"Let me guess – this is on the care and feeding of the tablicy?"*> The Polish word was the adopted name for the array, the big brothers of which were installed all over the hull of the *Angel*. Radschck was its genius designer and coined the term.

<*"Exactly."*> Well-schooled in his variant talent, Jonny's expression and body language gave no indication that the conversation was taking place. Likewise, he slowed his thoughts to about thrice verbal speed to ensure comprehension. <*"Since I'm the only pilot in the group who's been trained in the tactical use of the thing, I'm standing by to show them how it works. My 116 has it already, as you know."*>

She nodded. <*"Fine. I already know that stuff, too, since Phasmida's also equipped."*> She paused, withdrawing her consciousness briefly to think privately. <*"I'll want your evaluation of the other crews, how well they absorb the data. I also want you and Tahiwi to take the lead when we get to flight exercises. We can use Phasmida as the target, since she's about as slow and clumsy as an Ertainian cruiser."*>

She could feel the concern filtering through his thoughts. <*"Yes, ma'am, but that's not really my thing. Teaching is a role I don't have much experience in."*>

<*"That's on me, but you're the one with combat experience. Phasmida's not exactly a battle platform."*> She sent him a caricature image of her freighter with a turtle's legs and smiling face, and broke contact. There was something behind his statement she didn't quite catch, but she politely dismissed it from her mind.

She looked behind her and swept an arm forward. "Join the group, brothers – and thanks for taking such good care of my baby."

"Thank ye, mum." MacBrewster grinned at the compliment as they passed her and walked toward the lecture. Gomez also gave her a big smile and sketched a friendly salute.

Dani chose not to disturb the class; she was more than content with how the crews had responded to her directives. As she turned away a soft whistle caused her to look over her shoulder. The other Sprite glide overhead, its cone-shaped retro motivators melodically catching the wind, and settled on the lower landing pad next to her own. The hatch slid open and two Corpsmen, a pair of explorers back from a field trip, stepped out and headed for the headquarters hut.

The Sprite resealed and wafted upward, passed by Dani and came to ground in front of the hangar next to its sister. The pilot, the red-haired mechanic she had last seen in her lineup, spotted her and fisted her collarbone as she trotted into the hangar. Dani returned the salute with a smiling nod and tuned to gaze over the pond and the barren downward slope to the wilderness beyond.

On impulse she bent her knees and sprang upward while triggering her variant gift of levitation. She hovered for a moment to take in the view, then climbed toward the scattered gray-green clouds drifting through the birdless skies of Arcadia. In moments she was sailing high above the settlement and the hordes of flying insects, in her first free flight since she had arrived.

Unlike telekinetics, who could work their magic remotely, her levitation could only affect the tug of gravity around matter she was in physical contact with. Still, that was more than enough to indulge herself in the joy of flight, so she stole those few minutes to soar through the teal-blue skies above the virgin forest beyond the crater. After weeks of confinement within the freighter, she let herself savor the crisp, conifer-scented wind in her face.

A sharp-snouted, paddle-tailed lizard glided out of the sun and circled to look her over, then leisurely flapped twice and went about its business. It was a handsome creature, with a shimmering aquamarine body and two pairs of mottled green feathered wings. She shadowed it for a while, she and the eagle-sized raptor flying in nonchalant companionship, until something down in the trees caught its attention and it tucked its wings into a bulleting dive. She marveled at its camouflage as it disappeared toward the forest below.

Eventually her sense of duty prevailed, so she floated sedately back to the settlement and touched down outside her assigned quarters. Waiting for her inside were the computerized reports she had demanded from her charges. She had a lot of homework to do.

CHAPTER 10

It took two sets of knocks to break her concentration. She thought, <pause>, and dragged the mesh input-output headset from the tangle of her dreadlocks and dropped it on her tiny desk with a sigh. Only then did she feel the soft pressure on her mind: it was Jonny Cobb, just outside. She opened her mind enough to invite him through the door.

"I was wondering if you were ever coming up for air," he smiled as he wiped his feet on the door rug. The air from outdoors was noticeably cooler. Unknown to her, a stray storm cloud had drifted from the nearby mountains and muddied the grounds with a chilling autumn shower.

"My own fault for ordering four weeks of reports." She gestured to a chair near the front window. "These are clearly reconstructions – nobody kept their records up – but they're certainly thorough."

"Not surprising," he said as he took the seat. "There's been a lot of shop talk since you, um, introduced yourself. A pissed off African American woman is all kinds of motivation. And you gave them enough time to get their stories straight. I'm pretty sure it's all honest, since I took the liberty of helping them. They're too embarrassed to try to make themselves look good."

She chuckled. "Lesson learned, then." She stood and stretched away hours of desk work. "I appreciate your help – you have experience they don't, and it shows. Now, performance-wise, I can't fault them much, except for the ad hoc scheduling. They spent way too much time in the saddle doing duplicate sweeps. But when it came down to pulling the trigger on the raiders, they were fast, efficient, and deadly. Of course, seven Banshees against twelve pirate cruisers was serious overkill."

"No such thing in combat – even if you're organized, which they definitely were not. In my humble opinion, of course."

"Of course." She took a few steps across the cramped room that was her office, living room and kitchen combined, and pulled two bottles of water out of the countertop refrigerator she herself had delivered as cargo. Cobb nodded his thanks as he took one, and she popped the cap on her own. "From the combat reports it looks like they operated pretty well in flights of two except for MacBrewster, and he was the lone wolf who got hurt. So they're cool on the flight level, but not squadron or group."

He waved his bottle. "That's a training opportunity. Let's face it, only three of us eight pilots were armed forces, and only Badami and I have combat experience – and I'm a rejuve from the 'Nam era, so

I'm rusty as hell."

She nodded her understanding. Cobb was later in life when he was activated, and a Corps medical team of transmutators had shaved decades off his biological age. "So, let me run this by you. As soon as Feliks has installed all the baffles and they have some simulator time to adjust to the flux window, we'll work them through some scenarios in pairs for close order drill to give them a chance to get joined at the hip. Then we'll move on to squadrons of two flights and finally the full group of eight ships. We need to get them to the point where they won't be getting in each other's way regardless of the formation or the baffles." Built into the new baffle screens was a modification to leave a tiny, synchronized fluctuating gap in the coverage frequencies that would allow communication between the fighters' computers and crewmen.

He pursed his lips. "And how do you control all this, Group Commander?"

"Ah. A challenge." She grinned at him, but only got a raised eyebrow in reply. She sobered with a moue. "Ok, challenge accepted. Granted, I have no military experience, much less combat, but you know about my love of order and discipline. Lord Orion teaches us that, as long as you know the fundamentals and practice them until they're second nature, you can adapt them to any situation. I was a dance teacher, so I know how to nurture talent, create discipline, and blend complimentary skills into unified performance. And I'm not without ambitions of my own, so I've absorbed the theory of space combat tactics."

She sat back down at her desk. "And, Corpsman Ajax, I'm well aware that you participated in the development of those tactics. So as you challenge me, I challenge you."

He studied her for a moment, then said soberly, "I think it's time we compared notes, then, don't you?"

She nodded. "I agree. I'm going to be relying on you a lot." She set her water on the desk and loosened her mind shield to let him in. His mental touch was tentative at first, but as her willing reception encompassed her full consciousness his rapport became more and more open. The full story came flooding through.

Her eyes widened in shock.

Abruptly she snapped her mental door shut, jerked to her feet and stood rigid, fists clenched at her side, staring at nothing. It was long seconds before she could speak.

"Why... why didn't you tell me? We had weeks aboard my ship to prepare for this!"

He spread his hands in appeal. "Because we had no real idea what we'd find here. Lord Orion was hoping for the best, but he knows his people and pretty much expected the anarchy we found. The crews he left here weren't his best – he kept the four with the most combat experience with the *Angel*. He figured he'd need them over Ertain."

He leaned back in his chair, trying to convey an

impression of apology. "We kept my responsibility from you in the expectation that your great force of discipline would be necessary. Turns out it was, and you reacted just as Lord Orion hoped you would."

She glared at him, then cast herself into the love-seat backed against the hut's curved wall and threw a long leg over the armrest. "I feel like an idiot."

"No, no, no!" He shook his head vigorously. "If there's anyone you should to be mad at, it's me. It was my decision to hide in the ranks and let you be bad cop. What you've done, and what you're planning for the training, is exactly what these guys need."

"But it's sure to come out before very long that you and Marama aren't just an enhancement crew, Jonny."

"And it will – by the time they're trained. But it's better for the group dynamic that they don't know I was sent to command them until I've shown them I can. I need to prove myself by working my way up."

"So, it's still on me." She stretched full length, arms crossed under her breasts, shoulders high on one arm of the loveseat and ankles crossed far beyond the other end, glaring through the light curtains of the front window.

Jonny remained silent, giving her time to work it out. Finally, she threw her head back and heaved a huge sigh. "All right. Let's get started on the lesson plan." She opened her mind to him.

CHAPTER 11

The simulations were programmed into the new Com Central and beamed directly to the computers aboard the windowless Banshees. Since the vista outside a superlight warp sphere was an insanity-inducing sight from within it, no deep-space craft had a direct view to the outside. All the visuals the crews ever saw were from the ships' sensors, so the simulations could take place on the plateau in front of the hangar where all eight fighters were parked.

Initially the fighters worked in their customary two-ship flights, from which they got to know the advantages and limitations of the baffle screen in combat situations they were used to. They learned that while the baffles gave them a tremendous advantage in stealth, once they opened fire they were detectable because their streams of twenty-centimeter pulse spheres left a clear energy trail back to them. Three of the crews were simulated casualties before they learned to shoot fast and dodge faster. It took serious coordination between pilot and gunner/navigator, and leader and wingman, to synchronize the flight maneuvers.

Dani had assigned MacBrewster as wingman to Cobb, who gave him extra patience as the erstwhile lone wolf and his gunner were still a little skittish after their brush with nucleonic death. The highly detail-minded Scotsman quickly learned to trust the big American and the two with their gunners became a solid fire team. Thus, when the simulations progressed from two-ship flights to four-ship squadrons, Cobb had earned the position of leader of First Squadron.

Nasim Badami, the former MIG-21 pilot from India who had been the first to challenge *Phasmida*'s arrival, proved himself qualified to lead Second Squadron, partly on the radiopathic ability of his gunner, Roksana Sayanova. The blonde Russian proved adept at following the dizzying spectrum flux gap that allowed the fighters' computers to keep a firm grip on each other, and freely passed her discoveries and observations throughout the group. Radschck and Elser, themselves drilling Yan and his technical team in Com Central, tweaked and reasoned and prodded their equipment to capabilities well beyond the intended design thanks to Sayanova's practical input.

The spectrum flux synchronized a small, moving window of communication through the otherwise impervious baffle screens. It allowed voice and data exchange between the fighters and to ground control that was virtually undetectable by anyone without the pattern key. The complex simulations stressed the new technology to its limits before the fighters ever got off the ground.

And through it all, Dani rode herd with an iron will, tracking every move, every shot, every word, every adaptation through her I/O meshcap. Her pithy but encouraging critiques were immediate and to the point, sparing no egos as she prodded her diverse command into a steadily more synchronized team.

Initially, the sessions were four hours of drill followed by an hour of rest, during which the crews were not required to wear their flight suits. That quickly changed. As the training progressed, Dani varied both the length of the drills and the time off, simulating emergency situations against varying enemy strengths. The crews were forced to hit the deck, suit up, hook in and go right into combat at any moment of the day or night. As the Arcadian twenty-four hour day was twenty-five and a third Gaean hours long, that made for an exhausting schedule.

The ground crews, charged with prepping both the flight teams and their ships, pitched in with a determined will and steadily increased their speed and efficiency. Montrell Loiseau, the cheeky French telepath, proved his extroverted worth by coordinating the small contingent of mechanics to ensure that every pilot, every gunner, every Banshee hit the simulated ether ready to fight.

And the hangar crew were not alone; Yan, at Dani's tactful urging, not only trained himself in directing the operations of Com Central but volunteered much of his science staff for the many odd jobs that would improve the readiness of the combat team.

And it was working. Scramble time was reduced, test scenarios were perfected, and problems resolved at increasing speed and in improving unison. More, as the tests became progressively more complex, the crews themselves started adapting Dani's and Jonny's fundamental tactics to come up with their own imaginative solutions to each new trial.

At last, after nine days of grueling drill that only second-level minds could have endured, she was satisfied enough that she dismissed the exhausted company for a full twenty-four hours. Dani herself, more drained than any of them, wobbled in her flight from Com Central on the northeast ridge to her quarters and crashed fully clothed on her bed.

THE NEXT MORNING, cleaned up and more or less refreshed, Dani stepped out into the morning light, pulled in a deep breath of the wonderfully chilly air and ran her eyes over the landscape. She noticed with amusement that someone had put a set of gyrating mechanical scarecrows around the birdcage to protect the eight species of little migrants from being harassed by the local wildlife. Their container unit had been opened enough to allow the occupants some fresh air, and their song and movement had generated interest from all manner of small predators.

Sensor-guided forcefields protected the settlement from larger beasts, but anything smaller than a housecat could slip through and become a nuisance. So, half a dozen herky-jerky robots had been placed on tracks around the habitat to intercept them. Meanwhile the bug-eating nightingales and mockingbirds among the songsters were in danger of getting fat on the local diet. The Gaean insects stowed dormant in a cryogenic compartment beneath the bird cages were thus spared until they could be established in the *Angel's* park.

Dani launched herself and floated up to the flight barracks not far from the hangar, and strolled toward the mess hall innocently looking for a much-needed full-sized meal. She pushed through the swinging doors and stopped short, taken aback by the noisy room filled with men and women who had no current reason to like her very much. All sixteen of the flight group and nine of the fourteen ground crew were already at breakfast. The conversations were loud and animated, with forks waving in swoops and corkscrews as they talked shop between bites.

Badami looked up, froze, and announced her presence with a very loud and very un-military, "Oh, no!" Everyone stopped what they were doing and every eye clicked on her.

Dani burst into laughter, made heartier by the looks of relief as the diners visibly relaxed. She waved a hand as a multitude of irreverent and sometimes rude greetings welcomed her in.

Cobb rose and pulled out a vacant chair at his

round table for eight. "Welcome, Commander! I trust you slept as dead as we did." She groaned cheerfully as she settled in.

Sayanova, seated between her and Badami, poured her a cup of coffee from a steaming carafe. "I believe American term is 'hell week', madame professor. We all slept most of day." A pilot across the table spun the lazy susan to propel already ravaged serving platters in her direction.

"Try fitting a seventy-five inch body into a seventy-four inch bed." The coffee tasted heavenly. "I was comatose, even so. Thank y'all for keeping up with me."

Cobb snorted. "Hell, you can hardly accuse us of that. That was a rough week, ma'am."

She shook her head. "Call me Dani, please. Y'all know what they say about those who teach. You guys have the tough job." She speared a pair of venison sausage patties to start with. "I'm a good pilot, but handling one of those flying fleas takes a lot more talent than I've got."

"Speaking of which, when do we get to go up for reals?" a pilot called from a nearby table.

"Mph. Tomorrow," she said around a mouthful as she reached for a platter of crispy hash browns. She found she was ravenous. "I want a day for aaaallll of us to critique our performances."

A collective groan echoed through the room. She raised her voice. "Seriously. Dictate y'all's reports and upload them to the squad leaders – that includes you, Loiseau – by fifteen hundred hours and the four of us will compare notes. Y'all can expect our evaluations by ten hundred hours tomorrow. Then we'll go up."

"I hear you'll be up there as a target?" someone quipped. The laughter turned into a cheer that made her flush.

"Now hold on, there." She rotated her fork above her head and the room quickly quieted. "I know I've been driving you hard, but I have reason to."

"We suck!" A woman pilot's voice this time, which elicited a number of off-color suggestions along with the laughter.

Dani held up her hands, grinning nonetheless. "Besides that. But let me point out a couple of other things. First, I'm on borrowed time – Binary wants his freighter back and his brother wants his engineers. I go with them by default." She noticed the five missing ground personnel filing out of the kitchen, likely summoned from KP by Loiseau. "And second, which should probably be first: I shouldn't have to remind y'all that there are pirates out there. There are hundreds of pirate cruisers out there, and they know where we are."

She was speaking to silence now. She pushed her chair back and rose to face them.

"The last raid was almost four weeks ago and was pretty small. The Head of Ertain never heard back from them, so y'all can bet he's curious as hell. I'm surprised we haven't been jumped again already."

She searched the crowd, making eye contact with as many as were receptive. "Our new scanners can see them pretty far off, but that won't reduce their numbers any. That's up to us."

Her voice dropped in volume, the better to make her point. "You, brothers and sisters, are Arcadia's first, last and only line of defense. If we are not ready for them when they come, we lose this planet. And y'all can bet your sixes they will come."

She held her pause until every one of them was looking at her. She pursed her lips and shifted her feet to dispel some of the tension. "Sorry – didn't meant to sermonize. Let's finish breakfast and get back to work, okay? Fifteen hundred hours for y'all's reports. Ten hundred tomorrow, we meet in here for the evaluations. Tomorrow afternoon we put what we've learned into practice."

She resumed her seat, and sober conversations restarted around her as she picked up her fork. "Could somebody please slide me those rancheros? Lizard eggs, right?"

CHAPTER 12

Dani's tiny quarters were overcrowded as Yan, Radschck and Elser also chose to attend the briefing. The three were seated at the small dinette, while Badami and Loiseau shared the loveseat and Cobb kept his customary chair near the door.

Dani, at her desk, opened her eyes under the I/O meshcap covering her head and focused on Yan. "I'm glad you're taking a part, Kun-li. I'll be running the exercises from *Phasmida* with Max and Feliks, so we'll need you commanding Com Central to keep the sensor crew steady."

"I appreciate your trust," the engineer said. "As short-handed as we are, we'll all need to wear many hats after you three leave us. The practice will serve us well."

"I agree. I'll want to test the new jammer while we're up there, too. Lord Orion wants to keep our means of survival mysterious, in keeping with his god act during the big battle. The baffles will keep us stealthy, but we don't want the bad guys to get the word out if it's a protracted fight."

"And we definitely want to test whether the jamming spectrum will interfere with our own communications," Badami put in. "I for one don't want to feel alone out there."

"I don't see that happening," Max said. "The long-range tachyon and entanglement frequencies we'll be jamming use a different quantum range than our more local flux pattern, otherwise we'd be getting interference from all over the galaxy. And since our short-range coms are internal and not part of the tablicy, we can still punch through the interference."

Cobb grunted, "Trust but verify. Sorry, guys, but it's our butts on the line out there and we need to know for certain that we can maintain communications."

"And that's why we train," Dani flipped her open hand at him for emphasis. "We'll run a few trials with your new stealth tactics, Jonny – brilliant theories, by the way – and make sure we're properly glued together. And with Max and Feliks up top with me we'll be able to see if there's anything we know the Ertainians have that can catch up with the flux." She looked to Loiseau. "Are we ready to go, Montrell?"

"All the fighters are in top condition and fully provisioned, mademoiselle," the newly designated chief mechanic nodded. "Our two Sprites are rigged for search and rescue and will be standing by with my people as crew and the med techs on fast call." He gave an expansive Gallic shrug. "Like everyone else we are stretched thin, but as you can see from our reports we are fully prepared. I do request permission to add our recovery drill to the exercise."

"Absolutely," Dani nodded. "I'm putting you on

call to control the deployment from the hangar station at my signal." The Frenchman's chin rose. He had taken Dani's chewing-out very personally, especially since his own disrespectful behavior had helped to bring it on, and he had made it his own crusade to whip himself and the ground crew into shape. He had conceived the use of the Sprites as rescue craft and had taken the initiative to make it work.

"They have the baffle screens and flux communications, right?" Yan wanted to know.

Feliks nodded. "Yes, Montrell insisted, and we had plenty of spares. We can get your Sprite equipped when you're willing to let loose of it, Dani."

"It's not mine, it's Kun-li's. It's in my cargo manifest to leave behind. But I've got to say it's been great to have it aboard. I'll need to talk to Arden about letting me have one as a pin—"

Abruptly the I/O still in sync with her mind jabbed her, and simultaneously every wristpad in the room squawked an alarm.

"*PRIME ALERT. PRIME ALERT. SENSORS DETECT FOUR GROUPS OF FOUR TO SIX BOGEYS EACH APPROACHING —*"

"Scramble!" Dani shouted, simultaneously firing the command through her I/O meshcap. Whooping alarms went off all over the complex, and the forty-odd Corpsmen not on remote assignment leaped to their tasks.

Telepaths reached out to their designated targets, located them, and sent those locations to their assigned teleporters. One of them, a technician from Com Central, materialized, snatched for a grip on Yan and vanished. An instant later Domingo Gomez popped in and Cobb disappeared the same way. Badami, a teleporter himself, grabbed Loiseau and left to pick up Sayanova.

Dani had barely enough time to yank off her I/O before she felt a hand on her arm and found herself in her Sprite, with Radschck and Elser beside her. All three sprang to their stations, Dani to the pilot's seat, Max to navigation and Feliks to engineering. As Dani fired her engines her monitors came alive, and she saw an external view of mechanics swarming over the Banshees, prepping the ships for the crews suiting up in the locker rooms.

Dani did not wait for them; her place was aboard *Phasmida*. As soon as her lights were green she lifted off, and Max shot her a range and bearing to her ship. Feliks was already remotely waking up the freighter.

Not a word had been spoken since she had shouted her command, and Dani felt a surge of pride as she saw her brutal training bear sweet fruit. In only two weeks, the awkwardly patchwork militia of Arcadia had become an efficient, disciplined, unified fighting force worthy of the Omega Corps.

She switched from liftoff retros to drive three hundred meters off the surface and stood the Sprite on its tail. At a thousand meters they passed through the new camouflage dome that protected the colony from discovery with an illusion of an unpopulated crater pond. They gained speed rapidly and went supersonic at angels eighteen.

Dani glanced up and blinked twice at the ground com icon in the heads-up the computer held steady above her eye level. "Pi-Fang, sit report."

"*Coming to you now,*" Yan responded to his Corps name. Another icon flashed, and she blinked it to display the Com Central sensor scan on the lower half of her center monitor. "*We have five squadrons of six ships each decelerating in on retros from just under two light years, on a line with the present position of Planet 7 and slightly above the orbital plane.*" Her right-side monitor gave her the exact relative coordinates he was too unschooled to convey. "*The center squadron is farthest away and only came into view after the scramble order. The two on either side of it are nearest, and the outer two are mid-distance between, all covering an arc of about thirty degrees.*" Pause. "*We have positive confirmation from their screen pattern that they are Ertainian.*"

"Roger that." *Phasmida* shone as a fuzzy lacework through the stratosphere darkening the top of her monitor, and she adjusted her controls to intercept. The freighter abruptly vanished as Feliks woke up its defenses. The Sprite did not have a baffle screen, but she was confident the little craft was safely invisible against the backdrop of the planet. "What's the ETA at their present speed?"

"*The four nearer squadrons should cross the orbit of the fifth planet in a bit less than four hours, assum-*

ing they don't flip and backdrive before then. The Banshees are lifting off now."

She glanced at her chronometer. It was not quite five minutes from the scramble order. Not too bad at all, considering all the plumbing connections in those damnable suits. "Roger. I'm approaching *Phasmida* now, ETA two minutes scant. We should be up and running in five. I'll take strategic command then."

She scanned her display and glanced back at Feliks, who grimaced and shook his head. "Advise you maintain a global sweep. This group may not be alone – in fact, having them all come in from the same direction makes me nervous." Thirty ships constituted fifteen percent of an Ertainian fleet and may have been its picket force.

"Roger that." There was a pause as he passed the order to one of his techs. *"All Banshees have lifted and should be outbound by the time you link in."* He paused again, obviously unused to the stress of impending combat. *"Best of luck. Com Central listening out."*

"Roger, Com Central. Dragonfly back in five scant." She flipped the Sprite to decelerate for docking.

With the cargo gone the freighter was less than half the mass she had been. The only unincorporated equipment outside the cabin was the crane, firmly locked into its bay. Feliks triggered the center cargo hold to open for the Sprite, to balance its weight between the empty port and starboard chambers.

Dani backed the shuttle into the pressurized compartment and carefully positioned it so the landing struts could be secured automatically to the deck. The three Corpsmen piled out and raced through the airlock to the port chamber and up the stairs to the bridge, ignoring the computer's arrival announcement as the airlock hatches sealed behind them.

While Dani slid down the ladder to her quarters to don her pressure suit and Radschck finished powering up the sensor array, Elser policed the rest of the command module, its galley and the living quarters below to secure anything that might get jarred loose in combat. Then it was his turn to suit up as Dani literally flew to her pilot station, and when he was properly attired he took over for the engineer so he could do the same. Only when he was geared up did Feliks establish his tight-beamed contact with Com Central, and Dani eyed the heads-up icons projected around her head.

"Banshee Group. Group Leader Ajax, this is Dragonfly." Her address made official Cobb's presumed role as the Banshee group's tactical commander. "Position sit."

"*Accelerating past outer moon orbit now.*" Damn, those little birds were fast. The most distant of the seven small moons orbiting Arcadia was farther away than Luna from Gaea. "*Recommend plan Delta Bravo Two?*"

She ran the plan through her mind. It required them to split their forces, gambling on the immensely superior speed, stealth and punch of the Banshees to negate the enemy's numerical advantage. "Copy that. Banshee Group, view bandit squadrons as one through five port to starboard as they lay above the orbital plane. Flight Bravo, target Bandit One, Flight Alfa, Bandit Two, Flight Charlie, Bandit Four, Flight Delta, Bandit Five. Keep updating sensor data from Com Central to arrive bandit targets for simultaneous attack. Big Stick will keep an eye on Bandit Three." *Phasmida* was Big Stick. "Acknowledge."

The lead pilots of each flight repeated the orders. Bravo and Delta flights would run hell-bent to position themselves to meet the outermost hostiles, while the other two flights, Cobb and Badami in the lead, would reduce speed to be ready to strike their closer targets at the same time. That left the center squadron, hanging back far beyond the others, unobserved save for the shadowing *Phasmida*.

If all went according to plan – and she was uncomfortably aware that in combat, nothing went according to plan, ever – Cobb and Badami, her very best, would do their business and race off after that center squadron. Or, if a second force came in from another direction, the two squadron leaders would be close enough to the planet to defend in any direction, and flights Bravo and Delta would be redeployed as the situation warranted.

And of course, if hell froze over, the slow, clumsy, feebly armed *Phasmida* would fill the breach.

CHAPTER 13

Bravo and Delta flights, having the farthest distance to the intercept, drove at flank speed for two hours and were already flipped for deceleration by the time *Phasmida* slogged halfway to the orbit of the fifth planet. Alfa and Charlie were still under drive at their reduced speed, waiting to get closer before they spun to use their drive generators at full power.

Dani took *Phasmida* in the direction of the center flock of Ertainians at eighty percent of her top speed, certainly not to engage but to minimize the distance between the freighter and the broad pattern of her far more capable cohorts. Once in position, she cut the drive and drifted forward on momentum alone.

The four outer enemy squadrons started their backdrive halfway between the orbits of the sixth and fifth planets, coordinated to converge on Arcadia. If they followed standard doctrine, they would eventually flip to use their retros to complete the drop to maneuvering speed, then come in broadside first. What the more distant center group would do was still a mystery.

Feliks and Dani were in constant contact with

Com Central and kept the Banshees advised. The drive flares of the attacking ships were a steady glare in their screens, while the baffle flux allowed them to keep track of their own otherwise undetectable forces.

The green blips representing the defenders rapidly reduced the gap, and Cobb and Badami finally flipped their flights to meet their targets at the same time and speed as the outer flights. The minutes counted down.

Input from the fighters displayed on Dani's center monitor as the forces converged. The Ertainians were in an octahedral formation, with a lead cruiser four thousand kilometers ahead of a wide square of four and the sixth ship centered behind.

The ships were the same model as those the *Angel* had so easily shredded in battle. Each was an egg-shaped seventy meters of nanosteel, with three pairs of nucleonic cannons in equidistant turrets just forward of the thickest circumference and single guns similarly staggered fore and aft, twelve guns per ship. The octahedral formation gave them point-blank supporting fire without sacrificing maneuvering room.

Unfortunately for them, they were not fighting other cruisers. The formation gave the baffle-screened Banshees plenty of space to slip past their defenses undetected.

Jonny Cobb's voice did not betray his tension. "All flights, we're within their warp spheres. Relativistic speed and line of sight are stabilized. Check your decel to penetrate their formation in two minutes as of... mark. Be sure your course is to have the lead ship between you and the body of four outside you. Let them all pass, juke around their screens until they're all by." His center monitor in the cramped cockpit – he and Tahiwi were almost wearing the ten-meter fighter – gave him a good tactical view of all four flights. "Big Stick, Alfa Prime."

Dani was right there as he knew she would be. *"Alfa Prime, this is Big Stick. Com Central is on the line and standing by for your signal."*

"Roger. Penetration minus ninety seconds... mark. All flights, set target sensors and charge weapons. Mind your intervals and watch those screen diameters, I don't want anybody nudged." Cobb knew how jittery his inexperienced pilots had to be, and used his calm voice and routine reminders to settle them down. He wasted no worry on the steel-nerved Maori in the seat behind him; on his monitor he saw the tiny icon that showed her weapons to be armed and ready. He could imagine her tattooed chin twitching side to side as her only habitual hint of excitement.

"Sixty seconds out. Let's keep it tight, people. Mind your intervals and hang onto your mates until we break them up. Give those big engines of theirs plenty of room – don't get scorched going through. Thirty seconds." The back-driving cruisers were approaching them stern on as they used their main engines to decelerate. "I want you to reduce your coms to fifty in case any interference gets through. Twenty seconds. Check your speed, be sure you ease back to equal their velocity when you reach the rear of the formation. Ten seconds. Let me know when you're in position. Five... four... heeeere we go..."

Cobb, drifting backward relative to the enemy, saw MacBrewster skim past the other side of the lead ship, then it was his turn. With a few muttered words he changed his monitor from group view to his personal tactical, with his flight view in a smaller display. The two fighters slipped undetected into the formation and angled inward through the center square to skirt the screens of the four ships. In the cockpit behind him, Tahiwi tweaked the speedball under her left hand to lock her targeting crosshairs on the lead ship. Her right index finger rested next to the trigger on her joystick.

By the time MacBrewster had floated to a position beyond the bow of the last ship, both fighters were traveling at the same course and speed as the cruiser squadron. Cobb took a deep breath and calmly called, "Com Central, on my mark, execute..." ...he waited until he had amber go lights from each of the other flights in his heads up... "NOW!"

The receiver inside his helmet sizzled as the jammer created a system-wide hypersphere within which no long-range communications could be sent or received save those matching the flux pattern. "Alfa Two!" he called to check that his flux window was open.

"*Ready, sarr!*" MacBrewster responded instantly, his excited voice crackling slightly through the interference.

"Let 'er rip!"

Tahiwi pressed her trigger. From the twin barrels in the gimbaled nose of the Banshee blew alternating twenty-centimeter spheres of coherent molecular force a quarter-second apart, eight per second. At a significant fraction of the speed of light the spheres whizzed through the vacuum and slammed into the defensive screen of the lead ship eight thousand kilometers ahead.

Tahiwi's aim was perfect. Her shots followed each other in with millimetric precision. In less than a second the enemy's defensive screen was overloaded and the spheres bored into the cruiser's idle bow retros, digging deeper with each successive shot until the retro engines' power supply was hit. There was a brief flash of igniting oxygen, and abruptly the front quarter of the seventy-meter ship disintegrated into shards of tortured metal.

The cruiser staggered into a slow yaw, and Tahiwi twitched her guns to stitch a path of destruction from the bow to one of the primary gun batteries. Another, larger flash of shattering concussion, and the cruiser buckled inward like a broken egg, then spun wildly under the impetus of its still-blasting main engines. "Scratch one!" Tahiwi bawled.

But even before then, Cobb had stomped his drive, wrenched his stick and tickled his speedball, hurling his Banshee into a corkscrew spin and sending it tearing after one of the four center ships. In his monitor window he saw his wingman's point-blank target, the rearmost cruiser, violently come apart behind him. Over his com he heard Gomez howl, "*Uno mato!*" He knew MacBrewster was spinning his craft after his next assigned target.

In rapid succession he heard the other six Banshees of the group call out their success. Eight for eight, a good start.

In a matter of seconds his next target was within easy range for Tahiwi. The cruiser was turning to bring its main batteries toward the destruction behind it. Three bolts of hellfire blazed from one forward and a pair of broadside guns, followed by three more volleys. The near-solid blasts scorched the ether where his fighter would have been had he not changed course.

He blinked his general com icon. "Banshee group. They're on the prod. Don't linger over your shots. Fire and flit!" All seven pilots quickly acknowledged by blinking at their icons and sending a flash to his heads-up.

He blinked his internal. "Any time, Kohai."

By way of answer, Tahiwi sent a stream of spheres into the forward mass of the target ship. She ran her aim through the retro ring a third of the way back from the bow, then quit. In less than three seconds she had blown twenty-two holes in vital spots.

Cobb then did his part, whipping the fighter

upward and to the left, then boring in from another angle. The cruiser's answering fire missed again, and Tahiwi responded by ripping that gun battery clean out of its hull. The target spun wildly, and Cobb zipped into an arc that exposed the cruiser's stern and its drive engines to his gunner's weapons. Two seconds later the ship disintegrated under her fire. "Scratch two!" Already turning, Cobb located the third cruiser on his list and went after it. Over his flight com came Gomez shouting his second kill.

"*Group commander, this is Big Stick.*" The com was scratchy through the interference, but understandable.

"Big Stick, Ajax." His third target had turned to flee, and he directed his ship into a spiral as he chased to intercept.

Dani's voice was dangerously calm. "*I know y'all are busy and all, but things are getting interesting here. Right after the jammer started, Bandit Three flipped over and is accelerating flank speed toward the planet. Com Central has identified the lead and trailing ships as battleships, with twice the guns of a cruiser. If I don't get some help, Arcadia's going to get plastered.*"

His stomach cramped, and he heard Tahiwi mutter something in Maori. True to their ruthless form, the Ertainians had sacrificed their own people as a diversion. "Acknowledged. Banshee group. Bravo and Delta will continue operations. Alfa Two, Charlie Two, you're on your own. Finish off your bandit squadrons. Charlie Prime and Alfa Prime will flank speed to support Big Stick. Acknowledge." Seven green lights lined up at the top of his holographic heads-up, Badami's winking emphatically.

He blinked at his wingman's icon. "Sorry to leave you alone, Liam, but, um..."

"Not a problem, Skipper. I'll follow you as soon as I chase these buggers down. Give 'em hell, Yank."

"Roger that." Tahiwi fed him the course for a looping intercept with the distant enemy squadron's accelerating flight line. He curled into the trajectory and poured on the speed.

DANI STARED GRIMLY at the sensor results displayed on her left monitor. Bandit Three had ceased its full-bore acceleration and was bulleting in on momentum, with the leading twenty-four-gun battleship, one hundred ten meters of muscle, oriented broadside to the planet and the box of four twelve-gun cruisers bow forward for global defense. The trailing battleship followed them stern first on reduced backdrive.

At their current speed, they would whip past Arcadia's outer moons in two and a half hours. She expected them to flip again and reduce their approach speed to have time over the planet, but by then they would be well inside the orbit of the fifth planet and far too close to imagine that all six could be engaged by the hard-driving Banshees in time to save Arcadia from a devastating drive-by nucleonic bombardment.

So *Phasmida*, outgunned ninety-six to two, was powering to meet them.

Dani, vacuum helmet tipped back and dangling over her suit's environmental pack, slumped back in her pilot's seat and breathed deeply, trying to control the terror that seized on the brink of her consciousness. She forced herself to analyze their situation, to weigh each element, to mentally list the pros and cons in her eminently self-controlled manner. The discipline calmed her and allowed her to dispel her fears and look for solutions.

One thing came clearly to mind, the one thing she had available that the enemy could not possibly match: the two brilliantly inventive men behind her. She summoned all the calm and courage she could muster, then rose from her seat and faced her crew.

"Okay, guys, let's assess the situation."

Elser and Radschck swiveled their chairs and looked at her with wide-eyed attention. She could see the fear in Max's pale face, in Feliks's grinding jaw.

She leaned against the back of her chair and, somehow, smiled. "It's rough, but not as rough as it could be. Let's look at the bad guys first." She started ticking off her fingers. "One, there are six of them, and two are double the power of any mobile unit we've ever faced. We know the Confederation has battleships, though, and since the Ertainians stole their ship design from them we know their capabilities. Their mass makes them slower and less maneuverable, so they rely on firepower to be effective. That makes them nothing more than cruisers on steroids, right? And we know we can beat cruisers."

"Banshees can beat cruisers," Max corrected her tersely, tension making his German accent sharper. "They have twin twenty-centimeter batteries. We have two single twelve-centimeter guns pointing in opposite directions."

She waved it away. "We'll get to that." She kept her gaze steady as she ticked off another finger. "Second, they can't communicate with each other. We know the jammer not only prevents them from calling long distance, but Max was able to expand it on the fly to include their shortrange frequencies as well." She nodded to the German, who stared back without blinking. "We, on the other hand, can talk to each other, and because of that, help is on the way."

"But not before we engage," Feliks pointed out. "Even if the enemy reverse to decelerate right now we'll still have to intercept them before Cobb and Badami can get here."

Max nodded jerkily. "And they're only two Banshees."

"But they have us leading the way," she smiled, "and we can give a damned good accounting."

"How?" Max asked, and Feliks added, "Dani, we have two small guns that can't be fired in tandem. Our screens are barely enough to stop a meteor, much less a nucleonic bolt half a meter thick. And as much as I respect your baby, she's not that fast and she turns like a dump truck. What do we have to compete with a battleship?"

"We... have... each... other!" Like snapping a switch, her light demeanor was gone; the stern disciplinarian was back and vibrant with intensity. "Whoever told y'all we just sit at our consoles and let *Phasmida* do the work? She's here to serve *us*, not the other way around!"

She pushed away from her chair and stood to her full six foot three, feet apart and one hand on her hip. "Gentlemen, we are Corpsmen, with mental and physical abilities far beyond anyone we're ever likely to face. That's not just an edge. That's decisive!"

She let that sink in, and saw the wheels starting to turn as their eyes narrowed and their backs straightened. "Max. You're a computopath, with a direct read to everything within the quantum computer you helped design. You know the mainframe, you know diagnostics, targeting, sensors, relays, and every connection to every electronic millimeter of this ship. And with an I/O beanie you can direct it far faster than anyone else alive, and make it perform at its highest level."

She thumped her own sternum. "I'm a levitator, and everything I touch is at my command. I can become one with the controls, the drive, the retros, the very physical fabric of this ship. And you, Feliks, are an engineer and a telepath, with the knowledge and ability to link Max, the mind, and me, the body of this ship into a coherent single entity. We have exactly what we need to get the very best out of this ship and each other!"

She stepped between them, eyes flashing fire, and extended her hands. "Unite us!"

Max and Feliks rose together and reached for her and for each other. The three Corpsmen gripped hands, opened their minds, and became one.

CHAPTER 14

As soon as the squadron flipped to brake, *Phasmida* did the same to intercept. The ovoid enemy ships had far more powerful drive engines than the turtle-shaped freighter, but the tremendous difference in mass forced the Ertainian ships to begin their deceleration shortly after they passed the orbit of the fifth planet. That mass differential gave the skeletal Corps ship a considerable superiority in maneuverability despite the relatively weak retro array scattered over the girders of her container berths. *Phasmida* matched course and speed in short order and floated undetected through the octahedron, into the gap between the trailing battleship and the square of cruisers.

In full rapport, the three Corpsmen mentally ran through the ship to ensure they were truly ready for action. The Dani part of the blended mind was taken aback to notice that she had forgotten to depressurize the three airtight cargo holds. The Feliks part pumped the atmosphere out and into the tanks aft of the cabin. The Max part ensured that the potentially fire-feeding air tanks were properly shielded to protect them from a jarring impact. Feliks tugged at the perfectionist Dani's unsettled nerves so the three could again meld into a single mind. The perfect blend of talents got back down to business.

Max had an I/O meshcap covering his head, eschewing the safety of his vacuum suit helmet for direct contact with his beloved computer. Dani had her helmet on to get maximum efficiency from her heads-up displays, but her boots and gloves were empty on the floor so her bare hands and flexible dancer's feet could connect securely to the physicality of the ship. Feliks also went gloveless, preferring the dexterity of unencumbered fingers for his complex engineering board. All were securely cross belted to their seats.

Navigation sensors, targeting sensors and Com Central's remote view all contributed to the battle plan plotted and recorded in Twiggy's database. Three bodies twitched and swayed as the united mind rehearsed the opening moves of the ship's carefully choreographed dance. A communal check of the racing Banshees showed them to be at least an hour away.

The pilot, melded to her vessel as never before, eased her charge into a position where her stern's idle drive motivators pointed at an angle forward of the trailing battleship. *Phasmida* drifted up to the back-driving ship until they were within three hundred kilometers, knife range, of the blazing stern and Max's belly turret had a solid lock.

The dance began.

Twelve-centimeter spheres of molecular cohesion, four per second, were formed in the motivator of the gun turret, accelerated by rapidly flexing magnetic fields and slammed through the force-rifled barrel. The stream of fastballs pounded their way into and through the battleship's defensive screen and punched into the base of the drive engines. Several of the big blasters flared and died, forcing the ship into a slow spin away from its previous course.

They risked three seconds for the opening salvo, then Max ceased fire and Dani simultaneously stomped on the drive, flipping the ship into a spin that took it down and outside the octahedral formation. The battleship opened fire from two of its six broadside double turrets plus single guns from the ring between the rear retros and the drivers.

The blasts saturated the area where *Phasmida* had been, but she was already straightening out of her spin and heading for the cruiser on the far corner from their attack. The nearest cruiser also opened fire but was firing blind.

Meanwhile, a chain reaction had begun in the stern of the battleship. Pieces of shattered nanosteel peeled away from the concussion of internal explosions. The big ship was damaged, drifting toward the center of the formation because its backdrive was reduced, but it was far from out of action.

The Max part of the gestalt was already targeting the distant cruiser as Dani angled *Phasmida* to a spot ahead of it. Time crawled in their adrenalin-charged collective consciousness as the lumbering freighter strained to reach their next firing point. When the speed and distance matched the plan, she cut the drive, spun *Phasmida* so the top turret had a clear shot, then adjusted the angle of the ship for the next getaway.

Max, never bothering with a physical trigger, drove a thought through his meshcap and directed the gun to fire, allowing himself only two and a half seconds before he shut it down. The force spheres stitched the row of gimballed retros aft of the cruiser's thickest circumference, the first few taps disrupting the screen and the rest smashing through to the reactors and igniting a tremendous if brief fireball. Dani kicked the freighter into another driving turn.

The battleship and nearest cruiser both sent bolts into their wake, the cruiser's fire coming from an angle that barely missed *Phasmida*'s screens. A third ship from the relative bottom corner of the square took a shot of its own. Meanwhile the targeted cruiser crumpled like a paper ball as deep explosions split the ship nearly in half and the loss of its inertia absorption generators drove the powering stern into the suddenly inert bow.

Three of the four untouched ships, including the lead battleship, were now reacting to the threat, turning to bring their outer broadsides toward the global upper rear of the formation where they perceived the threat to be. *Phasmida* was actually looping through the inner circumference of the square to take aim at the higher cruiser, which had yet to fire a shot.

The choreographed script had reached its end. The freighter, battling far out of her weight class, had by stealth and artifice forced most of the squadron to redirect its momentum from its lethal rendezvous with Arcadia into an unpredictable defensive furball. From now on the action would be reaction, with the blended human and mechanical mentality of *Phasmida* analyzing the tactical situation to outwit the awakened enemy and keep the pressure on until help arrived.

Dani cautiously approached their next target from nearly behind it, again turning the ship's belly toward the cruiser with prow angled upward. As they powered past Max gave them ten spheres point blank into the drive assembly. The spheres lost their cohesion much more rapidly in the holocaust of the drive flare, but they held together long enough to penetrate to the main drive reactors. The ship bulged like an overinflated balloon and tore itself apart.

Dani drove upward and inward, spinning to show the thinnest profile to the rear battleship, which was still firing although drifting forward faster than the rest of the squadron.

But it was the cruiser at the bottom of the formation that got them.

Dani, so physically connected to her ship, shrieked in agony as deflector screens never meant for combat gave in to two hits ten meters apart. The container berth on the extremity of the port wing exploded into molten globules of ravaged nanosteel. Dani's left shoulder convulsed and her fingers twitched violently on her speedball, sending the ship into a wild frisbee spin. The baffle screen flickered briefly as two tablicy disks vaporized, but Max, despite the sharp pain in his head from losing the sensors, sent a furious command to the computer as Feliks rerouted power to bring the screen back online.

Dani rammed the joystick in her right hand hard forward and the topside retros forced the ship straight down. The vacuum above them was criss-crossed with a dozen bolts their brief appearance had encouraged. When they failed to connect, the surviving enemy ships expanded the target area and came perilously close to hitting them a second time.

Dani regained control of her spasming left arm and fought the spin. In desperation she reached out through the ship with her levitation and forced the port wing to slow, actually replacing the blown-away retros with her variant power, drawing on her synergy with the adrenalin-pumped Feliks and Max to augment her strength. When the freighter was at last on an even keel, she slammed her drive pedal to the deck, drilling the ship forward through the formation and away from the hellish nucleonic firestorm.

But the lead battleship was now close enough to be effective. By sheer chance, an eight-gun broadside flared from the monster and came straight at them in an expanding spread pattern. Warned by the razor-sharp Feliks, Dani threw full power of mind and mechanism into the bow underside retros and arrowed upward toward the perimeter of the spread.

Straight into a devastating blow.

The searing energy bolt sheared off meters of the bow, tore open the depressurized cargo bays to the vacuum of space and melted the nose off the Sprite. The gestalt mind staggered as the communications flux generator they were connected to through Max crashed offline. They were now blind and deaf, cut off from Com Central and Banshees both, and entirely on their own.

Dani, head pinging and half blinded from the psychic blow to her face, used the kinetic energy from the punch to augment the starboard keel retros and spun the freighter like a flipped coin. The crane, dislodged from its anchors by the massive hit, whirled away at right angles from their mean course, left the protection of the baffle screen and was obliterated by half a dozen bolts.

Feliks redirected auxiliary power to the sensors to re-enable most of their viewing and targeting capacity. Max spotted a cruiser that was driving toward them and used the split-second windows through *Phasmida*'s violent rotation to snap shots from each of his guns as they came to bear. Under the cover of the crane's spectacular destruction, he popped holes in the cruiser's bow and pummeled it into a barrel roll.

At Feliks's thought jab, Dani fired her stern drive and sent her spinning charge into a corkscrewing escape path, speeding away from the nucleonic bolts that saturated the space behind them. Max ceased firing to keep them undetected, waiting for his next chance to cause damage as they escaped from their latest sizzling frying pan.

The squadron's formation was a shambles. Max spotted the one cruiser still aimed at Arcadia and the still-dizzy Dani powered after it, momentarily ignoring the much closer lead battleship that was firing indiscriminate bolts through the surrounding space. They had no defense against such random peril, but for the moment the battleship was showing its bow to them and none of the assault was coming their way. Feliks worked furiously to strengthen the weakened tablicy systems that might leak their location.

Dani used both retros and levitation to get the spin under control at last. *Phasmida* laboriously glided within accurate firing range of the cruiser so stubbornly mission-bent. Max waited, waited for the range to close, then Dani cut the drive, dropped the freighter's stern so the top gun had a shot, and Max poured out his small but powerful spheres. Two seconds only, eight shots, and Dani punched the drive to run them clear.

The spheres were aimed precisely at a central gun battery, and the cruiser shuddered violently as its entire side cratered inward and it yawed from its course. Dani hurled *Phasmida* up and away from the scene, avoiding sporadic fire from the damaged rear battleship as it sailed past.

All but the lead battleship were now destroyed

or damaged, and that ship had apparently decided to cease fire until it had something to shoot at. The trailing battleship, its backdrive weakened by *Phasmida*'s first shots, flew on its greater momentum all the way through the formation and was spinning slowly offline from Arcadia, but the planet now showed a clear disk as the combat zone approached her through inertia alone. It was still in lethal peril from the undamaged battleship.

With nothing to maneuver the port wing and the bow but her own variant talent, Dani sent her battered freighter into an arching dive to sweep them past the battleship's menacing broadside for a shot at the vulnerable stern. All three Corpsmen felt a building surge of dread as they deliberately looped toward the heart of the enemy's offensive might. If their baffle screen so much as flickered...

Suddenly the battleship blossomed with a chain of bursting pits running rapidly from bow to stern, flaring with brilliant flashes of igniting atmosphere like a string of pearls the entire length of the ship. Barely a second later another series of fissures was gouged port to starboard through the row of primary gun batteries, erupting into even bigger craters as three of the six double turrets were blown out of its hull. The powerful ship came apart like a peeled banana.

Banshees!

An overwhelming rush of relief engulfed the melded mind that was the crew of *Phasmida*. Arcadia was saved.

CHAPTER 15

Nine days later the *Angel* glided into the Themis
system and threaded her way through the
remnants of the Second Battle for Arcadia.
Thanks to Com Central, Lord Orion was fully briefed
on all that occurred, but he had yet to speak to the
Corpsmen who had been most instrumental in the
victory.

The four squadrons of enemy the Banshees had
attacked were destroyed utterly, with a handful of
surviving crewmen retrieved by Loiseau's Sprites.
The center group, so devastated by an artless little
ship that was scarcely more than a collection of
Lincoln logs, fought on until the few survivors of one
helpless cruiser chose to surrender.

The prisoners were behind forcefields in one of the
many caves near Chelsea Pond. There they would
stay there until the Ertainian home world itself was
located, besieged and, as decreed by Orion, reduced
to unconditional surrender.

As for the victors, only *Phasmida* had suffered
serious damage, while two Banshees had taken graz-
ing hits to their shielding that knocked them spinning but caused no real harm. With the exception of

a few headaches, they had taken no casualties.

Every one of the fifty Corpsmen assigned to or around Arcadia got forty-eight hours of "shore leave" aboard the *Angel*, having a delightful holiday with the comfortable cabins, interstellar cuisine, top-notch recreation and entertainment, and the camaraderie of the intensely inquisitive and somewhat jealous men and women warriors of the mother ship.

The Banshee crews, including their newly confirmed Commander Jonny Cobb, floated their fighters into the *Angel*'s hangar deck. They were swarmed by their comrades and lacked for nothing during their stay. The ground crew, scientists and engineers from Chelsea Pond joined them via the freight-sized telebooth freshly installed on the surface. It took seven days to rotate the entire population through, and that included an interview and debriefing for each of them with Orion, Alpha and the appropriate department heads.

Dani had far more free time as Denny Connors' space-suited engineers and mechanics swarmed over *Phasmida*, working to repair the battle damage enough for her to get home to the Montana shipyard. The damaged Sprite would go with her, to have its vaporized nose replaced by a gun turret and serve as her pinnace. Dani was under orders to stay away from her beloved command to allow the engineers to work in peace.

Her reception from the *Angel* was sensational, even for one used to performing masterfully on stage.

A few times she was almost brought to tears by the overwhelming admiration and respect she received from the battle-wise Angelinos.

She was the last to be debriefed. Before her had gone Yan and Loiseau, Badami and Sayanova, Cobb and Tahiwi, Radschck and Elser. The interviews had taken place at various locations throughout the ship depending on the rank and comfort level of the interviewed. Dani was summoned to the High Lounge.

She was given thirty minutes' notice. She left her popular table in the crew's lounge outside the Park and hurried to her assigned quarters, where she was thrilled to see a Class-A uniform waiting for her. A power shower later she slid into the tailored gold-accented crimson turtleneck, black slacks and low-heeled matte black boots, and finally the flare shouldered nanosteel-blue jerkin with the Corps crest above the left breast and the four-inch black utility belt.

After a quick makeup session and adding the nanosteel-colored flat cap, she critiqued herself in the full-length mirror, unashamedly proud in the first full dress uniform she had ever had a chance to wear. The colors contrasted strikingly with her mid-dark skin while the form-fitting uniform flattered her tall, athletic form and the wide belt accented her long waist.

On a whim, she triggered a mental lock that only a variant mind could open. The nanosteel wirecloth uniform, another brilliant invention inspired by the lessons of the first battle for the planet, quickly transformed. Powered by tiny accumulators that gathered light and converted it into energy, the uniform seemed to come alive on her body. The flared shoulders of the collarless jerkin flowed up the back and sides of her head to meld with the flat cap. The sides formed ear cups that guarded her hearing. The folded peak of the cap in turn flowed down her face to reveal the golden reflective lenses that protected her eyes and the pentagonal apparatus over her nose and mouth that would purify the air she breathed. The face covering was crimson while the thicker portion protecting her skull retained the nanosteel blue.

The turtleneck unwound to reach up and meld with the new helmet, the cuffs transformed into flexible fitted gloves, and the hook-and-loop patches that secured the jerkin were reinforced by the same staunch closure as the helmet. The fabric, all of it woven from Corps-perfected nanosteel thread and further augmented by a lining of nanotech shock and energy absorbers from skullcap to boot soles, was now a suit of armor more protective than two centimeters of tungsten steel.

Only the Corps had the technology to pull off such an outfit, and damn, it looked *good*.

But that was not its only asset. She sent another thought to the suit's electronics and watched fascinated as she disappeared. Thousands of sensors on the surface of the armor scanned the environment and reflected what they saw in the reverse direction,

creating a chameleon effect that made her virtually invisible to the full spectrum from ultraviolet to
infrared. She looked in the mirror and saw the wall
behind her reflected there as if she did not exist. She
swung her arms experimentally and saw the merest
trace of distortion. Her giggle came from empty air.

Reluctantly, she cancelled the camouflage and
then the armor configuration and watched the ensem-
ble retract to its uniform mode. Still grinning, she
shrugged her shoulders to resettle the jerkin, then
decided to loop the cap through the belt since she
was indoors. She used her levitation to arrange her
cascade of shoulder-length dreadlocks, then executed
a dancer's spin cycle to test her freedom of motion.
Satisfied, she nodded to her reflection and strode out
the hatch to the nearby telebooth.

She stepped in and punched 1401 into the keyboard. Angela checked that the receiving booth was
clear, and Dani found herself looking out at the
double pocket hatch to the High Lounge across the
passageway. She checked her wristpad and saw that
she was twenty seconds early. Close enough. She
took a deep breath, straightened her shoulders, and
marched ahead.

The hatch panels whisked into the bulkheads and
she strode in. The deck stepped down from the hatch
platform to the richly carpeted floor, and there stood
Lord Orion at loose attention, himself in full dress
and looking as majestically commanding as his title
would presume. Lady Alpha, her spectacular beauty

deeply enriched by the form-fitting uniform, stood at his left shoulder. Senior Commanders Kodiak and Cobra were stationed behind them to the left and right. On the huge monitor at the far bulkhead were the images of Lord Commander Binary and Senior Commander Mercury, transmitted from Gaea.

Every bit of her self-confidence fluttered away. She was in the presence of legends.

She stamped to rigid attention. "Corpsman Dragonfly, commanding star freighter *Phasmida*, reporting as ordered, *sir!*" Her fist slapped to the Corps crest below her collarbone and her wide eyes focused on a spot between the Anson brothers on the screen.

All six of the commanders came to attention and Orion sharply returned her salute. "Stand easy, Corpsman. I think I'm the one who should be saluting you. Thanks to you, we still have a planet to settle."

She tried to relax and failed miserably. "I-I had a ton of help, sir."

"Which you trained." He smiled and beckoned her forward. "Please relax, Dani. We'd like to hear the story in your own words, but this isn't an inquest by any means."

Alpha gave her a dazzling grin and reached out a reassuring hand to touch her arm. "Especially since we've heard what happens when you get mad."

Dani giggled self-consciously and looked around at each of the others. Kalanev nodded deeply, a slight smile on his thin lips and a gleam of respect in his eyes. Connors met her gaze with a huge grin. On the monitor, Arden had a look of unabashed pride for her, and Jake, her immediate superior, placed his open palm on his Corps crest in a salute of pure respect. She bit her lip and looked away, trembling.

Jander turned his head and addressed the empty air. "Refreshments." A table dropped from the overhead to the center of the room, and Richard Ford and Gabriel Vargas popped in with trays laden with fruit drinks, ice, spirit decanters and finger food. The teleporters placed their burdens on the table and Vargas vanished. Ford, a fellow African American, caught Dani's eye and gave her a fierce grin and a hugely emphatic fist pump before he disappeared. It sent chills up her spine.

Jander was at the table. "I hear you have a taste for raspberry lemonade on ice with, shall we say, a dash of vodka. We aim to please." He built the tall glass and she accepted it gratefully. "You know how the High Lounge works? See how the soft wall contours upward? Just throw yourself at it and it'll conform to you." He demonstrated by sinking into the portside wall with an iced coffee and Kahlua. Vickie joined him there with a goblet of Chardonnay and a presenter's wrist flip inviting Dani to take the starboard side. She eased herself in and felt the tension flood from her muscles as the nanotech-controlled gel under the soft fabric molded itself to her body.

Pavel joined her further forward with spiked iced tea, and Connors, whose mass almost put him through the cushioning cells to the deck, settled in across from them with a huge stein of dark beer. Small circular tables descended from the overhead within reach of each of them. On the monitor, the Ansons were shown dropping into comfortable chairs with tall glasses in the arm rests.

"Now." Orion returned to business. "We'd like to hear your story in your own words. I'll follow along in your mind if that's okay..." Of course it was! "... but let's keep it verbal for your bosses on Gaea. Take your time and be thorough, please."

Vickie gave her an encouraging smile and a serene nod. "We want to hear everything."

And so, Dani talked. She started with her ship's maiden voyage from Gaea and the training of her passengers for emergencies, continued with delivering her cargo and whipping the Arcadian fighting force into shape, and ended with her gestalt's epic battle. She was frequently interrupted by questions and occasional clarifying probes by Vickie or Arden or the veteran warrior Pavel. Two hours and a few breaks for refills later, hoarse from talking and dizzy from concentration, she finally wandered to a stop and sat in the silence of exhaustion.

It was a while before Orion spoke. "I think that about covers it. Thank you, Dani, for a splendid narrative. I can tell you that everything you've said is corroborated by the others we've debriefed, and if anything you've been modest about your accomplishments. The entire Corps can learn from this."

She ducked her head at the praise, blinking the moisture from her eyes.

Vickie smiled softly. "First you channeled your exquisite artistry into effective coaching, and now you've transformed your teaching skills into proficient command. That takes a really special kind of adaptive genius."

Dani's lips quivered as she tried to smile.

Steele nodded deeply. "More than that, you reminded them of who we are, or who we're supposed to be. All of us went through boot camp and our core values were vigorously instilled. But most Corpsmen are specialists, and the concept of teamwork can be overlooked. Your command style brought those values back to us."

Dani could only stare at the floor.

"I'll second that," Jake Anson said quietly over the light years. "We're looking forward to having you back so we can pick your brains some more. You, my sister, are truly a treasure."

That did it. She couldn't help herself. The intensity, the exhaustion, the violent memories, the relief of ridding herself of all her fears and burdens, was too much. She gave a shuddering sob and burst into tears.

It was Denny, the big, strong teddy bear, who took her in his arms and helped her to let it go. Vickie, the consummate psychologist, surrounded her mind with a soothing warmth and comfort that eased the tension and brought her tenderly back to confidence.

She disengaged herself from Denny's gentle embrace and swiped at her face with the back of her hand. "I'm sorry...."

Steele handed her a linen napkin. "For what? There's nobody here who hasn't had that kind of moment. The human psyche wasn't designed to take this stuff lightly."

"I guess." She dabbed at her reddened eyes and managed a smile.

"For now," he continued, "you have the run of the ship until your freighter is repaired, then Jake and Arden can have the three of you back for further assignment. Though I doubt you'll be driving a truck much longer."

Arden from the monitor tapped his temple. "We're building some much more aggressive rides that'll need top-notch commanders. And you, dear lady, are definitely at the top of the list."

Jander nodded. "Agreed. The Omega Corps is soon to become a galactic power, and we'll need representatives of your caliber. So, get some rest – you'll be as harassed as the rest of us before long."

She grinned, spirits restored. "Believe it or not, I'm looking forward to it."

CHAPTER 16

Captain Hanash stepped into the austere office of the Head of Ertain, six-fingered hands balled together at his belly in the Ertainian form of attention. The Head sat motionless in his heavy chair behind the stark hexagonal table that was his desk. A computer terminal, archaic by Confederation or Gaean standards, took up the front angle of the table surrounded by stacks of printed reports.

The only other furnishings in the garage-sized space were a few wooden bin cabinets and a hodge-podge of pirated trophies on the walls and in corners. There were no windows that might permit an outside threat.

Nothing of a personal nature was visible. The Head was an absolute dictator who cared nothing for family, and every acquaintance was beneath him and by culture consigned to subservience. No one was even allowed to sit in his office.

The Head had aged, Hanash thought, ten years in six weeks. Not to wonder, since not only had almost six hundred ships and forty thousand men been lost from his orders, but the entire Plan, one hundred years of meticulous dictatorial effort under three

Heads in succession, had been negated in a cosmic instant.

The Head looked up slowly, his tired eyes none-theless snapping with power. "Report."

"The Alternate Plan has been put into effect, Your Supremacy. Four of the six rem– er, fleets have been scattered...."

"Remaining fleets, you were about to say?" The Head smiled grimly. "There is no need to mince words, Hanash. I am well aware of the facts." His use of his aide's single name with no title or rank would have been an insult from anyone else. From him, it was confirmation of his dominance.

"Forgive me, Your Supremacy. The First, Sixth, Seventh and Ninth Fleets have been broken up into their squadrons of six and are searching unmapped areas for advanced planets. Commerce raiding has ceased for now."

"Forever, Hanash. The Plan was ruined when the admirals let those two fugitives, the giant and the ghost, escape them on the planet of the black colos-sus. My only hope is to gain enough strength to con-quer the Confederation by force before they find us and try to steal our destiny. Now that our physical form is known the hope of economic takeover is lost to us." He smiled again, a sneer of absolute power that belied his words. "We must face the facts, Hanash."

The captain broke his stone-faced pose and dropped his hands to his waist. "But all that time, Your Supremacy, all our efforts...."

"Were wasted, Hanash. Our most recent intelligence has revealed the existence of some Omega Corps, from a race so far above ours that we are mice by comparison and led by a supernatural being called Orion. Our only hope is to appropriate the ships and the manpower to protect the Twin Planets from one ship and a few hundred men. Do you think we can do that easily, Hanash?"

"Of course, Your Supremacy!" The Head's gentle tone frightened him, but the habit of stroking his ego remained in full force.

"I'm glad you think so, very, very glad. Because that means my position as Head is secure. No one with your brains could possibly mount a successful coup."

Hanash's lemon yellow face paled to flaxen. "Y-Your Supremacy! I-I would never – "

"Silence!"

Hanash returned to attention and froze, eyes down, thin lips quivering.

The Head rolled back in his chair. "I did not gain my station by being stupid. I know you have pandered the information you are privy to as my aide. You have been telling people that I have discarded the Plan too soon, that I am getting careless with our heritage, too cautious with age. The only reason you are still alive, and them too, is that you spoke those thoughts in a pharsch house and you were so drunk on Khadditcz that none of them were sober enough to believe it."

He pushed forward and laid his hands flat on the desk. "We are fighting *gods*, Hanash, ghosts and wizards and phantoms that can disappear at will, men who can absorb lasers and females who can bend tigers to their whim – *tigers!*" Despite his anger, the fur that ran the length of his spine bristled as the atavistic fear of felines welled up within him, threatening to affect his control. "Now do you understand, perhaps, what we are up against? Or perhaps you would like to take an excursion to that planet and see for yourself?"

The captain's own fur stood on end. Two scouting expeditions had been sent to the planet of the black colossus and all had disappeared without a trace. His jaw jerked, but nothing came out. He could only quiver his head side to side in the negative.

The Head smiled, a terrible grimace without humor, and settled back in his chair. He had no intention of eliminating the flaccid Hanash over a few drunken words. Reinforcing his dominance would be enough. "Continue with your report, Hanash."

The captain swallowed, and again. "The c-captives are working on improving our ships, although they are as usual very s-slow." He paused for a deep breath to calm himself. "They are being built with stronger armament and screen generators and lesser drive potential, as ordered, and they will reinforce the Home Fleet. The Third and Fourth Fleets are in a cordon around the system."

"Conscription?"

"Every male beyond puberty is armed and in training. There is a guard for every ten slaves and a double complement of weapons crew for every Home Fleet unit."

"My, Hanash, you really are nervous. You fear the captives will revolt, now that we have had a set-back? I expected more intelligent mobilization plans from you. Halve the guard and put the cuts in the factories. 'Every man armed' is worthless if there are no ships to support them."

"As you say, Your Supremacy."

'Yes, Hanash, as I say. Do not ever try to presume on your position again, Hanash. Do not ever forget that there is only one Head, just one, and he is the power supreme. Dismissed!"

Hanash bowed almost to his knees and back-pedaled out of the office with his fists buried in his belly. The Head glared at him until the doors swept closed, then rubbed his tired eyes.

He would have felt much worse had he known that the *Angel* was already there, orbiting undetectable almost over his office – and that an invisible presence was watching his every move.

STEELE FINISHED THE ONLINE REVIEW of the Ertainian system and propped his feet up on his massive half-moon desk to reflect on it. First of all, Ertain had been right where he'd said it was – a fact that earned him plenty of extra sugar from Vickie, whose championing of him with Admiral Ganazan had made the ship's scuttlebutt richer for weeks.

They had also been partly right about the composition of the star system. Liev was indeed closer to the sun, but only sometimes. Ertain was actually a satellite, a moon, of huge and heavy Liev, the third planet of the five orbiting an orange star the natives called an unpronounceably slushy four syllables. Life was birthed and had grown to intelligence on Ertain somewhat sooner than on the gigantic mother planet.

When the Ertainians reached the threshold of interplanetary travel some six thousand years before, it was only natural that they would journey first to their neighbor, larger than Neptune, which dominated their sky. There they had found a hot, swampy expanse of volcanic land teeming with gigantic reptiles and tank tough insects, with a thick atmosphere rich in oxygen and sulfur. On a high plateau stretching farther than the entire diameter of Ertain a few hardy pioneers had settled and built their towns, surrounding themselves with stone walls forty feet high and twenty thick to keep out the ferocious lizards.

The Great War had isolated them, driving them backward through time until they were on more even terms with their cold-blooded neighbors. Now, two hundred or more generations after the first colony, no more than a few million lost souls glowered through the murky depths of that ready-made hell.

Ertain, in contrast, was a lovely planet of rich vegetation and vigorous life, speeding around Liev in a tight ellipse that kept day and night short but relatively even. The Great War had found the dominant species six billion strong, with colonies among the nearer stars and the pride of a war of extermination against the hated and feared felids found in another system.

The leader of the near-mythical bloodbath had returned in triumph and demanded the desk of the Head as his reward. His presumption caused the Great War that threw the Ertainians even farther back than the Lievans, doomed their highly dependent stellar colonies, and raised unfathomable scars on the few survivors. It stunted them physically and mentally, permanently poisoning their genes with the strong competitive instincts that had kept those few survivors alive.

The "Way of Power" – domination – was the virtue most highly cherished. The man with the greatest Way of Power was of necessity the Head; he was the only one of his generation able to reach and hold that position. As he was demonstrably the strongest his every word was law; his domination accepted without question. In every generation there was only *one* Head, from the violent political purge of his ascension to the renewed scramble after his death.

That would be the Omega Corps' point of attack.

Steele dropped his feet to the floor, rose and crossed the width of his office, past the small conference table and through the lounge to a hatch next to the couch. He passed through the pocket door into Vickie's place of business, a suite with the same layout but with a much softer and more harmonious decor.

The psychologist's serene headquarters had been taken over temporarily by Janus and his entourage. Janus, Mark Norwich, was unique in the Corps; Steele had labeled his variant ability "dyadic". He was able to split his ego into two parts. Half stayed with the Body, maintaining life and vitality. The other half existed as a free-roving, free-thinking Spirit, clairvoyant and clairaudient, able to go anywhere and undetectable by any but telepathic means. The two entities were mutually telepathic to vast but as yet unmeasured distances, and were in constant and unbreakable rapport.

That would make Janus the perfect spy except for one major drawback: when Janus split his ego, he also split his intellect. Instead of one highly intelligent variant, Steele had a couple of half-wits – one of whom was patently uncontrollable.

Controlling that free Spirit was the job of the Austrian telepath and psychologist, Gustav Kamerun. As good as the team was, they had not had enough practice prior to the *Angel*'s maiden voyage from Gaea and were left behind. But because of his need for an undetectable spy Steele had ordered the pair to travel to Arcadia aboard *Phasmida* to join the *Angel*'s company. With them came the songbirds for the park, and Feliks Radschck's modified tablicy discs that were now installed in the *Angel*'s complement of small craft.

Janus and his sweating Mentor were the authors of the intelligence report Steele had just read.

Also in the office was Wade Gayland, called the Mimic. His ability, too, was nearly unique among the Corpsmen. The *Angel*'s only multimorph was able to rearrange his body cells into whatever configuration he chose. He had masqueraded as the blue-skinned "Reed" on Dephlet; now he was lounging in one of Vickie's comfortable chairs while in rapport with Mentor, molding his features into those of the Head.

"I don't know what good this will do," Wade said when he saw Jander. His vocal cords already produced an exact replica of the Head's harsh voice and made speaking English difficult. "If I bring myself down to five feet I'll be too fat."

"You're a model, not an actor," Steele informed him. "I want you to assist while we transmute a few other folks."

"That I can do," the multimorph grinned.

Steele left the office, strode to the zero gravity tube in the passageway outside and shoved himself downward toward the ninth level. It felt good to be away from Dephlet and back in the *Angel*, without having to worry about a slip into a Gaean language or the disconcerting use of the uncanny powers his people so casually threw about. The less social exposure the inexperienced Corpsmen had, the better. That limited the danger to Spart, who had inadvertently broken the First Law by landing on Gaea to investigate the ultra-high-tech energies emitted by the ancient mechanism that activated the Gaeans' variant talents.

It also protected the general run of Gaeans. The few people who knew the Omega Corps hailed from Earth did not include the people of Earth — and the last thing they needed was a stampede of the curious to the Sol system. Eventually, with the development of Arcadia as their home base, those fears would fade and the Corpsmen would be able to roam freely.

He stopped his downward plunge with the hand-bar over the exit to the ninth deck and swung out into the passageway, then proceeded into the sickbay. He found Terry Kirkland in her cluttered private office. "Who'd you find, Doc?"

Terry grimaced; she took her profession too seriously to be called "Doc". "I've found three ghosts who might do; Fantasma, Wildflower and Bella."

Steele nodded as he brought the three women to mind. They had the high cheekbones and rounded chins, the long straight noses and broad foreheads under thick dark hair that would make the changeover relatively simple. More important, they were each possessed of an ego and individualism that would bring them through the identity change unscathed. "Very good. I'll talk to them individually, then send them to you for the technical briefing if they agree. I certainly don't want to order them to do this."

"I should hope not," the doctor sniffed. "I'm not sure I want to do it, either. Plastic surgery isn't my line – especially turning three women into one man."

"Just the face, Doctor. The rest they can keep." He winked with a grin and headed back to his office.

Hortensia Gutièrrez, the tiny Mexican ghost called Fantasma, was the first to agree, enthusiastically. The Kumeyaay tribeswoman had dragged herself out of the Baja and through to an engineering degree and still managed to retain a strong need to prove herself. Jander's offer was accepted with delight.

Next to agree was Janet Flowers, called Wildflower, a Cherokee from Oklahoma. An Army veteran who had made the height requirement by a quarter inch, and a martial arts devotee, she was an expert shot with everything from the bow to the rifle to the *Angel*'s primary armament. In combat she had the habit of announcing every hit with an ear-splitting, "*Next!*"

Medina Hussein was Iranian by birth and Californian by choice. She had worked her way to a geology degree with her skill as an exotic dancer – the traditional kind – thus her code name, Bella. Like the other two, she had battled sexist attitudes all her young life; she was more than happy to join in a scheme to drive a male dominant society to total insanity.

That misogyny was another product of the Great War. Because of atomic poisoning of the gene pool three out of four baby girls were born dead, or hideously deformed and ruthlessly put to death. Another aspect of the Way of Power was how many women a man could gain and hold. The Head and other high-ranking officials had a harem; the rank and file had a community female who was almost always pregnant. The only good thing about the system was that it had kept their population down to a reasonable level; otherwise, the Ertainians would have destroyed themselves in war at least once more.

The transmutational operation was set up in the largest operating theater in sickbay. In addition to Dr. Kirkland and her model, Gayland, the team that would do the primary work included three eidetics who would follow the operation in detail. Their perfect memories, plus Angela, would provide the information for the reversal process once the campaign was over. Several transmutators were also there to be prepared for other schemes. Each was linked by a telepath to Vickie, whose powerful mind would follow every shifting cell.

Wildflower was the first to go under the mental knife. Terry froze Janet's nervous system to hold her still, then started by altering the vocal cords. Twenty very carefully spent minutes later she reconnected the woman's body to her brain. "Let's try the voice, Jan."

"What do you want me to... Holy shit, is that me?" The former soldier's normally melodic voice had been replaced by a harsh tenor.

"That's you," Wade assured her – in exactly the same voice.

"Any pain, stiffness?" Terry asked.

"Not a bit," was the reply. "It feels the same as my old set, only… it vibrates more."

"Slower," Wade corrected. "Same as our species, an Ertainian male's voice is lower on the vibratory scale. She's normal, Terry."

"That's not the word I'd use," the doctor retorted, and the operation resumed.

By the time Janet's face, arms and upper torso were the Head's the ship was on the night shift.

She got shakily to her feet and walked to a mirror, and stared fascinated. She was a smaller version of the Mimic, perfect in every detail. "My hair…."

Terry chuckled – the ghost's knee-length mane was her most cherished possession. "It's still there. See the extra breadth of the shoulders?"

"And the extra thickness of the neck, and the streak of fur that runs all the way down your back," Wade added. "Terry followed my mimicking process exactly. There is no getting something for nothing. I can rearrange my cells, but I can't gain or lose weight. So, we pulled your hair inside and made it into a layer of protein under the skin, enlarging your shoulders, shortening the hair and blending your eyebrows into the hairline for the Head's fuzzy rug. The skin color was tougher; you'll find your, uh, private portions to be bone-white, completely drained of pigment."

Janet stared at herself dubiously, ran her now gnarled hands over where her breasts used to be, then triggered her spectrality. Every face in the room spread into a slow, tight smile. There, shimmering eerily even in the glaring light of the operating room, stood one of the three who would haunt the Head with his own ghost.

CHAPTER 17

Orion stepped from the Bridge passageway into Vickie's office and found Kamerun, eyes half closed, in rapport with the Spirit through the dozing Body of Janus. He aroused the telepath with a gentle pressure on the shoulder.

"Hi, Gus. Could you bring the Spirit back? I have something to show you both."

"Yes, sir." Gustav closed his eyes and, keeping one mental hand on the Spirit's leash, prodded the dormant Body awake. The aroused physical brain automatically reached out to the conscious, immaterial mind and drew the romping puppy that was the Spirit back to the Body. Seconds later Mark Norwich sat up on the couch and shook his head. When he reopened his eyes, they were filled with above-average intelligence.

"I'm back," he sighed. He preferred to think of Mark Norwich and Janus as two – or three – different people. "You wanted to show me something?"

"I need your opinion." He closed the passageway entrance in front of Vickie's antique rolltop desk and sidestepped to rap on the connecting hatch to his own office. The pocket door whisked open and Vickie entered, followed by three Heads, identically dressed in the original's uniform.

Gustav stared wide-eyed. "Marvelous," the psychologist breathed.

Janus nodded and rose, peering closely at the three ghosts. They fidgeted under his scrutiny, all the while trying to stay in arrogant character. "If the Spirit's memory serves me, I have to agree. Terry did a marvelous job."

Gustav also rose to stare. "The only problem I can foresee is one of psychology. If they're to act like the Head, we should get a more thorough psychological profile."

"But we can't do that through the Spirit," Vickie said, "and it's too risky to drop someone like you down there. You know better than I do that the Palace is crawling with guards. Besides, the whole point is that they *not* act like the real Head."

"For the most part, yes, but I'd think we'd at least want to capture some of his speech patterns. For one thing, his most frequently asked question is, 'What is going on here?' Sprinkling a few such catch phrases into their performances could enhance the illusion."

"That's a very good suggestion, Gustav. See what you two can gather up and we'll add them to the scripts."

"Speaking of gathering," Norwich cut in, "I think I've found your kicker."

Jander raised an eyebrow, then turned to the ghosts. "That's all for now, ladies. Go show off." They grinned in unison, an evil sight in their current form, and floated through the overhead toward the recreation area. "What have you got?"

"The Head is to review the Elite Guard – not the Palace Guard, but the larger body of troops they're chosen from. Here we have a thousand of the finest troops from all over the planet, packed shoulder to shoulder into an open-air stadium without a care in the world. I think if we can toss them around a bit, we'd give their top command nightmares."

"Let me see." Steele studied the layout recorded in Janus's mind, using mental search techniques learned from Vickie to untangle the Spirit's disjointed recollections. "That's it, then," he said. "Thank you, Mark."

He stepped to Vickie's rolltop desk and tapped a key. "Angela, locate Kodiak, Cobra, Hermes, Clarion and Panda, and request they come to my office immediately. Thank you." Angela acknowledged with two beeps.

Richard Ford took him at his word. Through the open connecting hatch they saw the teleporter appear before Steele had time to turn away. He brought his embryonic goatee into the other room.

Clarion nearly landed on his heels; David Malloye was also a teleporter. He had an almost unique distinction: in his days as an Israeli agent before joining the Corps he had come into face-to-face combat with the erstwhile Soviet agent, Pavel Kalanev, and survived.

His former enemy was next to arrive from his office down the passageway, followed by Denny from Engineering on the first deck.

Last to appear was the massive two hundred centimeters and one hundred fifty kilograms of Panomar Singh, the turbaned and bearded scion of a long line of Sikh warriors. Like Kalanev, Malloye and other older Corpsmen, the former weightlifter and security guard had had decades skimmed off his physiological age by the Corps medical staff after he was activated. There was a tigerish gleam in the telekinetic's eyes; he had been impatient to prove his mettle.

"Pavel, link with Janus and pass on the tactical view. Here's what I need you to do, and I guarantee you're not going to like it...."

THE OFFICERS STOOD ON the reviewing stage and glared with professional disapproval at the close-packed soldiers below. Between the ranks stamped the squad leaders, roaring equal parts command and rebuke, making certain that every piece of equipment from cross-strapped maroon tunic to laser rifle was mint perfect. The Head himself would arrive to review them in twenty minutes.

The pulse machine rifle was another combination of Jander Steele's brilliance in behavioral physics and Denny Connors' mechanical genius. Developed after the smaller pulse pistol, in general outline it looked a bit like an M-4 assault rifle complete with accessory mounts. The area before the trigger was enlarged to hold a magazine of eighteen power batteries, good for spurting a rolling total of nine hundred half-centimeter spheres of coherent force with the recoil of a pellet gun. The stock held a maze of microelectronics to create and propel the spheres.

Denny himself materialized with one in each nanosteel-gloved hand. He was teleported to the center of the stage, his gigantic frame popping into view just behind the senior officers standing near the edge of the platform. Two quick bursts from his terrible weapons and his field of fire was clear to the troops below.

Ford and Malloye flashed into being behind him, cleared the rest of the stage, then dashed into the wings, blasting down junior officers and technical personnel. Then they teleported under their own power to the front corners of the stands and opened fire on the already melting Elite Guard.

High in the grandstands lining either side of the square parade ground were Kalanev and Singh, flanking the body, their rattling weapons mowing down those who broke for cover. They worked from the edges in, trapping the long rows of troops between them.

Back and forth, the five destroyers waved their PMRs in ever-deepening arcs, tearing the Elite Guard into bloody spume and churning the grounds into boiling red dust. The chattering weapons and their screaming victims blended together, rocking the stadium with the sounds as well as the sights of total massacre. The Elite Guard, one thousand of the finest and bravest troops in all of Ertain, broke and ran, screaming, quaking, collapsing, bleeding, falling, dying before five men with spitting roaring butchering tearing mutilating death in their hands.

The few hundred who were able scrambled in mad panic for the faraway exit, jamming between the mighty pillars that had looked so handsome and martial a few moments before. Ford and Malloye executed the second phase, disappearing from the stage roof and rematerializing beside Kalanev and Singh, teleporting the two to the uppermost seats, then flashing themselves to the tops of those two pillars. With Connors behind and the teleporters above them, the Elite Guard died to a man. Not one of them fired a shot.

Meanwhile, Kalanev and Singh switched their PMRs from automatic to triple tap and began picking off the armed men in the streets below: police, soldiers, guards, anyone with a uniform and a gun. With the laser-optic sights reverse engineered from the Ertainians' own weapons, Pavel of the eagle eye was scoring hits as far as five kilometers away, yet his chilling killer's grin was absent. He went about his business with cold and methodical certainty, yet he had not the satisfaction of a man with a mission that he had shown in other battles.

Abruptly a shimmering lance of silver-red light blazed from a watchtower two kilometers away, barely missing his weapon and searing his neck below the chin – one of the few places not protected by the microtech-reinforced nanosteel fabric that covered the rest of his body.

Pavel spotted the sniper and smiled. He switched out his heavy battery pack with practiced speed, thumbed the PMR back to rapid fire and squeezed the trigger, moving the muzzle in a slow downward slant. The powerful spheres, which could punch through a centimeter of tungsten at that distance, cut through the stone tower with ease. The entire upper structure slid away and crumbled to the street, carrying its sniper with it. Pavel couched his rifle and nodded in satisfaction, then tapped his wristpad for his return to the ship.

Denny stared at the carnage before him, sickened to the soul. He was all for destroying these enemies of civilization, but this... this was stark, cold-blooded murder, the slaughter of intelligent beings who did not have the slightest chance of fighting back. He turned away, his nostrils filled with the rank odor of blood and feces and his shoulders slumped with the weight of hundreds. Mouth tight, he raised his eyes to the empty sky, breathing deeply to clear his nerves.

The image of the Head, four meters tall, glared down at him from the rear of the stage.

Denny tucked one of his PMRs under his left arm and trained the other rifle on the portrait. The spheres arched up, over and down. He studied the effect, and his jaw loosened. As Pavel had before him, he nodded once, then triggered his return to the *Angel*. On the huge portrait of the Head of Ertain, he had etched the horseshoe symbol of the Omega Corps.

He was the last to return to the ship. Pavel, who had traveled to the surface via one of the cargo teleporters below, was just pulling himself out of the aggie tube on the Bridge deck. Steele took his battle report out of his brain, then looked at the blistered skin on his neck. "You'd better go down to sickbay and get that checked."

Pavel shrugged and flexed his jaw. "It is nothing, Captain. A slight burn."

"A wound is a wound, tato. You know Chloe will remove the rest of your skin if you don't let her see it."

Pavel made a depreciating gesture, but his eyes turned soft. "Tato" meant "papa" in Ukrainian. It was the first time Steele had ever touched on that aspect of their relationship, and it sent a flush of warmth through him.

Not that he would ever admit it. "As you say, Captain." He inclined his head with a half-smile, then moved to the telebooth and tapped the keyboard to direct its energies to the ninth level.

Jander, who saw the change that one word had wrought, felt compelled to relieve the mood. "Tell her I said to give you a lollipop."

CHAPTER 18

Jander was half reclined in his office chair with his arms folded, staring at nothing, when the door chimed. He swiveled and set his clasped hands on his half-moon desk. "In."

Richard Ford poked his head around the edge of the pocket hatch. "Talk a minute, boss?"

"Of course, Richard." Steele rose and led his adjutant to his left, beyond the small conference table to a pair of contoured leather chairs facing the sofa on the far bulkhead.

Richard settled himself and slumped forward, staring at his hands. It was a long moment before he spoke.

"Jander, that was... messed up."

"I know." Steele shifted in his chair and rubbed an elbow. "But it was necessary."

"Was it, really? And even if it was, why me? I became a fighter from necessity, not for a profession. Sending Pavel, and David and Panda, I can understand. But Denny and me? It *hurt*, boss!"

"It bothered Pavel, too." Richard met his eyes, and Jander nodded. "Fact. I ordered him to do something he thought was behind him. I made him relive his ugly days as an assassin – and you know him well enough to know he hated himself then. And as Panomar Singh's first fight as a Corpsman it was a miserable flop. But it was necessary."

"How? For the luvva Mike, how can cold-blooded murder be necessary?"

Jander took a deep breath and released it slowly, holding the silence until Richard dropped his accusing eyes. When he spoke, it was with a calmness he did not feel.

"If a man kills another and is sent to the electric chair unarmed, is that murder?" He raised his hand as Richard made to speak. "I know, maybe the analogy doesn't strictly apply. The Elite Guard may have had nothing to do with the pirate activities unless you count guilt by association. But they served as an example, an effigy. It told the whole planet that the Omega Corps was knocking on the door.

"I chose this course because I wanted to announce our presence with a bang, with a psychological coup that would touch everyone. The Elite Guard came from every corner of every province, representing the finest Ertain has to offer. That is the first point: we destroyed the pick of the litter with five men and six guns.

"The second is that most of those men certainly had a family – or in Ertainian society, a gens – who will feel their loss. That is perhaps the cruelest kind of warfare, but it is one of the most effective. In every corner of Ertain the seeds of doubt have been sown.

There are tens of thousands throughout the planet and the fleets who will trust the policies of their government a little less than they did earlier this afternoon.

"The third is the impact on the ruling class itself, those who depended on the Elite Guard for protection and safety. In only a few minutes their security blanket was brutally torn away from them. They can't help but feel even more vulnerable now than they did after Arcadia."

Richard had relaxed a bit as he absorbed Jander's measured words. "Well, okay, I guess I can understand all that. But I still don't know why you used me."

"Because you're Black," Steele said bluntly. "And I used Denny because he's huge. That's why I required you to risk going down there with no head covering. You're both well-known standouts to the Ertainians. I felt it necessary to impress upon them that the Nemeses of Arcadia have caught up with them. Your color and Denny's size, Pavel's sharklike efficiency and David's teleporting, all are clear signs that it is the Omega Corps, the ones the Head himself has described as gods, who are at work here. And with the addition of Panomar, with his impressive size, red turban and heavy black beard, we have reminded them that what they have seen so far is but a few of our number.

"It was no coincidence that you all ended up in plain sight of the surveillance cameras and the populace, and that Denny could be seen and recorded in all his intimidating proportions in surroundings which would set off his relative size. I wanted you to be seen."

He sighed and massaged his neck with both hands. "I know how it felt, believe me. Remember, I myself was the cause of the deaths of several thousand on Arcadia. Even though it was the Ertainian high command that ordered that massacre, it was my fire-and-brimstone light show that gave them reason to do it. I regret that my gesture of mercy backfired, but I don't regret that it was better them than us. My demonstration was to scare them into leaving Arcadia alone, and except for a couple of raids it worked. And today's action was for the same reason, to make them fear us and, hopefully, shorten the war."

Richard leaned forward and propped his elbows on his thighs, rubbing his hands over his face as if to wash it. He raised his eyes with a shaky breath, then resumed staring at his hands.

"Okay, yeah. I think I know you pretty well by now, being your adjutant and all..."

"And friend," Jander interjected.

Richard gave him a fleeting smile. "And brother, yeah. And I know you never do anything without a hundred reasons. But..." He clasped his accusing hands and squeezed until the knuckles paled. "But don't ask me to do it again, hey?" He looked up and met Jander's eyes, pleading in every line of his drawn face.

Steele held his gaze for a moment, the slowly shook his head. "I can't promise you that," he said softly. "Nor can I take the time to explain my reasoning every time I give an order. You must assume good reasons exist whether you know them or not, and I must be able to trust that you will do as I require. While I encourage debate in strategy meetings, once I make a decision the Omega Corps ceases to be a democracy."

Richard lowered his head with a flicker of eyelids. "Yes, sir. Of course."

Jander drummed his fingers on his desk to refocus the mood. "That being said, you can always ask my reasoning after the fact if it'll help you to cope with the results. In this case, it's fairly simple. The few thousand lives that will be taken in our war of nerves are nothing compared to the hundreds of thousands, perhaps millions, who would die in a Confederation fleet attack. We must winnow the few for the ultimate salvation of the many, both friend and foe.

"I am not one to throw my weight around, you know that. I, we, are not fighting this war for our own gain, but because we are best equipped to fight it. The ultimate result of our efforts will be justice at minimum cost. That, and only that, is my goal."

Richard met his eyes again and slowly nodded in understanding, then added a tentative smile. "Yeah, if nothing else I know your goals – and if I didn't agree with them I wouldn't be here."

"None of you would be. Remember that the next

time you think of someone like Pavel. Under that icy exterior he's a compassionate man, just like you are. He may have molten steel for blood, but it's pumped by a heart like anybody else's." He smiled in return. "Why the goatee?"

"Cielo likes her man hairy." He grinned soberly, then stood to go. "I'll be on call, boss."

"Thank you, Richard. And don't forget, Vickie's right next door if you feel the need to talk it out."

Richard nodded. "Done there, been that. She helped me after Arcadia, or I'd still be lying awake nights." He came briefly to attention, then waved a hand at the sensor to open the hatch.

Jander watched the man leave, then returned to his desk and resumed the position he had held before, slouched in his chair with his arms folded, staring at nothing.

CHAPTER 19

The Head glared at his quaking aide in silence, feeling more than a little weak himself. If the attack had taken place a half hour later they both would have been among the first victims. "All of them?"

"Every man, Your Supremacy," Hanash said. "The weapons were so powerful that even non-mortal wounds proved fatal, from the sheer shock of impact. But fewer than ten percent died of such wounds. The rest were literally torn apart." He shifted his feet. "And not one projectile has been found."

"Verdict?"

"That the weapons used were of the same type as those turned against us on the planet of the black colossus. And the surveillance record confirms it. One of the attackers was probably the giant we chased for so long, another was the dark-skinned phantom. It is suspected that one or both of the light-skinned men were also from that planet. The big brown one with the facial hair and red helmet was unknown."

"So, they've caught up with us." The Head leaned back and rubbed his temples. "If we just had a little more time, another few months..."

"What good would it do?" Hanash whined dully. "There is no defense against people who disappear at will."

The Head raised his head and locked eyes with the captain. Ten seconds, twenty, he held that Medusa stare, until Hanash was forced to drop his eyes.

"We are not giving up, Hanash," he said quietly. "They can be killed. It is known that the dark man was severely wounded before; it takes only one well-placed bolt or bullet to make them die, just like you and me. They beat us before, yes, but that was when we were just a few thousand. Now we are billions, and we are strong."

He rose, ivory-faced yet calm. "Arm every man, every boy over ten, even the females. For the first Ertainian or Lievan to positively kill a member of the Omega Corps I will have a place at my side as my personal bodyguard – be he man, child or female. For any man, child or female who fails to shoot or fall at the appearance of a member of the Omega Corps there will be the severest punishment." He sat again, drained. "The entire system is hereafter on defense alert. See to it."

Hanash bowed vacantly at the dismissal, then turned to leave.

"Hanash!" the Head roared. "Who am I?

The Captain spun back and jerked to attention, pressing his fists into his belly. His fur stood on end as he realized he had made a lethal blunder: he had turned his back on the Head.

Terrified, Hanash spoke by rote. "There is only one Head, and you are he, and he is the power supreme!"

The Head glared at him. "You may be my confidential aide, but if you think you're irreplaceable you are sadly mistaken. One more hint of insubordination and you will be retired, permanently! Go!"

Hanash bowed again, fists in his gut, and remained doubled over until he had backed well beyond the door.

STEELE SAT IN HIS OFFICE behind his desk, waiting for Tsin Li-san to complete the connection. When Nil Spart, casually dressed for once, appeared on his center monitor, he greeted him with a smile. "Good evening, Admiral."

"Fleet Admiral, if you please, and it's the middle of the night here." He noticed that Orion, like himself, was sitting in front of a display case filled with books, trophies and memorabilia. He was warmed by the friendly atmosphere of the meeting. "How goes the battle?"

"Well enough. We've made the opening move."

Spart waited for him to continue, then pursed his lips as he realized that Orion would say no more. "Hm. Well, Arani has learnt a few things that might interest you. There was indeed a portly passenger on board the ship with Hamar – the original Hamar – and there was also a reclusive Dwatan with his tail amputated. Does that suggest anything to you?"

"An Ertainian in a fur coat – hiding in the skin of a species he loathes. Perfect camouflage."

Spart bowed his head. "Perfect deduction. That individual was a second-class passenger named TuŜyæ et cetera, and continued on to D'Wech!tiŜ, a Dwatan planet, where he disappeared. The original Hamar debarked on Larkant, carrying the name Zanga Silten."

"That sounds very Lievan. Ertainians and Lievans have a single name preceded by an occupational title, but they gave him two to mimic the Sabarian style. How puckishly imaginative that they used real names. Dead end, then?"

"So it appears. This was five years ago, remember, and the new Silten has slimmed down to a new life, wife and strife. Oh, and there has been no sign of Ertainian-looking Ertainians on Dephlet, D'Wech!tiŜ or anywhere else – recently. But there were some up to a few weeks ago when pirate activity was common."

Jander shifted forward and nudged his coffee cup out of the line of sight. "I'm not at all surprised. With the neutralization of the Plan the Head recalled every ship and every man for new orders. The spies probably went underground."

"What plan is that?"

Steele leaned back and locked his hands behind his neck. "About a hundred years ago there appeared on Ertain a spaceship, filled with technical marvels the Ertainians hadn't seen even in their heyday. Sound familiar?"

"Quite. Fifty years later a similar ship landed on Sfor and started their space age."

It was Jander's turn to nod. "Nothing wrong with your reasoning, either, Nil. Yes, our mysterious visitors again. Not the same ship, of course, since they were both slaughtered, but the same blatant violation of your First Law. Only the Ertainians didn't slaughter the crew immediately like the Sforans did. They bled them dry first – science, technology, economics, history, everything you always wanted to know about the Confederation."

Spart stiffened, his eyes hardening. "You mean it was a Confederation ship?"

"An armed merchant – crewed by Sabarian stock, no less. Unfortunately, the Ertainians weren't interested in their genealogy or even their motives. Their identities are unknown."

"Not for long." Spart reached for a touch tablet to his right and typed with the force of irritation. "Arani will track them down, or you'll have to make good on your promise of finding her a job." He fired off the note and scowled again at the screen. "So, what is this Plan?"

"To build a powerful fleet of fast ships and send them out commerce raiding. A variety of captures were encouraged, in order to get the finest and most desirable goods possible. Their spies were everywhere, reporting cargos, routes and schedules, setting up the merchant ships for their attack squadrons. Select liners and private craft were also captured, stealing the best brains of the Confederation as slaves."

"You're talking industrial piracy."

"On a grand scale. The object of all this was to stockpile and duplicate the best the Confederation had to offer, then come in like a lion and undercut all competitors – and as you know, the Confederation trade laws make room for advanced societies that can trade equally with the Confederation members. Imagine one planet, one system, with machine tools as good as the Hasgondi, nanoelectronics as good as Squn, metallurgy equal to that of Nokilo, architectural material as fine as the Dwatans', and so forth – at a fraction of the price."

Spart made clicking sounds with his tongue. "They'd destroy the whole trade system, ruin entire planetary economies, spread chaos everywhere."

"And step in with their powerful fleets to restore order," Jander finished. "Even if the products were obvious knockoffs, as are their ships, the Confederation government is too ponderous to enact new trade laws in time to avert such an oblique threat. Hell, there could even be planetary revolts, secessions, even civil war within the Confederation as treaties were broken, contracts ripped up, commercial rivalries intensified..."

Start crossed his arms and thought blackly for a moment. "You know, it just might have worked? A nice, clean economic coup, virtually bloodless for the Ertainians."

"And it was well on its way to working – until they

tried to snatch this little *Angel* we dangled in front of them. The only thing that could possibly harm the Plan is if someone established a link between the pirate attacks and the smart, technologically superior Ertainians. When Kodiak and Nebula saw them in the flesh and lived, the work of a hundred years was compromised with one gut punch."

Spart nodded vigorously. "If those two are typical of your Corpsmen, I'm bloody glad you're the good guys. So, what are the Ertainians doing now? Surely they're not sitting on their avaricious little arses waiting for us to find them?"

"Surely not. All this time they had an Alternate Plan, that is, to seek out small empires and single worlds to conquer, technologically superior worlds they could enslave to build a navy not even the Confederation could match. What they could not take by guile they were determined to take by force."

Spart scratched at his jaw. "Why? Why are they so bloody determined to knock us off?"

"Because you think you're better than they are — or so they assume. Their entire society is based on a policy of upmanship that makes the mating season of the Eleakan vek!põt look like a kid's birthday party. Their most respected character trait is the ability to dominate others. They were determined to destroy the greatest interspecies alliance in the known galaxy simply to prove to themselves that they could do it."

He shrugged and sank back into his chair. "I humbly admit we've shaken their assumption of superiority rather badly, but they're determined to fight even us to the death. The Confederation is well and truly off the hook; the Ertainians have found an even bigger fish to gaffe."

"Little do they know. And when you've properly worked them over, there in the wings is the Confederation, bigger than ever and wide awake."

"And ready to do exactly the same thing they were planning to do to you – put out the fire and scatter the ashes."

Spart smiled crookedly and nodded. "Okay, Orion, you knock them down and we'll fall on them. Our distinguished Admiral Mati Ganazan is itching to regain the self-esteem Lady Alpha so casually stripped her of. Was that necessary, by the way?"

Steele almost winced at that familiar word. "It was. You'll see the reasoning when we're done. My word to Alpha basically meant, 'knock her down a peg'. When Mati takes over she'll do it our way."

"If I didn't know better, I'd swear that was your ego talking. But I know better than anyone that you see things a thousand brains in concert would never notice. I'll make sure she follows your instructions to the letter."

"You trust me more than I do sometimes. I hope you're right."

"Right?" Spart snorted. "In the eyes of the law I'm a traitor and a felon ten times over – and I can imagine your score. And here I sit, promising to make a rogue out of the best combat admiral in the Fleet, hand-picked by the Director – who is also a traitor." He chuckled again. "What next?"

"A Confederation fleet of seven hundred capital ships at the beck and call of a man from a barbarian planet. The subversion of an unaligned sovereign government. The persecution of four billion people – "

Spart held up his hands. "Enough – I'll see it on the vids. Good luck, you unspeakable rogue."

"Thank you, scoundrel." Steele cut the connection with a grin, feeling better than he had in days.

CHAPTER 20

The team consisted of Terry Kirkland, Ann Whitney and Vanessa Lozano, known as Guardiana, an equally lovely and dangerous Italian telepath. Her job was to make sure the two transmutators, Chloe and Sabrina, remained undisturbed. She stood just inside the door of the makeshift morgue near the Palace with her pulse pistols set to subsonic speed, whisper-silent guns of deadly accuracy. Her mind quested powerfully outward, probing the corridors of the refrigerated hall and keeping a mental ear on the three Ertainian guards outside the door as well.

Ann, deliberately kept busy to help her over the grief of losing her husband Zach, and her department chief paced quietly through the morgue, staring at each of the dead guardsmen in turn. Occasionally Terry would point significantly at one of them, and Ann would nod. From one end of the grisly hall to the other the finger and the nod occurred nineteen times. Starting at the far end, with one of the women on either side of the hall, they worked their way back toward the door.

STEELE LAY ON HIS BACK in the sweet grass, soothing his soul with the sighing of the breeze in the leaves overhead. The newly established birds whistled and sang as they flitted from the ten-meter trees to their feeders or to hunt the bugs that breeped in the natural grasses. The squirrels that had lived there from the outset added their chittering voices to the natural sounds of a springtime meadow.

Missing from the park was any sign of Leyla, the sabertoothed tiger. Despite the efforts of a pool of zootelepaths to tame her, the giant cat had proven too destructive to keep aboard. After a tearful farewell from Sharon Gibson, she was set loose on Arcadia to rejoin her pride. Not surprisingly, the park had become more popular since.

The *Angel*'s park was dedicated to Zach Whitney and Freddie Soames, and one small material item, one cherished possession of each, was interred beneath their names in a corner plot. Under three other markers in that shaded garden corner there were three other buried packages: Bill Wize, Elga Mançon, Simon Crawley. In this small piece of Gaea in a giant starship, five of her children had come to rest.

Vickie glided softly through the grass and settled beside her man. "I swear, you brood more than anyone I've ever met."

He smiled and opened his eyes. Even without probing he could tell she was worried about him, disturbed by the burden of command that weighed so heavily upon him. He reflected on her reaction toward Admiral Ganazan: like a lioness defending her cub. Gods help anyone who ever tried to kill him.

"I'm not brooding. It just so happens I'm relaxing for the first time in weeks." He reached up and pulled her down beside him. "Of course, if you don't think I have the right to relax...."

"Oh, silly think." She snuggled closer and ran her fingers over his neck. "As a matter of fact, I took it upon myself to do a little planning of my own, just so's you could cool your heels for a minute."

"Oh, boy. I can imagine the kind of scheme your ziggy little mind could cook up. Tell me about it."

"Okay." She looked up as a curious goldfinch, fully recovered from the trauma of its trip as *Phasmida* cargo, flitted to a twig, gave her a quick once-over, tweeped a single rising note in greeting and flew off. "So, what's the ugliest word in the English language?"

"Rape. No question. Why?"

She took a deep breath to steel herself for the next step. "So what do you think the Ertainians do with their female captives?"

She felt him stiffen. "But they're of different species!"

"So? They're female, which are in short supply in these parts. Even Kanitaks are female half the time. And Sabarians are fairly close in appearance to Ertainians, and tall, stately Sabarian women are very highly prized."

"Prized," he spat.

"Prized. They're given as rewards, passed from hand to eager hand, bought and sold at tremendously high prices, even black-marketed. And the Head himself has a fine harem, sixty-eight at last count, chosen of the loveliest taken. And when he's done with them, he gives them to the Palace Guard...."

"Cut it out." The words came roughly through gritted teeth. "What is your plan?"

She rubbed his chest as if to massage away his anguish. "For heaven's sake, when are you going to learn you can share my mind anytime you like?"

THE PALACE COURTYARD was dark and empty of guards, but the intruders nonetheless moved with as much stealth as possible. Even Denny Connors, all seven hundred twenty pounds of him, made barely a sound. With two telepaths on guard to cover them in the huge space, he and his number two, Hal Summers, slipped down the line of elaborate VTOLs used by the Head and his highest aides.

"Here it is," Kodiak whispered hoarsely. He motioned the Canadian toward a powerful-looking craft set apart from the others. "The Head's personal chariot."

Hal was not a man of many words. He simply jerked his head and tapped a message on his wrist-pad. A few seconds later a complex electronic assembly appeared in mid-air. He caught it telekinetically and wafted it toward his chief. The screwdriver end of Denny's antique plierench popped open a panel it had taken an expensive instrument to close, and he and Hal gentled the awkward mechanism into place. Wires, cables and circuit boards appeared from its innards and Hal snaked them through the ship.

They labored for half an hour, testing and retesting every delicate connection, then Denny closed the panel with a firm rap of his palm. The engineers collected their cover force and departed as quietly as they had come.

COBRA FOUND STEELE in the gym watching a fencing match. When not on duty or specific assignment the members of the Omega Corps were free to do as they wished, even under yellow alert – provided they were ready to jump at five seconds' notice. Steele himself had just finished working out his hostilities by being thrown around the room by Osamu Arai. His brown belt had proven no match for the Japanese technician who, along with the currently very occupied Wildflower, served as the *Angel*'s primary martial arts instructor. Now Jander was waiting to take on the winner of the saber match in front of him.

"You wished to see the report on captives as soon as it was ready, Captain," Kalanev opened without fanfare. He passed a tablet to Steele's proffered hand.

"Thank you, Pavel." He watched a particularly good parry – he suspected the fencer was using her clairvoyance – then glanced at the tablet. He was back with the match without missing a stroke. "Do you have the location of this mixed batch of VIPs?"

"To the millimeter. I suspected you might wish to rescue them."

"Not unless necessary. I want to save the space for those in immediate danger. I'm having the twenty-third level turned into a barracks – that's our empty deck, remember – but it won't hold more than a few hundred by shoehorn. This says there are over twenty thousand Confederation captives."

"Would 'immediate danger' include paranoid catatonia?"

He glanced up with a frown. "The Ygnians, of course."

"Fifteen of them." The four-eyed, six-limned centaurs of Ygun were reclusive to the point of asceticism; they and their three descendant planets had joined the Confederation more for the protection it afforded than for its brotherhood. "There were originally several score of them, but the others either committed hibernation suicide or were vivisected."

Steele slapped the tablet against his thigh in disgust. "These Ertainians are rapidly losing their appeal. We'll bring the centaurs up tonight."

"We will have to wait until mid-morning. They are on the other side of the planet. Two other races are in some distress: the Squns are suffering from the gravity and the Nokilonians from the cold."

"I'm afraid there's nothing we can do for them at

present. I don't see any Eleakans here."

"The Ertainians killed them all in self-defense – if you can call it that. None of them was able to accept the condition of slavery and attacked their guards at the slightest opportunity. As endothermic reptiles they are much stronger than other species, therefore gunning them down was the only choice."

"And the others? How are the holding up?"

"Those of Sabarian stock are reacting as any Gaean would; they have confidence in the Confederation and are waiting more or less patiently for rescue. There are a few examples of sabotage – very clever ones, at that – but in the main they are keeping to the standard minimum of cooperation. The Hasgondi are as usual quite peaceful, although they take as many guards as the others. Otherwise, they would simply sit down and do nothing. The Leosans are acting dumb; suddenly their memories are unnaturally poor. Dwatans are very few; most males were slaughtered for looking too catlike, and the females were raped and mutilated to death for the same reason."

His gritted teeth belied the steadiness of his voice.

"Fthlonians also have heavy fur, but they are not subject to nearly as much brutality. Female Fthlonians are small enough and humanoid enough to be passed around, regrettably. Kanitaks are wisely selecting to be male, and are vying with each other in bungling the simplest jobs. The little Karani are always managing to escape; being nocturnal they have ample opportunity. Unfortunately, when they are caught they are punished severely, but that does not stop them from trying. The others, Nokilonians and Squns, are marginally cooperative because they receive bearable living conditions if they do so."

"Ugh. They're the most valuable from a technology standpoint, along with the Hasgondi. We'd better keep an eye on them and snatch any who are working on anything too sensitive. And I want to bring the poor Dwatans up with the Ygnians if we can get at them. They're too damned cute to have to go through that. I wish we could rescue all the females, but we simply don't have the resources." He scrolled to the last page in the tablet file. "What's this non-Confed bunch?"

"There is one species from beyond the Confederation, the crew of a ship which happened into Ertainian reach. These people are called Æzants and are marsupial. They were on an exploration cruise and got lost, just as we did on our initial voyage. Their holdings consist of one planet and a small colony at the nearest habitable star, some scores of parsecs farther away from Confederation space."

"Interesting. What were they doing 'way out here?"

"They were testing their brand-new nucleonic drive fed by solar accumulation. I find it intriguing that so many species have settled upon that same system."

"Better that than having everybody with a zero-point gravity drive like ours. The extra speed and mobility that gives us is worth its weight in parsnips."

Pavel actually cracked a smile. "I may take issue with the vegetables, but I agree with you in practicality – and upon consideration your metaphor is quite apt. When Denver and Chelsea elected to retreat to a stronghold on Arcadia, they sacrificed their greatest weapon, the element of surprise. With our small numbers we should never accept a defensive role."

"'Damn the torpidity, full speed ahead!' Thanks, Pavel, I'll remember it." He stretched to his feet. "Well, so much for my saber match. I want to be available for the pickup. So, let's try to get some sleep."

"I will accept that. However, I would request that you first review the supply situation in sickbay."

"How's that?"

"Dr. Kirkland has no lollipops."

CHAPTER 21

It was a terrible sight. The thousand bodies were laid out in the cold of a climate-controlled assembly hall that had been cleared to serve as a morgue. It fell to their former comrades to identify them.

Captain Hanash moved almost reverently toward the first body and removed the shroud. The men with him checked the uniform insignia and leafed through the books they carried in search of the face.

"Pusra, trooper." The shroud was replaced, a tag was filled out and laid on the dead man's chest, and the three moved on.

"This one I know," Hanash said quietly. "He is Siver, a squad leader." Again the tag, again the short journey to the next covered body. Hanash stared into face after empty face and waited for the name, waited for the tag. Every one of them reminded him of his resentment, that the Head had relegated this macabre task to him as the accepted bearer of bad news.

His morning report had been full of bad news. The city's traffic control computer had been infected during the night; the signals at each busy intersection had been changing virtually at random. Dozens of accidents, some injuries and a few fatalities had been the result. Their best analysts, a full score of them, had thus far been unable to clear the virus; meanwhile hundreds of troops were being tied up as traffic cops.

In another city half a continent away the radio stations had been provided with a tremendous power surge; thousands had been temporarily deafened and many radio receivers and loudspeakers had been blown out.

In an army camp every single motorized vehicle had been turned onto its roof. In another the larder had been cleaned out and a full regiment had gone to assembly hungry. In still another the records office had been wiped clean.

And in the largest city's largest airport a deep crater was discovered in the primary runway, with no clue of how it got there. There had been no explosion and no flash of light.

"Chokilonis, group leader." There were many others, childish, annoying pranks that bothered rather than seriously harmed. This Orion was playing with them. Hanash and the Head both could see his strategy. He was methodically giving them the jitters, putting them all into an attitude of, "What next?" These silent, always unexplained, often impossible practical jokes were but the harbingers, the opening touches, of what they knew would be a terrifying war of nerves.

They would lose. Hanash knew they would lose. The gods were laughing at them now, but before too long they would weary of their sport. And then they would step on them.

"Ghelas, trooper." The tag was laid on the shattered chest and the three moved on. Hanash stepped to the next corpse and gently pulled back the shroud. He stared down at yet another face immobilized by death.

And screamed.

VERY FEW OUTSIDE the Palace knew the details. They thought the panic within was greater than was warranted, but they were nonetheless overcome by the grief the news brought with it.

The word spread like the wind through the city, to the news outlets, across the full width of Ertain and into the cordoning ships and through the void to Liev. Everywhere the reaction was the same: men wept and bells tolled; radios and loudspeakers blared dirges; the entire population of two planets went into instant and stricken mourning. The Head was dead.

Deep in the confines of his sanctum, the Head was almost the last to know. In the sheer panic of finding the Head among the corpses in the morgue no one thought to check his office. Why bother? There was only one Head. Only Hanash could have told them that His Supremacy was still alive; in fact, he had told them. That was why he was under restraint.

The Head discovered the fact of his own demise soon after his secretary entered his office unannounced. Alas, Janus was not present to record his reaction. It was known that the Head did not have the courtesy to make him comfortable before stalking out of the office to find the reason for his collapse.

"Guard! What is going on here?" The guard snapped to attention by instinct alone, then recognized the voice. His momentum slammed him back against the wall, his knees buckled and he fell face forward to the stone floor.

The Head stared dumbfounded for seconds, then stomped to the fallen man, whose fists were still clenched at his stomach as he lay flat on his face. "What is going on here?" he bellowed again. "Has everyone gone mad?"

He looked up at the sound of rapid feet, then stood glaring as General Slichen, the top officer of the Elite and Palace Guards, rushed around the corner.

The General skidded to a halt and barely kept from collapsing himself. "Y-y-y-your S-s-supremacy! B-b-bu-but, but, b-but...."

The Head did not trust himself to speak. With studied slowness he squared his shoulders and stamped menacingly toward Slichen, face livid and fists clenched. Shoving his face within a few inches of the General, he hissed, "Yesssss?"

"B-bu-but you're dead, y-yo...." Slichen sputtered to a whispering halt, trembling in every cell.

The Head stepped back and took his time absorbing that information, then calculated the most scathing reply possible.

"Oh, really!"

Slichen blinked, then loosed his pent-up lungs in one tremendous explosion, doubling over and managing somehow to keep from spitting in his sovereign's face. His complexion turned from khaki to lemon to burnt orange. He finally managed to gasp, "There must be s-some mistake, Your Supremacy."

"I'm glad you agree," he growled viciously. He was regaining some measure of control. "Guard! Find Hanash. I want him here at once!"

The guard picked himself up and sidled away, then stopped abruptly and twisted back to attention. "But who shall I say is asking, Your Supremacy? Everyone thinks you're dead!"

The Head glared at him in disbelief. "Everyone?"

The General supported himself against a wall, Head or no Head. "It's true, Your Supremacy. I saw your – um, the body myself."

The Head turned his baleful eyes on the General. "Where?"

"In the morgue, packed in with the, uh, the Elite Guard. Hanash and his assistants discovered the, um, body." He blinked and lowered his eyes. "He went a little mad at the sight, Your Supremacy."

"No wonder, since he had seen me alive but a few moments before." He frowned, his mind spinning. "Forget that order, guard. I would see this body myself. The resemblance must be remarkable."

"More than remarkable, Your Supremacy, perfect," Slichen told him. "Even to the scar on your upper lip, and the gap in the left side of your brow fur. Perfect."

"Too perfect," the Head responded angrily. "It's a trick of that cat-hearted bastard, Orion. It has to be."

He glared at the General. "Slichen, you will call in the Palace Guard and give them the news, then see to it that the 'rumor' of my good health reaches the outside – the sooner the better. As soon as there is a definite reaction, I will give a televised speech, live, which will convince them beyond doubt. And while you're at it, find out who, if anyone, tried to advance themselves as my successor. I want any such effort identified and quashed immediately. Clear?"

"Yes, Your Supremacy." He bowed and rushed away, scuttling sideways so as not to show his back.

HANASH, WITH A DAZED AND SOMEWHAT haunted look on his face, stood with the Head and Slichen and stared down at the corpse. The Head had ordered his aide's release when he learned that he had been slumped helpless on the floor while his assistants had fled and screamed the news to everyone they met. The assistants had already been executed.

The Head, who had stared at that face a dozen times a day all his life, could only marvel at the perfect copy. "Who was he – originally?"

"There is no way of knowing yet, Your Supremacy."

The captain's voice was fuzzy with sedatives. "Even the teeth and retina patterns are yours. We'll have to tally the others to find out who's missing."

"Get on it, then. I have to give that speech before the entire system goes crazy." He saw Hanash wince at the word and snorted in disgust.

The Head and Slichen left the morgue and strode to the broadcast studio in another outbuilding. Within ten minutes he was patched into every station on both planets, and the broadcast was beamed to every ship in the system. Attendance was compulsory and virtually unanimous; any time the Head saw fit to speak to his people the entire Twin Planets dropped everything and listened.

He glared into the camera with the haughty stare that was well known to everyone, the visual proof of his Way of Power. "People of Ertain, people of Liev, you well know who I am. I am your Head; I am your leader. I am the only one with that title and that distinction. There is only one Head, and he is me.

"Earlier today there were rumors of my untimely demise; you know as you see me that they are false. The Head is living, and he will continue to live and lead you in your battle against those who seek to destroy us and our Way of Power.

"Who are these people? Some call them gods, some ghosts and demons and stealers of minds. To those few of you who persist in labeling them thus, I say you are fools. You would give us all into their hands for fear of your lives. They are not gods; they can be killed. They are not mystics; they breathe, and they can be killed. They are not demons; they live, they breathe, and they *can! Be! Killed!*"

He leaned forward and spat the words, drilling them through the lens and the microphones and into the ears of billions. He demanded with his tone and with his simmering eyes that they be believed, that they be not doubted.

He tossed his head in dismissal. "Who are they? They are tricksters, trying in vain to confuse us. They are cowards, hiding behind a series of childish pranks they think we cannot comprehend. They are fools, imagining they can defeat us without a battle, without a test of strength they *know* they cannot win.

"*I* understand their tricks. I see their cowardly strategy. I know what they are trying to do. They are trying to turn us against ourselves and each other. They are trying to force us to fear them. They want us to think them so much greater than we that we will give up without a fight. And knowing as I do, I can lead you to victory!"

He sat back with a cruel and knowing sneer, and the cameraman took the cue to move in closer. "Omega Corps, I know you are watching me. I know you can hear and understand my every word. Now I want you to hear and understand this: I defy you to your face. I dare you to try your strength against mine. All your childish pranks, all your so-called ghosts and demons, are as nothing compared to the Way of Power we of Ertain possess. We will meet you on any battlefield you choose and defeat you utterly. We will take all your supposed torments and return a mocking smile, a laugh of derision.

"We understand you, Corpsmen, and we know we cannot lose. We cannot lose because we cannot be frightened like sniveling slaves, we cannot be used like mindless females. Not only will we defy you and your puny power, but we will stand on your corpses and reach upward to the stars!"

His voice was not raised; his haughty sneer did not change. The words left his lips with calm and chilling certainty, the certainty of a man who knows that his words are prophetic. In the pause, his people copied that mocking smile, that knowing gleam. Now they understood; now they realized what was going on. And now that they knew they could face it like their Head could: as Ertainians, as the destined conquerors of the galaxy.

The camera backed off, reuniting the Head with the general audience. "People of the Twin Planets, your future is secure. The fates have given to us the Way of Power, the means to achieve our chosen role in the galaxy. The Way of Power was not given to this cowardly gang of tricksters; it was not given to that motley collection of foolish weaklings called the Confederation. It was given to *us!* And that very fact is the enduring proof that we are worthy of it. We need only to use it as it should be used, as the foundation of our greatness.

"You, the people, are the depository of that power,

you are the foundation of that greatness. Give to me your power, your greatness, and I will give you the empire you so richly deserve. You need only to act as true Ertainians and follow your Head. And I, the Head of Ertain, will focus your power through mine, guide it with my own unrivaled power, and direct it toward our enemies. Time and again I have proven myself worthy of the power within me, the Way of Power that has made me your Head. You need only to believe in my power, believe the truth in my words, and we shall triumph!"

The transmission ceased. Tsin cut the connection and turned to look at Orion, who sat quiescent at the rear of the Bridge. Steele met his eyes, then gave an almost infinitesimal shrug.

Everything was working perfectly.

CHAPTER 22

<*I am free. I am safe. I may return.*"> Vickie drove the hypnotic impulse deep, far into the subconscious, down into the lowest reaches of the Ygnian's mind, seeking to stimulate a new will to live from deep within.

The mind remained empty.

"No response so far." Terry Kirkland stared darkly into the Ygnian's odd physiognomy, searching with her microvoyance for any sign of quickening pulse or increasing oxygen that would nurture the dormant cells of the brain. "You haven't reached her."

Vickie withdrew a bit as she reviewed all she had been able to learn about Ygnian catatonia. Most of the six-limned mammals of Ygun had the ability to hibernate; the extreme elliptical orbit of their home planet made it a virtual necessity. The intelligent denizens had refined this into a type of self-hypnosis far in advance of the meditative practices of Gaea. They used it only in times of great danger, when they had decided that there was no hope of escape.

Rather than suffer, a Ygnian withdrew. The shut-out was so complete that the body could be eaten alive and the mind would never know it. And in all the long history of Ygun no one had ever returned from that state; it was an early form of death, and death was the inevitable result.

Then again, none of them had met Lady Alpha.

Vickie tried again. <*"I am safe. The time of suffering is behind me. The need for peace is past. There is comfort without; there is life and hope and freedom. There is only death within, and death is not yet my fate."*>

"Response!" Terry rapped. "You're reaching her. Lay it on!"

Vickie bit her lip and concentrated. <*"My time of death has not yet come. I thought I saw the signs of death, I thought I saw the need for the ultimate peace, but I was wrong, wrong! I live, and I have long life ahead. I can return! I can be free!"*>

She could see it now, deeper than she had ever seen into anyone; that tiny spark of life that never failed, never gave up hope until the fragile shell without had abandoned it. No living being, from the tiniest organism to the most massive behemoth, could extinguish it by will alone. Only the death of the body could do that, and the Ygnian's body was still alive. Vickie clutched at that spark and nurtured it, giving of her own mental energy to make it grow. And no intelligent being save one could resist the hypnotic power of Lady Alpha.

The pulse quickened; the breath deepened. The pure oxygen rushed through the lung-feeding tube, through the bloodstream and into the starved brain.

And the brain accepted it gratefully, at long last convinced of the desire for life. The Ygnian lived, and the two pairs of eyes fluttered their lids into her natural hibernation.

Terry sighed and exchanged grateful looks with Vickie, the penultimate doctor and the ultimate psychologist.

Gustav Kamerun, whose experience with Spirit had brought him in as a consultant, caught their thoughts. "But then again, the Omega Corps specializes in the impossible."

PHASE ONE CONTINUED without change, despite the Ertainians' renewed will to resist. Jander had been surprised by the early results in any case; he had expected frustration but had not presumed to engender so much fear this early in the campaign. Thus the "childish pranks" still served their purpose.

On the night side of the planet all the street signs on a major thoroughfare were switched with those from another half the planet away.

The Secret Police discovered their confidential files on highly placed people missing and were deluged by questions from the information media that has received them.

The cause of a massive power blackout was found to be thousands of mice, or rather their Ertainian analogs, which had dashed madly through underground conduits and chewed through every wire they could reach.

At a sports arena the kickball suddenly came alive, attacking the players and caroming through the stands, leaving bruises on scores of stampeding spectators.

A full division on parade stared in shock as a young soldier walked stiffly to the reviewing stand, swung the stock of his unloaded laser rifle and deprived the commanding general of four of his teeth.

One city's public address system ordered every citizen to drop whatever he was doing and return home immediately. Everyone obeyed; no one ever learned why.

Another town was paralyzed when a violently objectionably odor began pouring out of every smoke-stack, filling the city with gut-spewing fumes.

Deep in the bowels of an iron mine, every metal-lic tool suddenly went haywire, bending, twisting, smashing into walls and workers as the iron depos-its were subjected to wild fluctuations of magnetism. Buttons, rivets and bits of ore became deadly and destructive missiles as the operation was literally torn apart.

Every merchant ship in a major harbor was immo-bilized when a massive carpet of seaweed drifted in and wound itself around the entire bay.

The storage tanks at a principal refinery were provided with new valve controls that made the flow impossible to turn off.

And in the place of the fifteen rescued Ygnians

and the two dozen tortured but stubbornly surviving Dwatans, their guards found thirty-nine manikins filled with unprocessed sewage – manikins whose shells disintegrated at the slightest touch.

There were smaller actions, also, annoying incidents that struck the high and the low alike. The Corpsmen approached Phase One as a contest, and every one of them came up with more than one ingenious contribution.

And thanks to those hundreds of brilliant minds the campaign was telling. Police stations and military posts were swamped with complaints and reports; armed soldiers were dispatched to one trouble spot after another far too late and totally impotent. Hundreds of thousands of the Head's "depositories of power" found themselves powerless to do anything but try to regain their aplomb – and wait for the next nuisance. The torture went on all seventeen Gaean hours of each Ertainian day, everywhere on the globe.

The Head crumpled stiffly on the edge of his bed nest and buried his head in his hands, heaving a tremendous sigh. The ordinary citizen's frustration was nothing compared to his. He had hoped that his challenge would bring this Orion into the open, but the cat-loving bastard had simply ignored him and gone about his business with glib and ruthless efficiency.

Hanash had been reduced to giving him hourly reports of the atrocities, even though the Head knew his aide was close to the breaking point. The discovery of nineteen perfect replicas of his leader's face on bodies of the Elite Guard had left the captain incapable of feeling alarm from the other reports. But that same shock had made him a hollow shell, barely sentient, capable now only of a job of clerical level.

<*"Hi, Heddy-baby."*>

The words were so impossible that at first, they did not even register. The Head sat stolid, breathing deeply.

<*"Hey, you little yella tomcat, I'm talkin' to you!"*>

That registered. The voice was deep, resonant, mocking, and the insult was the worst any Ertainian could ever receive – fighting words. The Head stiffened and staggered to his feet, eyes wide and staring into every corner. He was alone.

<*"Wassamatta, mustard-mug? Can't find your head?"*> The voice chuckled wickedly.

The Head spun in a full circle, questing everywhere with no success. "Where are you? Who are you?"

<*"What difference does it make, puss-puss? You couldn't do anything if you knew."*> The deep chuckle continued, rising in volume, filling the suite with mocking derision.

"Guard!" he shouted. "GUAAARD!"

The chuckle rose to a horrible, booming laugh. It rocked the room, rippling off the walls and coiling through the curtains like a living thing. It went on and on, ever louder, ever more evil, crashing through his brain and deafening him from within. He clutched at his head and screamed, eyes screwed tightly shut until the lights leaped within his skull, adding to the agony and tearing at his head from without. He fell to his knees and screamed again and again, rocking back and forth in agony, trying to drown out the insane laughter, wanting to run and unable to move, wanting to hide, wanting to die.

The laughter abruptly ceased, leaving him in the middle of a scream. Just that suddenly, the only sound in the room was his own hoarse voice.

He stayed there on his knees, sobbing, gasping air into his burning lungs. He dragged his trembling hands from his head down to his throat, then clutched his arms tightly around his chest. The pain was there, in his chest, from the screaming. There was not even a dull ache within his skull.

He opened his eyes and stared around him, amazed to see the room exactly as it had been... how long ago? The chronometer told him it had been three minutes, but that could not be right. It had been hours.

He staggered to his feet and swayed over to his bed nest, collapsing exhausted into its satin luxury. He forced his brain – his incredibly clear, untortured brain – to work on his ordeal.

It had to be Orion, of course, attacking him through his own brain. The "voice", not actual sound but resonating within his mind, had been low and deep, that of a giant. He thought of the giant who had done them so much damage in the past. Could he project his thoughts? Unlikely – he would certainly have used that talent on the planet of the black colossus. It was someone else, perhaps, projecting his thoughts for him. Or was it only his imagination?

One item did not fit. He sat up and pushed a button at the side of his nest, then sagged, waiting. It took the Captain of the Guards seven seconds to step soundlessly into the room. "At your service, Your Supremacy."

The Head stared at him dully. "Didn't you hear my call?"

"No, Your Supremacy." He thought the Head looked a little strange. "The computer is keyed to respond to the word 'guard' and notify me immediately. Perhaps it is... out of order."

The Head smiled tiredly. "Or has been tampered with. You will see to it in the morning."

"Of course, Your Supremacy. Is there anything else?"

"No, that is all." He saw the man hesitate. "Yes?"

The Captain shifted uncomfortably. "If you would forgive me, Your Supremacy, you look... despondent. Perhaps a woman, to ease your mind?"

"No, not tonight. I am too fatigued." He saw the almost imperceptible change of expression. "Choose one for yourself and your men."

The Captain brightened. "Thank you, Your Supremacy. I am sure they will appreciate it." He bowed low, then backed hastily from the room.

The Head sighed and closed his eyes. He had to force Orion into the open; he had no other alternative. He must be forced to battle on equal terms.

He remembered that booming laugh, and shivered.

CHAPTER 23

The Captain of the Guard collected four of his men and told them the good news. Grinning in anticipation, the five almost ran to the Sabarian harem. A word to the three suddenly jealous guards outside and they passed through the doors.

The Captain feasted his eyes on the dozens of tall, beautiful women, the pick of months of commerce raiding, and licked his lips at their fearful expressions. No woman had ever returned to the harem after answering the Head's call. Not to wonder, since the Captain had a score of off-duty men every night. Few of these beauties, genetically weaker than the smaller Ertainian men, survived past ten or twelve.

The Captain rubbed his hands together. "Good news, ladies. The Head wants no company tonight."

He grinned as he watched their reactions, the heaving sighs, a few sobs of relief. "Instead," he went on in his slushy Sabarian, "one of you will have the privilege of pleasuring me and my men – no need to wait for your party."

The relief turned to dread. He chuckled, enjoying their terror and deliberately adding to it. "That's right, girls, we can get right to the real fun!"

The naked women cowered back, huddling on the dirty mats they tried to sleep on, twisting together as far from their beastly tormentors as they could hide. They knew it would do them no good, but horror knows no logic. These once-proud ladies, the daughters of the equalitarian society of Sabar, had experienced the ultimate degradation – carnal slavery. They were sheep, cared for and kept for one thing, fed and handled and herded and prepared for slaughter. Thinking sheep, sheep that knew exactly what their final fate would certainly be.

The Captain licked his lips again as he studied them. Cream and tan and brown, all at least a head taller than he, many of them heavier, with their long blonde or brown hair flowing across their shoulders in uncaring tatters. He searched lewdly for an exception; since he would be first tonight, he wanted something special.

His eyes alighted on a woman much darker than the others, whose tight curls were cropped close to her lovely face. Her lips were full and sensuous, her youthfully taut body curved with a ripeness the scrawny Ertainian women would never know. And oddly, this one had a little spirit remaining. Her eyes, squeezed tight in a glare of feral hatred, never left his face.

He motioned to his men. "Cut that one out, the dark one."

The men grinned and stalked toward the milling women. The pitiful creatures wailed and packed even tighter against the wall, folding themselves and covering their breasts as the guards advanced on them. The four chuckled and joked as they looked over the squirming pile, pointing to and discussing the womanly merits of one sobbing girl after another with practiced and degrading vulgarity. A shriek rent the air as a guard reached in to check something, and they howled their mirth at the reaction.

Abruptly two of them pounced, grabbed the arms of the dark beauty and wrenched her out of the pile. She screamed, not a wail of despair but of pure, unsullied fury, as she was dragged from the huddle and wrestled, snarling and scratching, back to the Captain.

The other women ceased their wails and slowly raised their heads, knowing they were safe for another night and wanting to have one last glimpse of the poor sacrifice of tonight. With dull eyes and quivering lips they watched a spectacle that only a few of them, those who had survived from the beginning, could remember. The dark girl was actually opposing her fate. She would not helplessly give in to them. The sheep in the corner stared fascinated.

One of the guards already had a trophy of the night, a set of bright red scratches down his left cheek. Two others had strong, cruel grips on her arms, and needed all their strength to handle the unusually vigorous captive. The woman paused in her struggles as they came up to the Captain, and glared at him in wild-eyed hatred.

"Well, well, well," he slurred, drooling with excitement. "I thought all you little mice had lost your fight. It'll be nice to have some sport for once."

"Stuff it, *panya!*" The Captain did not recognize the word, but he certainly recognized the spittle that came with it. He recoiled in surprise, then stepped forward and slashed the back of his hand upward into her mouth.

The woman rocked backward from the blow and used its momentum to lash out a kick. The ball of her foot caught him high on the thigh, very close to the mark.

The guard with the bloody cheek stepped behind her and drove his fist under her ribs. She gasped and sagged, head down, dripping blood from a gash in her lip. The Captain flexed his thigh and brought his hand up again, catching her nose with his palm. With a surprisingly quick move, she ducked away from most of it and sank her teeth into his thumb.

The Captain howled and stepped back, gaping incredulously at his lacerated hand. The girl spat again and drew in great gasps of air, her wild eyes cutting into his without the slightest sign of defeat.

"You little..." He stamped forward and swung back and forth again and again, catching her face with palm or backhand with every full-powered blow. Her head rocked side to side, spraying blood and sweat in wide arcs, jerking the men on her arms like puppets until one of them lost his grip. The next blow spun her away, and she sprawled face down on the floor.

The captain paced furiously over and kicked, feeling a rib give under his boot. The woman grunted and flinched away, then glared through misted eyes straight up at him. She grinned ferally, a horribly gruesome parody of humor, and gritted, "You'll have to kill me, *panya!*" She spat a gob of bloody phlegm onto his boot.

The Captain reached for her with a snarl, then stopped. He gave her a slow sneer and growled, "Oh, no, little mouse. You don't get off that easy. You'll die, all right, but like all the others, under a score of Ertain's best! Pick her up!"

The grinning guards grabbed her cruelly by the arms and legs and carried her, still writhing madly, out the door. The women cowering against the wall stared breathless until it slammed closed, then broke into excited and suddenly alive whispering.

Through the corridors they struggled, the woman gasping with every painful move, yet still alive and fighting. The men shifted their grips time and again as her sweated and bloody flesh squirmed in their hands, yet they held, and followed their Captain to the guard barracks room.

The officer slammed and locked the door behind them. Twenty or more heavily breathing guardsmen crowded around to stare at their surprisingly active catch. The four guards heaved, and the woman crashed with cruel force onto a nest of old blankets already bloodstained from similar use.

She dragged herself into a corner, still glaring redly. "You said you were first, *panya?*"

The Captain tore at his tunic, his eyes dilated, his words breathless with lust. "You bet I am, little mouse – and I might leave some for the rest!"

The woman wiped her bloody lips with a bruised and sweaty forearm and drew herself to her knees. "You're first, then!" she snarled, and then she... changed.

It must be understood that the average Ertainian loathes cats. They hate them and they fear them, with an instinctive aversion unknown to any other intelligent species. An armed Ertainian will instantly shoot at anything remotely feline, and not stop until the corpse is unrecognizable. An unarmed Ertainian will collapse, screaming, and huddle completely helpless until he is convinced there is no longer a danger. The fear is involuntary, totally debilitating, and so intense that the only human who could possibly understand it would be a bona fide lunatic.

Cielo Kiaga was a meta-panther. And she *hated* Ertainians....

THE SCREAMS OF THE GUARDS outside sent the women into another huddling scramble to the end of the seraglio. They stared wide-eyed at each other, and a few, emboldened by Cielo's resistance, glared fearfully yet defiantly at the door.

Abruptly it slammed open, and there stood the

woman they had never expected to see again, dripping blood. A few of them shrieked at the sight.

"Relax, girls," Cielo grinned airily and shook her arms like a swimmer. "None of this is mine." She pointed behind her at a downed torso visible through the door. It was torn open as if caught by a chainsaw.

One of the women, a tall blonde bolder than the others, spoke in a quavering voice, "But, but you were hurt!"

Cielo shrugged. "My kind can repair any physical damage in a few seconds. I'm Raankhak, of the Omega Corps." As it always did, her chin rose proudly at the title.

"*Omega Corps...!*" The room buzzed with excited whispers as one of the more recent captures told the others what the words meant.

Cielo ignored them. "You on the line, Janus? We're ready."

The women stared at her; she had spoken to empty air.

In the center of the room a large booth appeared, with a uniformed woman visible through the transparent sides. The abrupt arrival caused another chorus of shrieks and gasps.

Vickie stepped out and smiled reassuringly. "It's all right now. I'm Lady Alpha, First Officer of the Omega Corps cruiser *Angel*. We've come to get you out of here."

A few women swooned to their knees. Most of the others simply stared in shock, unbelieving. It was impossible; miracles did not happen.

Vickie rushed to speak again before the inevitable reaction took hold. "We'll have to hurry. This booth will transport you to our flagship, where you will be cared for until this is over. Hurry, now!"

She stepped forward and started pulling girls out of the huddle and pushing them toward Cielo, who in turn packed them into the booth. Reaction was setting in; most of those who touched either woman did not want to let go.

When a dozen or so were crowded into the tele-booth Vickie said, "One of you punch that button by the door. Quickly, now."

It was done, and the occupants vanished. Those ready to enter shrank back with gasps of alarm.

Cielo gestured them forward. "Come on, kittens, do you think we'd go to all this trouble just to inciner-ate you? Let's go!" She started cramming in the next batch.

Suddenly the harem door was crowded with a half dozen staring guards. They could have had no idea what was going on, but the condition of the corpses outside and the sight of one woman fully clothed were enough to set them into action. They scrambled into the room and leveled their lasers.

Vickie cursed herself for not keeping watch, then mentally chided Janus for the same, but that took only a corner of her mind. She dodged aside and threw all three of her variant talents into the soldiers as a woman behind her fell to a hurried shot. Two of the guards stopped dead in their tracks and screamed at the pain in their brains, and Vickie remote-controlled their lasers to cut them down. Then the lasers whipped around by themselves to kill the two immobilized by her telekinesis, then she dropped the guns and turned to the wounded girl.

Cielo had taken care of the rest. Reflexes two seconds ahead of instant triggered her metamorphosis, and she leaped full onto one of the soldiers. Her gleaming teeth and powerful claws ripped into him, then she was off and onto the other. Both were dead in seconds, victims of one hundred forty pounds of lightning-fast black panther.

Cielo hit the floor in a soundless crouch – the first time her paws had touched the floor since her initial leap – and turned her fierce amber eyes on Alpha's victims. She considered mauling them on general principles, then decided that even she had had enough. The near-fatal wounding of her man on Arcadia had been more than avenged. She flicked her tail in dismissal and padded toward the door.

"It's okay now, Raankhak," Vickie called. "Janus will keep watch, or I'll spank him, Spirit and all. I need your help here." The panther sat down, and a leisurely three seconds later the woman stood up.

Cielo used her bloody hands to hustle more women into the telebooth while Vickie kneeled over the wounded girl. The blonde who had first spoken to Raankhak crouched beside her. "Can I help? I... used to be a trauma nurse..."

Vickie gave her a quick scan. "Welcome back to the profession, Lieutenant Galen," she smiled. "Thank *you*."

"Thank you," the woman responded feelingly. "I haven't acted much like an officer lately."

"I imagine that if I were in your shoes, I'd act the same."

"I'm not wearing any shoes – and I can't imagine you in them, anyway," she retorted. "You, or your furry friend over there." She shuddered. "I should have known she wasn't one of us, from her wrists. I'm surprised the guards didn't see it."

"That was me," Vicki told her. "I have a hypnotic talent that suppressed their perceptions. We wanted Raankhak to have her fun – it's bound to scare the feces out of the survivors."

"I know." Galen pressed her hand against the victim's laser wound to staunch the weak flow of blood. "I wish she'd visited that... *Head!*"

"The Head still has his uses – in fact, we engineered things so that he wouldn't want a woman tonight." They helped the girl to the telebooth and propped her in with the next batch.

Galen stepped in with her patient. "When the time comes," she said with a chilling lack of emotion, "I'd like the privilege."

"You'd have to fight me for it – and I'd have to fight Lord Orion." She pointed at the button. "Punch it." Galen did so, and the women vanished.

Vickie turned away and found herself staring at

the dead guards. She took in a sharp breath, feeling more than a little queasy. The suddenness of the attack and her lethal reaction to it had shaken her much more than she had expected. However much she despised the Ertainians and their vicious culture, however many thousands of them her command decisions had killed in action over Arcadia, this was the first time she had ever personally taken a life. It wrenched her compassionate soul to the core. Her belly quivered in spasmodic reaction as the fetid stench of violent death penetrated her every physical sense.

For a moment her breath caught in her throat as she fought the urge to vomit, but then her psychic gifts took over. She sensed the joyous relief of the rescued women as they eagerly awaited their freedom; she recalled the shock and pain of the wounded girl counterbalanced by her overwhelming gratitude; she felt the ferocious satisfaction of the glowing Cielo, who had deliberately invited her enemies to do their worst and had wreaked righteous vengeance in return. She drank it all in, savored it, allowed it to sooth her shattered nerves and wash away her guilt. With a quick shake of her head, she went back to work.

It took seven loads to clear the room. The Corpsmen forced themselves to ignore the filth and the bruises the captives had endured, working instead to keep them organized and moving. Vickie used her lilting voice and soothing telehypnosis to try to transition them from their months of trauma, while the combat-sated Cielo maintained a cheerful banter as she pushed them one by one into the booth.

The sobs and hysterical giggles diminished with each sendoff as Vickie was able to narrow her focus to the fewer victims. She and Cielo slipped in with the last five women, took a last look at the rancid bedding the captives had been forced to share, then Vickie reached for a button high above the door that would take the entire assembly back to the *Angel*. An instant later, and for the first time in far too many months, the Head's seraglio was empty.

CHAPTER 24

"In." Jander looked up from the array of monitors on his desk as Terry entered his office and flopped into a chair. "You look tired, Doctor."

She sighed. "Try rehabilitating fifteen confirmed suicides sometime. It was all Vickie and I could do to convince them they were alive."

He chuckled. "I assume you succeeded."

"Barely. Three of them withdrew again when we turned our backs and had to be put under hypnotic compulsion to stay awake. The rest are fairly convinced, but the slightest shock could put them under again. That's besides malnutrition and dehydration from the coma. For now, I've got them wired for sound – they're not going anywhere. I figured that guards would freak them out again."

"Suppose we have that Sabarian lieutenant talk to them?"

"Vickie already thought of that, but that particular lady is a little too gung-ho. Besides, she's too quick – one glance at any of our open machinery and we'd have one less secret."

He grimaced with a nod. "That's what I'm afraid of, with this refugee business. We'll have to convince those ex-slaves that they're still prisoners, at least as far as a free run of the *Angel* is concerned. Deck twenty-three is empty of goodies, so they're confined there – and Angela has safeguards and alarms at every telebooth outlet, staircase, elevator and Jefferies tube in case any of them slip by, so they might as well be in a Confederation barracks."

She nodded. "Since Sabarian adults are severely lactose intolerant, we're feeding them from the comestibles we picked up on Dephlet. But if we keep them too much longer, I'll have to come up with a lactase supplement that fits their generic metabolism. It's amazing how much we Gaeans use dairy products."

"How about the Dwatans?"

"They're tough little critters, already wanting to get out. Still, it will take a long time for them to recover from the hell they've been through. Every one of them had their tails literally torn off. Can you even imagine that?" She shuddered.

Jander shook his head in sympathy. "Add that to the Ertainians' bill. What's their prognosis?"

"We can grow them new ones, but it'll take six hours and a team of three doctors plus support to do it. And I'm not sure they'll ever have full use of them again. But I've scheduled one a day for the next month. That's on top of all the broken bones, muscle tears, nerve damage and other trauma."

"Damn. That breaks my heart. Do whatever you can."

"You don't have to tell me that. We've already

synthesized a plasma compatible with their copper-based blue blood. Most of them are hypocupremic from bad diet and blood loss, so they're on heavy supplements. They'll also need a lot of physical therapy. They're all in traction for now whether they need it or not, just so they'll stay put."

Her wry smile became a grimace. "That last is really questionable ethics. Hippocrates would turn over in his grave."

"He'll be spinning like a top before we're done — we're entering Phase Two. Soon we'll set the ghosts loose, and you can start wholesale Head-making."

"I'd better get some sleep, then." She rose and stretched, then looked back at him. "How are you holding up, Jander?"

He smiled. "You and I are very much alike in that, Terry. We both worry too much about everyone else."

"That's not an answer."

"Well, carry it one step further, then. I, like you, can still get a good night's sleep."

She studied him intently, then grinned. "Touché. Okay, giant-killer. You provide the bodies, I'll provide the Heads." Her step was lighter when she left.

CHAPTER 25

The "one and only" Head sighed as he leaned over his table-desk and planted his chin in his hand. He had been awakened from his exhausted slumber in the middle of the night by General Slichen, who looked ghastly entering his third day without sleep. The news he had brought was even worse: The Palace was hip deep in blood; his entire Sabarian harem had been spirited away; and worst, a full third of the Palace Guard had been literally shredded by cats. He repressed a shudder. *Cats!*

Captain Hanash stood at attention in front of him, his face entirely blank, his voice dead. "Orion's pranks are becoming more destructive. Dozens of bombs were spread around Moleg City, producing impenetrable black smoke that caused the population to sneeze for hours. A cruiser from the Kæzig spaceyards took off by itself and crashed into an arms factory, destroying both with high casualties. The sewers in Sreake backed up...."

"Enough, Hanash, enough." The words were barely audible. *Shredded!* He looked up. "Prepare my aircar for a move. I'll be going to the Summer Palace for a while. This one is no longer safe. You will come with me. Instruct that all reports are to be forwarded there." He sighed again. "Get busy, Hanash, don't just stand there."

"Yes, Your Supremacy." He bowed, barely more than a nod, and backed out.

Preparations were made in little more than an hour. The Head, accompanied by his driver, Hanash and half a dozen guards, strode through the courtyard and piled into the aircar that was warmed up and ready. With a throaty roaring hiss, the VTOL rose into the empty sky.

Other than a few security craft and military vehicles, the Palace entourage owned the air. In the hundred years since the Ertainian renaissance the general populace had benefited little; most of them were still stuck in the petrochemical travel age.

Which gave the Omega Corps that much more room to work.

Hal Summers, dour as usual in contrast to the huge grin of anticipation on Denny's face, sat at his board in Engineering with a speedball beneath his left hand and a joystick in his right. He watched the ascent through his telepathic link to Mentor, who had Spirit ready to follow the action.

When the aircar reached a height of two kilometers Hal tapped a key to activate the equipment they had installed a few nights before. He twitched the speedball experimentally and watched satisfied as the aircar yawed as if in turbulence. Then he reared back, took a deep breath, and threw both fingers and mind into his controls.

Thanks to the efficient internal gravity the Head and his retinue felt no physical effects, but the expansive windows showed them exactly what was going on. The car quadrupled its speed, arched out of the city into the farmland beyond and arrowed straight for the ground.

"*DRIVERRR!*" the Head bawled. "What is going on here?!?"

"I'm out of control, Y' S'prem'cy!" the pilot howled.

"I know that, idiot! Get it back!" The comic-opera tone of the exchange was lost to him.

"I can't, sir!" the driver's response was a wail of despair, but the Head barely heard the words. He could only stare fascinated as the ground rushed toward them with terrifying speed. Oh, stars, that it would end like this. If only he had a few more weeks...

The aircar slowed as if regretting its rash action and stopped barely a foot from the ground. It hung there for a few seconds, nose down, then hopped up a few meters and dropped again, its ineffectual engines sputtering feebly. It repeated its little dance, looking for all the world as if it were trying to find a hole to fly through. Giving up, it flipped over and bulleted toward the horizon – upside down. The occupants stared at the ground less than two meters above their heads, their speed – three times the speed the car was designed for – tearing up the country turf and leaving a furrow behind them.

Summers warmed to his job. The craft barrel-rolled several times, then shot straight up, looping over the open fields in ever more complex maneuvers. It nearly tore off the roof of a farmhouse, had a private gymkhana through an orchard, dived on a herd of farm animals, took a quick bath in a lake, whipped through haystacks and flattened grain fields, and all the while rose and fell at dizzying speeds. Behind Hal and his controls, a rapidly growing peanut gallery vied with each other in calling out suggestions, while the car's interior became very foul indeed.

After ten minutes of hair-raising gyrations they were nearly back where they had started, screaming through the streets of the capitol city. Hal was an expert by this time, choosing the smallest possible holes through which to bullet the stately craft. Narrow streets between office buildings that happened to line up correctly were his favorite targets, with low bridges and clover-leafs tied for second.

At last Summers took the car back up to two kilometers and cut power to the remote controlled zero point drive. The craft dropped like a stone, then hurled back upward as its turbine engines growled back to life and the madly fighting pilot realized he was back in control.

The Head panted through the malodorous air and swiped at his brow fur with shaking fingers as the pilot brought the car to a hovering halt above the Palace. Hanash and the guards too began to breathe, their mouths and clothing foul from their bodies' reactions. Only the Head and the pilot had managed to overcome the terror and nausea.

"Back to the Palace, driver," the Head sighed resignedly. "Apparently we will not be allowed to leave."

In the *Angel* far above, Mentor passed the word to Summers, and the engineer touched a series of keys. The extra drive assembly, hard-wired to make it a single connected unit, was teleported back to the ship.

CHAPTER 26

Jander had chosen to take his dinner in the crew lounge rather than the mess hall, the better to gauge the mood of his off-duty Corpsmen. He was not disappointed. The friendly gaming, casual conversations, spontaneous laughter and a few instances of romance reassured him that their morale was high and their lives properly oriented. He got the sense that they had come to see the *Angel* as their harbor and haven, and not just a means of transport and adventure. They were family, and this was home. And having Dad in the room changed their demeanor not one bit.

He saw Vickie's touch in all of it, and he felt the warmth of her presence all around him. He drank it in, allowing himself a few moments of carefree gratitude.

Gabriel Vargas, a Brazilian pulse gunner recruited by Ford as his apprentice yeoman, teleported in and presented an oval plate resplendent with grilled steak in red wine mushroom sauce, Mexican street corn and potatoes au gratin. "Your dinner, senhor." He vanished and came back two seconds later with a steaming mug. "And your coffee." He placed it inches from Jander's right hand.

Steele picked it up, sipped and grimaced. "Come on, Gabé, I could make better coffee with my socks."

"Me desculpe, meu Capitão. I forgot you have a special blend." Corpsman Kinkajou flashed his luxuriously mustachioed grin, taking Steele's remark with the humor he knew was intended. He took the offending item and vanished.

Jander cut off a bite of steak in mushroom sauce and forked it into his mouth, then stopped chewing with an odd look on his face.

Gabé returned with a fresh mug and saw the look. "Doohickey steak, senhor. We cut a few out of the herd when we stampeded it. Do you like it?"

"It's really good. Kind of halfway between pork and veal." He took another bite. "Doohickey" was another of the ubiquitous puns the Corps was guilty of, referring to the animal's huge teeth and rapid digestive system. Several kilometers of fencing had been removed from a grass range, and the ship's four werewolves plus a dozen ghosts and a few levitators had stampeded the food animals, nineteen thousand of them, to all points of the compass. "I assume Science cleared this as edible?"

"Sí, senhor. I'm told Ertain has left-handed proteins. I have no idea what that means except that we can eat it."

Steele nodded. "It's called chirality. Gaea has left-handed amino acid-based proteins, along with right-handed sugars, so we can metabolize just about anything else that does. So does Arcadia, by the way, with the caveat that it also has some heavy metals we could do without, but not enough to hurt us."

Gabé's eyes unfocused for a second as he committed that information to memory, then bowed with a smile.

Richard popped in, gave Gabé an upward nod and stepped into Steele's line of sight.

Jander took another bite and continued around it. "We ought to, umph, acquire more of these critters for the freezer. No reason to go completely unrewarded for this mission."

"Can do." Richard pulled out the tablet he always carried and tapped away, inserting the note between "drop in on the ladies" and "check the candy supply". The self-appointed duties of Orion's intrepid adjutant were many and varied.

Vargas, a onetime rancheiro among other things, stepped in. "Suppose we gather up a few as breeding stock for Arcadia? They'd be happy with the grass there, and we'd have them close at hand."

Jander shook his head emphatically. "Absolutely not. We don't want to do anything more to harm the natural ecology there. If even a few of them get loose and go feral, they'd multiply like rabbits and we could cause some real harm to the environment. It's bad enough to have us there – look at what the first contact already did to the bug population. No, I won't risk it." His voice had raised with his annoyance.

Vargas shied away a bit, then decided to stay

despite the suddenly electric air.

Ford, much more fearless through his familiarity with Jander, shifted his feet but held his ground. "Sure, boss. I know you're right and all, but if you don't mind me saying so, it's not like you to dump like that. Something big goin' on?"

Jander sighed and slumped back from the table. "I apologize, Gabé. I am otherwise pissed, yes. I'll let Pavel tell it." He pointed with his fork toward the hatch. The two turned in time to see the Ukrainian stride in.

"From the anxious looks directed at me I would deduce that you already have my news. Ertain has found the Æzant system, and their Seventh Fleet is converging on it."

"Damn," Jander grunted. "Pavel, I wish you were wrong for once. There goes the whole campaign plan – we can't allow those poor guys to become slaves. Command level meeting in the briefing room in thirty minutes."

"Yessir." Richard vanished to spread the news. Gabé felt the energy of the jump through the special sixth sense every teleporter seemed to have and followed on his heels.

Pavel sat down across the table. "I am quite surprised we have accomplished as much as we have before something like this happened."

"So is everybody else, to be honest." Jander sensed a pressure on his leg, followed by a series of pinpricks ascending his calf. He reached a hand down to meet the head of Cinnamon, his tortoise-shell cat, who spent plenty of time in the lounge promoting strokes and treats while her person was otherwise occupied. She butted his hand with a low-pitched plurr-rp and hopped into his lap to inspect his dinner.

He held Cindy back with a soft forcefield while he sliced off a small bite of steak for her. It was gone in an instant. Two other cats, of the forty or so on board along with dozens of other small pets, crouched nearby but did not contest the queen's elite standing. "How soon can you get the Æzant captain up here?"

"Allow us fifteen minutes," Pavel told him. "He is incarcerated with other high-ranking officers in a penal complex just outside the capital. I will send Guardiana with Kinkajou. Their very attractive-ness may serve as an advantage in convincing the other prisoners that they must remain there." The classically beautiful Italian and the equally striking Brazilian were well trained in pathport team tactics, including behavior calculated to assuage the shock their sudden appearance always engendered. "And his crew?"

"We'll leave them. The disappearance of the whole bunch could tip our hand." He cut a bite of steak for himself and lifted it toward his mouth over Cindy's swipe. "Have Vanessa indoctrinate the captain in Sabarian language, and we'll have Alpha create a mental block to prevent him from retaining anything worth remembering. I'll interview him as soon as the meeting is over."

He chewed reflexively. "Correction – when the firefight is over."

CHAPTER 27

Steele settled into his chair and looked down the long rows of faces at the conference table and along the walls. The multi-faceted campaign against Ertain called for an almost unwieldy command team, but he welcomed the contributions of every one of them. He knew without a doubt that their collective input would save lives.

"I apologize to those of you who were off-duty," he began, "but recent events have just thrown our schedule into the wood chipper. So it's all hands on deck to adjust accordingly.

"The original plan, as you know, was to avoid full-scale battle unless necessary. Given time, our war of nerves would have compelled the Head to withdraw his fleets from deep space without much bloodshed. Given time, the Twin Planets would have become so paranoid that the population at large would have demanded the strongest possible defense, which would mean recalling the fleets and setting them up for a Confederation blockade. Given time.

"Unfortunately, the Ertainian Seventh Fleet has stumbled upon the Æzant system. Here we have a peaceful race of budding astronauts just past the threshold of interstellar travel, with the technology and numbers to provide Ertain with slave fleets."

He looked to Pavel, who nodded. "The Æzant industrial base, under compulsion, could begin turning out completed warships in a few months. If we prolong the siege of Ertain for much longer than that, the Seventh Fleet could provide enough overseers to control a thousand Æzant-manned ships. Ignoring for the moment the deplorable thought of a race enslaved, a fleet of that size could wreak considerable havoc, perhaps even instigate revolt within a pacified Ertain."

"Which leaves us with two tasks," Jander took the lead again. "First, we have to take the *Angel* to Æzant and hope we aren't faced with a fait accompli. Second, we have to speed up the recall of the other fleets to keep the Head from sending additional forces to supplement the Seventh.

"So instead of avoiding battle, we give them a bellyful. We take the first page of Phase Three for today, then zip over to Æzant while Ertain catches her breath. While we're gone, Alpha will have as many people as the *Angel* can spare in our newly established Ertainian hideout to continue Phase Two in our absence. We'll retain the necessary engineering, weaponry and bridge personnel to fight the ship, and keep our Confederation passengers under lock and key. Questions?"

"What if the Ertainians have already occupied Æzant?"

"That depends on how thorough the occupation is. If small, the Æzants should be able to handle it themselves as long as the fleet is compromised. If there is a powerful force on the planet, we may have to call in the Confederation for the job – which I don't want to do, for appearance's sake. I hope to avoid that by entering the system slowly and giving the Ertainians plenty of time to mobilize. If they follow general orders, they'll have every ship and every man aloft to meet us."

"How many will you leave with me?" Vickie had managed to accept that her husband was going to "dive into danger" without her again, although it was clear from her smoldering hazel eyes that she did not like it.

"All the personnel associated with Phase Two who are in Terry's science department, minus a squad in sick bay to take care of our patients. And you'll get all the auxiliary craft except two Sprites and as many ghosts as we can spare. I want the attacks on Liev to begin immediately, and ghosts are unencumbered by gravity."

He saw the storm warnings in Denny's eyes – he would be separated from his bride – and went on hurriedly, "That means we'll all be sacrificing some comfort – among other things, we're losing our best cooks – but I want to give you as much muscle as possible." Denny's mouth snapped shut.

The byplay was not lost on his own wife. "But that deprives you of your most effective ground force."

"Ertain's four billion are a bigger headache than the Seventh Fleet's ten thousand. Besides, I'm keeping most of the teleporters, because I anticipate we'll need plenty of fast evacuation work. Actually, I wish I could give you more, but with fifteen percent of our complement and two thirds of our Banshees guarding Arcadia I can only leave two Sprites, four Banshees and a hundred Corpsmen with you. It's an awkward division, but it's the one most likely to enable us to do both jobs." She nodded acceptance, and Denny grudgingly copied her. Jander turned to the table at large. "Anything else?"

Janet Flowers, who was wearing a large name tag to bypass the fact that she looked exactly like the Head, asked in her raspy Head's voice, "Suppose we're discovered down there? Some of their stolen technology could detect our shielding and blow our cover, and without the *Angel* we won't have a bugout."

"Excellent point, Wildflower. Kitsune!" He turned to the sensors chief, who flashed her trademark grin. "See how fast you can find an alternate hidey-hole they can retreat to. Try to find a place with enough natural cover so that they won't need a lot of shielding." Yukio bobbed her head and turned her eyes to Tsin Li-san. The telepath connected with her to keep her posted on the meeting as she turned transparent and wafted through the wall toward the Bridge.

"Thank you, Janet. Any more thoughts?"

There was nothing. "Very well. Alpha, you and Chloe will get your party moved down as soon as possible. I want you on the surface before we stir them up, so there's no chance of your being discovered in transit." He stood. "Dismissed."

Vickie came up to him as the room cleared, her brilliant eyes filled to capacity. "Don't get into too much trouble, okay, fella?"

He smiled and traced her jawline with his fingertips. "The *Angel*'s a small planet, hon. We'll be fine. I'm a lot more worried about leaving you without her support. I'm not going do anything that would risk stranding you here, believe me."

Her lips parted as she leaned into his gentle touch. "I know. You're leaving me with enough muscle to take over this planet if we have to, but..." She took his hand in both of hers and studied it intently, as if searching his palm for the right words. "Well..."

"You don't have to say it," he said softly. "I expect you to finish the job if I fail, as I would if... anything happened to you." He pulled her close, breathing deeply the fragrance of her hair. "It doesn't mean I love you less. We have a job to do, and we must see it through no matter what." He leaned back and lifted her chin with a finger, "Don't apologize for courage, my love. Just watch over your own, too, okay? Keep our family safe... no matter what."

She tried a whimsical smile. "Don't worry about that, darling – and I can show you a whole bunch of rodents who'll wish they'd never heard of either one of us!"

STEELE NODDED FROM his command chair, and several things happened simultaneously. Nwoye Lam, the helmsman, punched the key which teleported the otherwise motionless *Angel* to a position fifteen thousand kilometers above the Ertainian capitol city; Mealla O'Hearne, who had taken over as primary armaments officer upon Kalanev's promotion, cut the baffle screens, opened the gunports and directed her gunners to run out their weapons; Tsin Li-san triggered the connections which not only cut into the Head's intercom circuit, but also preempted the entire planets-spanning address system. In less than a second the *Angel* was visible to all, and Steele's voice could be heard by billions.

He created forcefields within his own throat and mouth to make his Ertainian more understandable. "To the Head of Ertain, to the people of the Twin Planets, greetings. This is Orion, Lord of the Omega Corps."

He paused to let that sink in, and caught the thoughts of Kurino at her sensors station. They were already attracting fire from the Home Fleet.

"Forgive me for interrupting you in these interesting times, but it has been brought to my attention that you have chosen to pit your strength and resources against those of the Omega Corps."

<*"The screens are already radiating at twenty-three percent of capacity,"*> Yukio informed him.

The ghost was concentrating on her console's readouts and displaying the results in her mind for his convenience.

"I grant that there is some reason for the overconfidence that would cause your supposition of invincibility. Up until now you have been allowed a reasonably easy time of it as far as your minor conquests are concerned. I am forced to admit that the initial success of your Plan was largely due to my inattention to the matter."

<*"Forty-four percent."*> The Japanese was getting concerned.

"Being a peaceful man, it is difficult for me to understand how an intelligent species such as yours could be so violently antisocial. But now, my subordinates have brought the scope of the problem to my attention, and I am taking this opportunity to try to make you see reason."

<*"Sixty-two percent."*>

"I am pleased with how my subordinates have handled this affair so far. I instructed them initially to harass you a bit, to give you an idea of the relative powers involved."

<*"Seventy-nine percent."*> Kitsune was openly anxious.

"Regrettably, it seems that you have proven incapable of heeding warnings of a subtle nature. As a result, I have felt compelled to bring my flagship here to show you more forcefully the futility of continuing this struggle."

<*"Ninety-seven percent."*> One more gun would overload their screens.

"Observe." He chopped a signal, and O'Hearne gratefully gave her gunners the order to open fire. The *Angel* exploded into life, and the ships outside her screens exploded into oblivion.

Steele breathed a tiny sigh of relief as the ship's pulse and beam weapons cut loose. He had cut it suicidally close. He could imagine how Vickie, safe in her hideout on the surface, must have felt – he need not worry about her fingernails on his back for a while. He ran his eyes over the full-coverage monitors that showed the cataclysmic scene without.

Defensively the *Angel* could withstand eighty-two and a fraction Ertainian nucleonic cannons; offensively the margin was irresistibly greater. He followed the lines of double-tap pulse spheres, each glowing with seven kilotons' worth of nuclear destruction, as they bored through screens and into nanosteel to erupt within the attacking warships. One or two such hits and the gunner could sway the spitting weapon to another ship.

The beam projectors too were proving their worth; the continuous hollow rods of force sliced completely through their targets and beyond, spearing two or even three ships at a time. Screens ruptured; inertial compensators failed; engine rooms and gun batteries exploded to consume internal atmospheres. Ertainians and Lievans alike became crisped, crushed and flared so swiftly they were unaware they died. In less than two minutes the pressure against the *Angel*'s screens dropped to zero.

But that was not the end. The eighty-four mighty weapons could reach five times farther than any type of nucleonic cannon. The scores of warships barreling through space toward the *Angel* found themselves being torn to pieces far outside their own range, helpless to reply. The gunners turned their weapons to all points of the galactic compass, shifting here and there with casual and practiced ease, until the only other object in sight within three hundred thousand kilometers was the planet itself.

Steele gave the signal to cease fire, then went on as casually as before. "Your Home Fleet has now been depleted by a matter of... " he read Mealla's mind and continued without a break, "...one hundred forty-seven ships. Granted that is only a small fraction of your number, but I trust I have made a point of sorts."

<*"Sixteen percent."*> Incredibly, the Ertainians who had been behind the planet were boring in to renew the fight.

Steele sighed audibly in mock resignation. "Oh, no, I see that I have not. I'm afraid there's nothing for it but to allow my subordinates to continue their harassment on a larger scale, in the hope that you will eventually see reason."

<*"Forty-two percent."*>

"I will instruct them to go easy on you for the time being. You do as a people have some measure of promise, despite your Head's willingness to continue a hopeless struggle. I regret the inevitable loss of life that will incur, but until you express a willingness to join the more civilized planets in peaceful endeavors you must be contained."

<*"Eighty percent."*>

"Thank you for your attention, and I hope our next meeting will be on friendlier basis." He jerked his thumb across his throat, and the *Angel*'s entrance was reversed. In an instant they were teleported a hundred thousand kilometers away and rendered undetectable. Three brain-pinging leaps later and they were outside the corridor between the Twin Planets. Lam threw his fingers and telekinetic mind into his helm console and the *Angel* headed for deeper space.

Li-san yelped and spun in his chair. "The Head's responding, sir!"

Steele was thoroughly astonished – the Head did not impress him as the type to shove his arm into a fireplace – but that did not disrupt the working of his brain. "Full planet broadcast! Full ship's circuit, two-way, except sick bay wardroom. Follow my lead, everyone – and remember, Ertainian language only! Jinwu, watch for my signals!" He flipped his index finger up and down.

He sat up in his chair and listened tensely as the Head's harsh voice cut through the ship. His first signal was one finger up, telling Tsin to let the Head talk.

"*To Orion and his childish crew, greetings.*" The words were slurred through sneering lips. "*May I be the first to congratulate you on your fireworks display. The fact that there none of my ships were in the vicinity did not detract from the beauty of the spectacle.*"

Steele cut him off with a laugh. The Head was playing right into his hands – apparently, in his arrogance, he was not expecting a rebuttal. Jander's finger dropped and Tsin cut the Head's transmission. The Ertainian leader's antiquated equipment sounded an audible blip, forcing him to accept that his opponent was in control.

"An interesting fiction, my small friend, especially as it implies that you allowed my cruiser to come so close to your planet without interference. Your incompetence is revealed either way – I seem to recall that it is your duty to protect the people of the Twin Planets." He raised his finger.

Blip. "*Of course it is, and it always shall be!*" The Head's voice drawled as he sought desperately to fabricate a response. "*However, it is also my duty as supreme commander to protect my forces from cowardly attacks...*"

Jander shifted forward in his chair. The finger dropped. "Oh, I see. Well, then, if you were aware of the attack and have time to withdraw your air-tight cordon, something your commanders might take issue with, why did you not regroup to oppose me?" He chuckled again, and a few of the bridge personnel followed his lead and joined in. Finger up. Blip.

262   ◆   Keith Huntsman

The Head sputtered a bit, then caught himself. *"It is my will to save my forces until you are compelled to battle on equal terms. Your childish pranks are of no consequence."*

"I'm sure the people of Moleg City will be happy to know that their problem is nothing to sneeze at." Jander waved his arms, and the crew obediently snickered. Kalanev, behind him in the second chair, raised a few eyebrows by emitting something like a breathy rasp.

The Head's temper was suffering badly. *"I forbid you to question my statements! We of the Twin Planets recognize you for the coward you are, and we do not shrink from meeting you on any terms you choose!"*

He had to raise his voice to be heard. The crew was really getting the hang of it. Unintelligible remarks loaded with derisive sarcasm came from throughout the ship, barely out of range of the communicators. Even the Sabarian women on the twenty-third level were entering into the spirit of the thing.

Finger down. "Let's be reasonable, son," Jander chided. "We've been kicking your loutish ass all over space, and all you've been able to do in response is scramble around like mice. And as for meeting you in full-scale battle, my subordinates took you on twice before today and sailed away unscathed. We have beaten you at every turn, and we shall continue to do so until you recognize the futility and beg for peace." The crew in the background expressed their eagerness to be let loose. Finger up.

Blip. *"Do your worst, Orion!"* the Head snarled hotly. He was wild with fury at this humiliating treatment. *"Forget any hope of easy victory – I am not a fool to be frightened by sleight-of-hand. We defy you to the end! Ours is the Way of Power, and it is the Way of Power that will carry us to victory! In a month, in a year, in a hundred years, when your puny power is broken and your people destroyed, we will still be strong and undaunted – and we will be there to take our rightful place over your corpse!"*

He was met with guffaws. Finger down. Steele, his voice still calmly taunting, spoke over the noise. "You are a stubborn man, my small friend. We really have no intention of destroying you – as I have said, your people do show some measure of promise. Our task is, and has been, to purge you of your antisocial attitude toward other species. If Ertain is destroyed it will be your foolish pride that destroys it. Perhaps if you were removed…." He paused as if considering the notion. "Um, no. We are not here to disrupt your political system. You may retain your position for as long as your people agree to your incompetence. Granted, your removal might make peace more likely, but it is the people of Ertain who must make that choice." Finger up.

Blip. *"They have made their choice!"* the Head snarled. *"There is only one man worthy to be the Head of Ertain, and he is me!"*

Steele grinned in satisfaction. That was what he had wanted to hear – and broadcast. Finger down.

"Very well, let us assume that the populace hangs on your every word – so to speak. All you need to do right now is reconsider, and admit that you have erred. Nothing could be simpler – as you have already learned from our conversation it is much easier to admit the truth than to fabricate a lie..." Finger up.

"*I have not lied!*" the Head shouted. "*And I have not erred! It is implicit in my very station that my decisions are unalterably correct. I am the Head of Ertain, and mine is the power supreme!*"

He was jeered by the entire crew. Steele gave him a few seconds of it, then dropped the finger again. "How quaint. I don't recall ever hearing such mighty delusions of grandeur in all my travels. Among my people such airs are known only to the incurably insane." Finger up.

The Head spluttered, "*You dare –* "

Finger down. "Not at all – there's no daring involved. I'm merely making a professional observation. But no matter." He made his voice imply a shrug. "This has been an enlightening conversation, son – not to say entertaining – but as I'm sure you know I'm a busy man. I hope that the next time I appear over your planet you are more coherent in your outlook. Until then, farewell." Finger up.

"*I am not fin –* " Finger down, with a jab for emphasis. Tsin cut the multiple connection, chopping off the Head both in the *Angel* and on the planets.

Steele sat back and grinned airily. "Orion to crew, and guests. Very well done. You may stand down.

Thank you, Jinwu. Helm, set our course for Æzant."

He grinned at the cheers. He had gained immeasurably, and the Head had suffered an immeasurable loss. To Orion fell the great prize – morale.

CHAPTER 28

The Æzant people were bobtailed and hairless marsupials, who commonly wore flaring skorts cinched just above the hip and close-fitting jackets that covered the back but left the pouched midriff exposed. Unlike most baldish intelligences they got away with such minimal clothing because their home world was quite warm with almost no axial tilt and therefore no seasons. Both sexes possessed thick-skinned abdominal pouches, slightly darker than the tawny skin on the rest of the body, but only the females had the functional capacity to carry and nurture the young. Their narrow shoulders and long skulls with sharply pointed chins gave them an elfish look.

Steele interviewed the Æzant captain in the High Lounge directly above the bridge, on the fourteenth level. The hexagonal lounge was the nearest thing to a throne room the *Angel* had and was the epitome of luxury. The funnel-shaped central deck extended from the double hatch and spread wide as it approached the far bulkhead, that end holding a small stage with a well-equipped entertainment center.

On either side of the funnel, the thick silky carpeting extended upward in a gentle curve from twenty centimeters above the deck almost to the overhead. Hidden beneath the concave surface of the wall carpet were hundreds of thousands of nanoprocessors coordinating millions of gel cells, which molded themselves to the contours of any physical form. One had only to leap or lean into the curved section to construct a perfectly tailored, fabulously comfortable chaise lounge.

The Æzant accepted the invitation to sit rather dubiously, wondering how he would contrive to get up again. He wriggled experimentally and felt the gel cells realign beneath him, pushing him gently to his feet. He bared his broad, curved teeth and settled in again. "Fascinating."

"Glad you like it, En'tal," Jander smiled in return. He spoke in Sabarian, in which the Æzant had been mechanically educated. In return he had learned to understand the captain's language, a bubbling hiss no human could articulate. "As you may have guessed by now, we of the Omega Corps take our relaxation whenever we can and designed our flagship accordingly."

"And you deserve every minute of it, Lord Orion," En'tal responded. "The Sabarian ladies on the higher deck told me much about you."

"In that case we can dispense with the introductions." He paused as Vargas appeared from nowhere with a tray, handed Steele his coffee, teleported across the room and presented the Æzant with what was to him an exotically delicious and mildly intoxicating beverage, coconut milk. His duty done; the mustachioed Brazilian disappeared.

En'tal was fully occupied for several seconds. "I can see that even the most impossible things I have heard may be true. That was one of the two who rescued me from my prison not long ago. Can you in fact turn yourself into predatory animals?"

"Only a small number of us have that ability; our talents vary." Jander blinked at sensors above him that summoned a pair of drop trays from the overhead and placed his cup on the one nearer to him. "But there will be a time to answer your questions later. I'm afraid I must quiz you on the problem facing us both."

En'tal nodded. "Of course. You refer to the Ertainian invasion of our home world, of which I have been informed. But with you aiding our cause I have no fears."

Steele pursed his lips, concerned by the conviction he saw through his telepathic link with Guardiana one deck above them. He decided to shake the awed captain up a bit.

"Ah, yes. The reports I've received on your people indicate that you can be complacent. I regret to point out that Ertain comprises a serious threat – but if you choose to accept whatever happens with equanimity our resources may be of greater value elsewhere."

The Æzant stiffened. "Complacent peoples do not

indulge in pioneering flights into the unknown, as my command was doing. I said 'cause' and I meant it." He set down his half-consumed beverage with a forceful click.

"Then you must remember that freedom must be bought, not taken for granted. I will give you whatever aid I can, but ultimately the fate of your planet rests in your hands."

"What is your price?" En'tal's voice was tight.

"I will secure your freedom if you will safeguard it." He let that sink in. "We will enter your system, probably fight a battle, and leave again. Undoubtedly there will be survivors from the Ertainian force, but we cannot pause to root them out. If your people allow them to regain their strength and renew the attack when we are gone, we will not be responsible for the outcome. To use one of your own expressions, we have our own pouch to fill."

En'tal's flat face was expressionless. "That's all you want – to fight for us?"

"When did I say that? I want to end the menace of Ertain. When we leave the Æzant system the menace there will be compromised. Whether it recurs is your worry. I am doing it not only because your people would otherwise be enslaved, but because those slaves would be the property of Ertain – and in a few months I'd be fighting you."

He raised his hand to forestall En'tal's protest. "And don't think you could affect a viable resistance – ask the ladies upstairs. The Ertainians are the most vicious thugs ever to acquire a brain. You would have no chance. As of now there are two hundred-odd ships and some ten thousand men converging there. After they had beaten you down – and they will, barring our interference – there would soon be a hundred thousand more to make sure you stay beaten. If they are allowed the slightest foothold you can be certain they would crush you."

"Like hell they would!" En'tal shoved himself to his feet, broad teeth bared. "You've lived in the clouds far too long. There is more than talent and technology that can win a fight, and whatever it takes we of Æzant have in full measure!"

Narrow jaw working, he paced furiously in ever tightening circles. "You just get me there – even if you do no more than that and let them take us, we will never admit defeat! We may have to work for them, maybe even fight for them – but someday, somehow, we will be free!"

"Bravo!" Jander rose and clapped the Æzant on the shoulder. "Now I know we're on the right side. You are absolutely right, Captain. You bet we'll help you, any way we can."

En'tal glared at him, then turned away and hissed a few morphologically impossible positions.

Jander grinned and waited him out. "I've heard that before, more or less. People seem to stay awake nights trying to find new ways to describe me."

The Æzant scowled, then rubbed his eyes and made his species' wheezing equivalent of a chuckle.

"I'm not at all surprised. That was rough, Milord."

"Goes with the title. I can't afford to coddle anyone." Jander smiled and tugged at his belt, mimicking the Æzant gesture of opening the pouch to a friend. "Forgive me, En'tal, but I had to see what you are made of. You've been so dazed by all you've seen that your true nature was difficult to plumb. You have our support, I assure you."

He tapped his wristpad, and Vargas popped in to refill their cups and as quickly disappeared. "Now, Captain, shall we get down to business?"

En'tal made a chair, studying the mental chameleon that was his host. "One more question, if you please. Tell me about your Stellar Confederation."

"First of all, it's not 'our' Confederation." Jander nonchalantly tossed himself into the opposite wall without spilling a drop of coffee. "In our opinion, aligning the Omega Corps with any galactic union would upset the balance of power and possibly create more strife than there is already – which is plenty. The Omega Corps is strictly independent, giving aid to any race or society that needs help with a problem beyond their capacity. You might call us free-lance trouble-shooters, loaning our talents for whatever causes we believe have merit. The Confederation is so important, however, that I prefer to work with it personally. There is only this one ship in this sector of space, but it is crewed by the elite of my species."

He mentally patted himself on the back; he had his line of bull down solid. Words like "cruiser" and "this ship" and "flagship" hinted at overwhelming power somewhere else. In fact, except for the three hundred Corpsmen on Gaea, the *Angel* was unsupported.

"The most numerous group in the Confederation is the Sabarian species, with the mother planet and twenty-three independent children or grandchildren as members. They have had star flight for over six hundred years. Three hundred years ago they joined with the Hasgondi bloc of ten planets and the Leosan bloc of seven to form the embryonic Confederation.

"The alliance has grown to include eleven species and eighty-four planets, plus nineteen colonies dependent on various members and three species in dependent status until they qualify for membership. They also covertly protect a number of underdeveloped planets from interference so that they may develop normally.

"The government is located on Dephlet, a planet developed specifically to be the capitol of the Confederation. It is headed by a Director, selected from a pool of candidates by a series of electromechanical tests, and confirmed by vote of confidence.

"The legislative branch is the Stellar Council, consisting of three delegates from each of the member planets. The Council has administrative control over the planetary members, but that control does not extend to their laws or societies. The central government manages trade agreements and interplanetary relations, handles affairs with other galactic powers and protects the members with the Fleet.

Otherwise, planets maintain local governance within the Confederation."

"That sounds very sensible," En'tal said. "And how does a society qualify for membership?"

"Once a species has developed a means of interstellar travel, they are eligible for consideration as dependents, a precondition for membership. It's voluntary, of course. The requirements for consideration vary according to the qualities of the petitioner, but generally they include economic stability, a centralized government of some sort, and some military potential.

"Dependents have no voice in the Council, but they have controlled travel and trade, Fleet protection and technical advice. There is no coercion or pressure of any kind, if you exclude trade relations. Members of course maintain favorable trade policies with each other within Confederation guidelines. It's up to each dependent whether they allow travel visitors.

"Once the dependent reaches a competitive level of commerce and interaction, it may apply for membership. It must be accepted by a three-quarters majority of member planets. When the trade, government and legal details are worked out, it turns its armed fleet over to the Confederation complete with crews, for service wherever needed.

"The Confederation maintains the Fleet along with the central government with revenues levied from the members according to their means.

Merchant vessels, along with science, exploration or any other independently operated ships are allowed autonomy and are not subject to any Fleet participation unless drafted in an emergency.

"Joining the Confederation is never a question of getting something for nothing. In a union of equals everyone pulls equal weight. That by itself is an excellent reason for joining. You will have the company and protection of friends, friends who will help you in any way they can, friends you can count on to fight for you if they must – as long as you are willing to do the same for them. Just as you are strengthened and bettered by the alliance, so shall they be."

En'tal listened spellbound, a bit overwhelmed by the scope of it. "So, you would recommend we accept dependent status?"

"That's not my call, but if my species were in your position we would definitely consider it." He settled a bit and sipped at his coffee, wryly admitting to himself that Gaea was so far outside the ballpark they could barely see the lights.

"Of course, my recommendation is academic. If your government expresses an interest, we'll convey your location to them as a courtesy. As soon as Ertain is neutralized and occupied by Confederation forces they are certain to send a delegation to treat with your leaders, and you can learn about them first-hand."

"You mean, you won't occupy Ertain yourself?"

"With what? One ship and two hundred sixty crew?

I can't do that anymore than I can post a guard over Æzant. We have recently discovered an unclaimed planet in this sector, just outside the Confederation sphere, which we plan to turn into an advanced base. That's where the rest of my crew is, and the development will take most of our energy for quite a while.

"But Æzant is the problem right now." He leaned up to the drop table and set down his cup. "Tell me about your planetary defenses."

En'tal sighed. "What defenses? Æzant has been under central government for generations. All our most powerful weapons were scrapped or consigned to museums centuries ago."

"I was afraid of that. Ertain will have an easy time of it. It's a wonder you haven't been located in all those centuries as it is." He thought for a moment. "Police?"

"Strong. Crime is always a problem. They're the only group under arms, though, and they aren't strong enough to repulse a determined global attack." He hesitated, then went on, "Let's face it. Our largest weapons you could fit into your pouch if you had one. Our resistance would be token indeed. With the head start they've got, the Ertainians might already be in control."

"Cheer up," Jander smiled. "The Omega Corps specializes in the impossible. We'll have your planet back in a week." He added in his mind, *I hope.*

AS PLANNED, THE *ANGEL* loafed into the Æzant system unbaffled and at a leisurely speed, and it was clear the Seventh Fleet had seen her. Ships came boiling from the planet's surface by the score, leaving only a few on the ground to hold key positions. The fleet powered out to half a million kilometers and grouped into a bowl formation, with the lip of the half sphere spreading outward to flank the *Angel* as she approached. There they waited, knowing the *Angel* would come to them.

As soon as the big ship penetrated the warp sphere of the fleet, Tsin activated the jamming impulse that would prevent the enemy from communicating with Ertain or any of the other roaming fleets. The *Angel's* eighty-four guns were manned and ready, and eight telebooths were crewed to hurl fission bombs through quantum entanglement into the enemy ships.

Steele, with Cobra in one flanking chair and En'tal in the other, listened to the reports from the two baffle-shielded Sprites he had sent ahead. The Ertainians had completed their conquest days before, using a combination of ultimatum and example to complete the takeover of Æzant in short order. Town-sized sheets of cooling lava demonstrated the ruthlessness of their campaign.

En'tal sobbed quietly at the horrible damage. "And you thought we would not fight!"

Kalanev, as cold and as hard as he outwardly was, sighed in sympathy. "They will pay for this, my friend, in full."

"Pay attention, Cobra, there's something happening down there." Steele stared tensely at the big screen.

"I am very much awake, Captain."

Steele was instantly sorry to have spoken, but his whirling mind was fully occupied. The fleet was breaking the bowl formation as the *Angel* approached the lip. The bottom of the bowl quickly flared out to skirt the horizon of the planet, while the lip curled inward toward Æzant rather than continue the flanking maneuver. What in the world were they doing?

Suddenly he jerked erect, the hair on the back of his neck tingling. "Helm! Bear down – get us in there, fast! Gunnery – prepare to open fire!" The *Angel*'s gun ports spiraled open and ran out their barrels as she bulleted forward.

But they were too late. The fleet, all two hundred-plus units, roared down to the surface in a carefully preset pattern. Long before the *Angel* made it into maximum range every ship had grounded – smack in the center of a city.

Steele slammed his armrest with his fist and released a few of his rare curses. "The one thing they could have done!"

"You must admit it is effective," Kalanev repaid him for his rebuke. "It is our splendid luck to get a commander who knows when to disobey orders."

Jander growled, much less for the comment than for being tactically outfoxed. There was no way they could attack the fleet now; to do so would burn hun-

278 Keith Huntsman

dreds of square kilometers out of the cities and kill hundreds of thousands of Æzant innocents.

"Report from the Sprites, Milord," Tsin called. "The crews are scattering to the four winds, leaving only a few guards locked inside each ship. It could take weeks to dig them out."

"And every city, every citizen is a hostage," Steele gritted. "If we attack the crews the ships will burn entire city blocks – and if we attack the ships the crews could wipe out tens of thousands. Damn!"

"Then there's nothing you can do?" En'tal moaned.

Jander thumped his armrest rhythmically, his brow knotted. "You know better than that, Captain, I made a promise to you. But we'll have to ask your people to do a larger portion of the work. We don't have the numbers at present."

"Anything you need, Lord Orion. But the cities…"

"Are in no danger if the ships aren't there." Steele was silent for several seconds. "If we neutralize the ships the disembarked crews will be unsupported. Hostages may still die, but with quick action the damage can be kept to a minimum. We can get rid of the ships and tell you where the troops are hiding. Can you take it from there?"

"Just watch us!" En'tal responded through gritted teeth. "But how can you get rid of the ships?"

By way of answer Steele smacked his chair again. "Angela, full broadcast save sick bay wardroom." He waited a breath until Angela flashed acknowledgement on his console.

"Attention all, including our Sabarian guests. We are going to steal a fleet..."

CHAPTER 29

To conserve his teleporting strength Richard Ford walked into the cargo hold instead of jumping. Most of the hold was curtained off to conceal its contents, so that anything noticeably Gaean or high-tech was hidden from their Sabarian "guests". The exception was the area around the hold's loading zone that included the huge telebooth. The sixty-eight former captives had already been exposed to that technology during their rescue, and since it was vital to the task at hand there was no harm in allowing them a glimpse of it.

Nearby stood a mock-up of an Ertainian cruiser's helm station, and before it were a number of Gaean and Sabarian fledgling pilots getting last-minute instructions. Richard joined the group, since he would be one with them.

After three days of mind-bending preparation Lord Orion's audacious and dangerous plan was about to be executed.

Denny Connors planted his bucket-sized fists on his hips and scowled down at his students. "Number one!" he roared in Sabarian.

"Depress the seven red switches to engage drive

engines!" He was answered by a ragged chorus.

"Number *one!*" This time the response was in crisper unison.

"Number two!"

"Depress the blue switch to synchronize engine pressure...." Ford joined in, digging the answers from his mechanically educated mind and eying the laser-highlighted location of the switch on the console. In another hold Hal Summers would be holding forth in front of another model, bending his psyche all out of shape with the necessity of speech. Other engineers or experienced pilots, two of them Sabarian, harangued other Greek choruses in other holds, training two hundred-plus men and women most of whom had never even seen a control room. And the entire plan depended on each of them getting the prize off the planet's surface within a few minutes of taking over – without a mistake, without a collision, without a loss.

No chance, Richard thought, no chance in hell.

He belted out number eight: "Slide the white lever to engage screens!" This was a very engaging operation, he mused. He made a mental note to try that one on the boss; Steele loved a bad pun.

"Attention, all personnel. This is Lord Orion." Denny raised his hands. The hold became as silent as an elevator. *"We will be certain of our time. It is seven twenty-one Dephlet standard as of... now."* Ford gave the Squn-built chronometer in his Corps wristpad a casual glance; a timepiece perfected by

the elite microminiature electronics experts of the galaxy, there was more chance of his 'porting power failing than that of his watch losing a nanosecond of Dephlet Standard, Kohana Mean, Greenwich Mean or Montana Mountain time.

Steele let a few seconds slip by, then continued, "*Here is the latest report from the surface. All Ertainian groups are maintaining their positions, and all have been thoroughly and secretly surrounded by Æzant police forces.*"

That was a relief; it had been pretty tricky convincing the planet's local gendarme that Cobra's telepaths had accurate information.

"*Thus, Operation Shoplift will commence at seven forty-five.*"

The room buzzed. Richard felt a chill travel up his spine, even though he knew that he would be safer than any other teleporter. He was to be Pavel's partner, and that was like having Jesus on your keychain. Better – Jesus was probably a lousy shot.

"*Pathport teams will take your stations in fifteen minutes,*" Orion continued. "*I caution you to be sure of your links – a few practice jumps might be appropriate.*"

That was the least of Richard's worries; the Kalanev-Ford pathport team was legendary. Unfortunately, that very expertise meant that they would have more targets than anyone else. He looked around to the other two pairs that would be jumping off from this station. Vanessa Lozano with Gabriel

Vargas vanished as he saw them, and Tsin Li-san and engineer Gunnar Ormsson, an amusing half meter of difference between their heights, put their backs together and followed close behind. Another duo winked in and out from another station as they tested their connection.

The Sabarians in the crowd watched the flickering Corpsmen with emotions ranging from alarm to awe to hilarity. Richard could not help but wonder which of the strong reactions might rear up to compromise the mission.

Steele, unmindful of his active crew – since teleportation was instantaneous the practicing teams would not miss a word – continued calmly, "*Remember to check every corner of every ship. The pilots will be defenseless when they take over and must be assured of their safety. They'll have plenty of other things to think about.*"

The novice pilots around him tittered nervously. Ford could see through the boss's tactics – do your worrying now; you won't have time later.

"*Pilots, be lined up and on your toes. We must get you to your ships as soon as is safely possible. The enemy will be close by and you don't want visitors. So... be... ready!*

"*I wish you all the best of luck, and I'll see you at the rendezvous. Orion out.*"

Pavel stepped up behind him with his shark's grin already in place. "This is a task to my liking!"

He shrugged out of his jacket to reveal the jumpsuit beneath – "jumpsuit" being the literal style. In contrast to the dense nanosteel wire cloth reinforced with shock absorbers that armored the rest of the outfit, the back was a thin net designed to allow the skin contact that a pathport team needed to connect.

Richard forced a grin in return. "I gotta admit there's a charm to fighting against odds. But think of Jander, providing top cover with only eighteen people in this barn."

Pavel's right hand patted the Omega Corps insignia beneath his left shoulder. "Lord Orion can more than take care of himself – "

"All *RIGHT!*" Connors bellowed at the top of his lungs, stunning even the Ukrainian into silence. "We have time for one more run-through before the lid blows off. Number *ONE!*"

"*ALL STATIONS, REPORT.*" Steele was on the Bridge, ready at the helm, accompanied only by Kurino Yukio at sensors, Mealla O'Hearne covering communications, and Mealla's equally ginger twin brother Quinn, a metallurgist by trade but currently manning analytics.

In the cargo hold Anton Gastogne muttered into his headset microphone, then sat tense at the telebooth controls. One of the last Corpsmen to be activated before the *Angel* left Gaea, the former surveyor's job was to send the pathport teams to the precise locations from which they were to begin their assault, then teleport a pilot into each control room they cleared. Angela had the locations locked in, but it was the telebooth operators who would choose the safest time to transmit their living cargo as the *Angel* spun swiftly around the planet at the limit of teleport range. Lives depended on every delicate touch to his control board. He did a final check of his power levels, then took a deep breath and calmly steeled himself for the most vitally precise mission of his young life.

Richard, with Pavel's wiry shoulders pressed against his burly back, sent the mental command that pulled the layered padding of nanosteel from his shoulders and reconfigured it into a full helmet and mask that sealed itself to the fabric at his neck. The cuffs at his wrists expanded to add the flexible but tough gloves. The suit was permeated with nano-processors programmed to react instantly to a hit from a solid or energy weapon, while the netting on his back was infused to help maintain the connection between the teammates.

The suit was designed to protect the wearer head to foot from anything short of a tank killer. Richard took a deep breath and exhaled slowly, trying to convince himself of that. He well remembered the Ertainian copper slug that had slammed into his bare chest on Arcadia a very few months before. The rugged, mentally synchronized skinsuits represented the lesson learned from the injury he had barely survived.

He sighed again. This is it, he thought, and

286 ◆ Keith Huntsman

answered himself cynically, I knew you'd say that. He heard Pavel chuckle in his mind and ears. Together, already in sync, they unlimbered the pulse pistols from their battery-laden utility belts and settled them ready in their hands.

"*Ten seconds,*" Steele said, his voice a soothing drone. "*Remember your assignments, be sure of your targets. Six seconds. Good hunting, Corpsmen. Two, one... go!*"

They were off. Ford, hyped as he was, felt the millisecond's difference between natural and mechanical teleportation, then he found himself in an enemy cruiser's control room. His right gun spat out a triple tap with one squeeze, and an Ertainian who happened to be in the way fell before it. Pavel's pistols ripped twice, and Richard saw in his brain the next destination. He triggered his power, and another pirate in the ship's engine room spun to the deck. Yet another point of reference and another body, with Pavel adding to the score. Then they were done with this ship and it was time to move on. Jump...

Almost on their heels, a pilot arrived from a telebooth in the *Angel* and reached for the helm to sequence the ship for liftoff.

Their next landing was in a hotel, and the four weapons discharged together. Linked as he was to the Ukrainian, Richard was able to keep score. Five in the ship, seven here. Nine thousand, nine hundred eighty-eight to go.

Another jump, a police station that served as a

halfway point to the next target, then on to another control room. Three. Wardroom. One. Engine room. One. Jump, a native conference room with Ertainians to target and Æzants to spare, pow kapow pow pow, nine. Jump, hallway, blast, three. Jump to a midway point between targets, jump again. Another control room. Two. Jump...

It was just like Arcadia. One split second he was in one crowd, then the assassin at his back spotted the next target and passed on the destination and they jumped and fired and went on. The mind link was nothing like ordinary telepathic conversation. It was as if he and Pavel were one two-headed dragon, ambushing their victims and spitting fire, always in perfect accord with the same brain waves and experience and destination.

Yet there was a part of his being, that part which made him an individual, that stayed aloof and looked on amazed, astonished that he could become one with this uncanny killer at his back... jump, a double tap as the battery ran out of charge... jump, a halfway point, reload, you fool, you cannot kill with an empty gun... who was Pavel telling... Pavel would say pistol, not gun... drop both weapons into their holsters, flick out and store the spent batteries, slap in a fresh pair, another fifty shots each without reloading... draw the guns... jump, two triple taps...

... Jump... another control room... how many... how many ships with new Gaean or Sabarian pilots, how many more to become so... how many small groups of Ertainian terrorists to cut down nullify annihilate in the fastest time with the tiniest delay and move on and secure the ships but don't try to kill all the other pirates just knock them off balance and give the cops a chance jump move on but secure the ships check every corner the pilots will be defense-less jump blast reload jump blast jump move on...

<"... *Yours is free, this one is mine.*"> Abruptly the mind link became conversation. <"*Good luck, my friend.*">

<"*Same to you, bro'.*"> He pulled his shoulders away and jumped, landing alone in the ship he was to pilot. Shoot, this was nothin' like his old yella cab. Secure the ship; the pilot will have enough worries....

"Cool it, bucko," he said aloud, angrily. The frenzy of combat was clinging to his brain like a spider, and he felt his face contorted into a snarl. He forced his muscles to relax, and his mind relaxed with them. He heaved a tremendous, shuddering sigh, thought his mask and helmet back to their camouflaged place on his shoulders and looked around the inward-facing circle of bridge stations to find the helm console. Red switches, number one.

He pulled the dead Ertainian out of the way and sat down at the control board in the bloody chair too small for his Gaean body. The ship came alive under his still-gloved hands, and he remembered that he had missed five times with his left hand and twice with his right. He needed more target practice. Pavel, he knew, had not missed a mark.

The drive roared, and he hurriedly cut the power a bit. Pay attention, man, this town is messed up enough. Number four.

They were all coming back to him in pieces, damn his great variant memory, the stunned and stricken faces, the falling bodies, the blood-spattered walls where the pulse pistols' spheres of pure force had gone clear through and kept on going. Number seven. In his mind's eye he saw the Æzant woman, naked and dead, her small marsupial genitals brutally torn and bloody. In an instant of rage he had pumped seven triple taps into that Ertainian bastard, and Cielo had torn twenty-nine of his ilk to bloody fragments, bless her feral heart. She said they tasted foul.

The ship shuddered under his unpracticed hands and lifted sullenly, and Richard was reminded of his first driving lesson. It had been a big red Buick, and he found out later that his friend had stolen it. Jeez, that had scared him. He'd survived South Queens for fifteen years without joining a gang, and here he was, driving a stolen pimpmobile.

The viewscreens slowly darkened as he left the planet's atmosphere behind. What was that? The proximity alarm. The hologram within the circle of control stations popped up to show another space-ship spinning end over end straight toward him.

He locked his controls and teleported, arriving upside down in the other control room. The artificial gravity took over and he landed hard on his padded shoulder.

A shriek told him that the Sabarian pilot had discovered him. "Chill out, lady," he growled, then switched to Sabarian. "What's the problem? That's my coffin you're bearing down on."

She helped him up and literally shoved him toward the console. "I don't know! I lost control!"

"Yeah, I noticed that item." He scanned the board, trying to appear knowledgeable. To his relief he found the problem. "Here it is – you forgot number six. This panel of levers synchronizes the retros to stabilize the drive." He made the correction, joysticked the ship out of its dizzying flip and set it back on course, just in time to view his own cruiser whizzing by the bow. "By the numbers, girl. You're doing fine."

She flattened herself against his bicep and beamed up into his eyes. "Oh, thank you, so much!" she gushed, and started an electric slide across his chest. Oh crud, he thought ruefully, Cielo's feline senses will pick up on this for sure. He hoped she remembered that the Head had not picked these girls for their brains.

He gently disentangled himself from the Sabarian's outrageously flexible double-wristed hands. "Listen, you should have seen my takeoff. A blind Lievan could have done better." He grinned engagingly. "We're all in the same boat – so to speak. Which reminds me, I'd better get back to my own ride before we get too far away."

He finally managed to free himself and maneuvered her into the pilot's seat. "By the numbers, sugar. See you later." He jumped.

He felt the odd tugging which told him he was nearing the end of his range, then he was back in his own control room. Another few kilometers and he would have been sucking stardust. He settled in and checked his course, deciding it was safe to leave it on automatic pilot for a few more minutes. He glanced at the screens and saw that the Sabarian was in reasonably good control, then searched for others. There was one quite close, probably Pavel's, puttering along like a pussycat. That guy could do anything with ruthless efficiency, including pilot a strange craft without a hitch.

He looked ahead and saw the *Angel* slide into view from behind the moonless planet, the clean, faceted disco ball of a ship looking huge and beautiful. He saw a silvery beam flick out and push one of the egg-shaped Ertainian cruisers out of its collision course, then the smaller ship jerked away into a carefully prescribed position. That would be Denny at the controls, or Hal or Nwoye, taking over to park the cruiser with all the ease of veterans – which they definitely were not. All they had was almost instinctive mechanical skill, pure genius.

He flipped off the autopilot and spun his charge to decelerate with the main engines, noticing with more than a little anxiety that the Sabarian was wobbling quite a bit from using her forward retros to brake. There were egg-shaped ships all around them now, being handled with wildly varying degrees of skill, all being juggled like beans in the crowded space. He increased his backdrive to slow his momentum and give the less able pilots goofing room.

"*Hermes.*" It was Li-san, back in the *Angel* at his com station, tapping into his earbud.

"Hey, bro'. Wanna get me out of this can?"

"*We certainly do. We need you. I've been telling some of these idiots to stand off until we get a better pilot.*"

"No way you can mean me!" Richard certainly did not consider his horrible takeoff as any indication of greatness.

"*Yeah, you. You ought to see some of these yú-rén. A lot of them couldn't hit water if they were paddling a canoe.*"

He could see the truth of that all around him. "Maybe you're right. Lousy is better than suicidal. I'm coming in." He sighed and jiggled the drive.

CHAPTER 30

Vickie sat back in her chair and untangled the meshcap from her rumpled hair. Her small desk was nestled in a shallow alcove in the wall of the cavern, but the echoes from all the activity in the lofty space left her with a dull headache.

Above them was half a kilometer of limestone that rose as an uninhabited island in the southern Ertainian ocean, within teleporting distance of the mainland. The air was still a little dusty from the ventilation shafts they had drilled to supplement the single entrance.

As much as she missed the comfort of the *Angel*, Vickie missed Angela even more. Eight of her small force were in a cavern closer to the surface, monitoring the Ertainian military, government and civilian communications systems and categorizing the intercepted data into files the away teams could use. Another five were dedicated to maintaining the relatively small quantum plasma computer, all coding to update the systems and organize the constantly expanding data load. Angela could have done all that by herself with almost no monitoring.

Three engineers were stationed across from her

engaged in maintaining the cave's infrastructure and screening. They also operated the big teleporter platform in the center of the cavern. Pairs of well-armed Corpsmen took turns patrolling the island above, and three three-person crews were dedicated to the busy Sprites hangared in a surface niche. Another eight crewed the four Banshees with four more people as ground support, hidden away in another cavern when not on harassing missions. Another four Corpsmen maintained their alternate hideout in a mountain range three thousand kilometers northwest, standing ready to teleport everything off the island. All told, her force was cut by almost fifty percent just to keep the operation running. And all of them had to sleep sometime.

Terry Kirkland saw her come up for air, crossed the uneven floor and pulled up a folding chair to join her. "Let me tell you, being your second in command is no picnic."

Vickie smiled wanly and reached for a water bottle. "Wanna swap?"

"Oh, gods, no. Forget I mentioned it." She twisted to stretch her back. "Why don't you get a good meal and some shuteye? Assignments are all out for the next twenty hours, and in a few days we have the big hit on Liev. I assume you want to be reasonably fresh for that."

"You bet. I want to see those dragons of theirs — especially after the ghosts blast a few breaches in the town walls. Should be fun."

"Well, even with your telekinetic talents, handling the triple gravity won't be a picnic. You'll need to be in top form."

"I know. I'll turn in as soon as the three ratketeers put on their performance this afternoon. They've been setting it up for a week."

"I know they've been gone a lot."

"Yeah. Hortensia gave an open-air speech at an army camp a few days ago, exhorting the soldiers to support her against the present regime. And Medina did the speech bit one better at a Fleet base, giving the second half of the speech in Farsi – and the audience applauded every word."

Terry chuckled. "And I know Janet's been doing smaller gigs here and there, saying things that would be high treason from anyone else but the Head."

"So, the real Head broadcast a speech last night while you were off duty, telling the world to beware impostors, don't believe the treason, check with the Palace if there's a question of who's talking, et cetera. Which perfectly sets up today's performance in the city of Nuschgich."

"With all three of them. I wish I could see it."

Vickie tapped her temple. "Feel free to listen in. I'm going to monitor it to be sure they get back okay."

Terry stifled a yawn. "They're ghosts. What can happen?"

"Knock on wood. They're going to be corporeal for a lot of it, and even though the Head isn't to be touched there's bound to be a lot of chaos. The Spirit is keeping an eye on them, but you know how tough it is to keep him focused."

"I know. Gustav is practically mainlining Robusta coffee. I'm pulling him and Janus out of the line for a solid eight hours after this."

"No argument from me, which is partly why I want to monitor. I'll be ready if they need help, but I want Gus to take the lead." Vickie's yawn was fully formed. "We have a telepath in the ratketeers' local hideout to coordinate them, but we don't have telepaths to spare for a combo link from here to there. The Spirit's our only direct observer."

"Okay, but as a doctor, I have to say we're pushing everybody way too hard."

"Can't be helped. We have to keep up the pressure. We can't let them guess only thirty percent of us are here..." She raised a hand to halt herself. "Of course, you know that. I must be tired if I'm bossplaining."

Terry laughed. "And I'm docsplaining. You know you need food and sleep. It's part of my job to see that you get it."

"Okay, mommy. I can eat while I'm waiting for the ratketeers to come online."

"Good. Meanwhile I'll make sure the team is ready for the bank virus job in the capitol, then I can watch the show." She stood and shoved the chair to the side.

"Works for me." Vickie used the table to pull herself up, then spread her feet wide and bent to flatten her palms on the cave floor, careful not to show her derrière to the room at large. The stitch in her lower back told her she needed to hit the pool when the *Angel* returned. "See you in a little while."

"Then you get at least seven hours sleep. Doctor's orders." Terry gave her a mock glower.

"Just go." Vickie shooed her away with a backhand wave, powered off her meshcap and headed for the commissary across the cavern.

She was back at her makeshift desk finishing her doohickey stew when Mentor called from his isolated alcove in another passage of the cave. <*"Hi, Lady. The girls are in position and the show's about to start. The Spirit has a ringside seat."*>

Vickie took a last bite and shoved the tray away. <*"Sounds good, Gustav. I'll observe from the Body's brain so I share your direct link to the Spirit, but it's your show."*>

<*"I'm more cameraman than director, but I appreciate the respect. Let me set the scene: Wildflower is about to enter a pharsch house across the street from the Grand Plaza and bang elbows with the common folk. Act One begins."*>

<*"Got it. I'm watching."*> Vickie sent a mental invitation to Terry, who hurried over and resumed her chair. The doctor grabbed Vickie's meshcap to send a record of the performance to the computer.

Another pop of Vickie's mind alerted Wade Gayland, who was on call in case his voice talents were needed. The Mimic was stationed in the Communications cavern near the surface of the island complex. He strolled into his sound stage wearing the face, throat and uniform of Captain Hanash and took a seat behind a hexagonal Ertainian desk. The backdrop behind him was a duplicate of Hanash's Palace office, constructed somewhat larger than life to offset the Mimic's greater size.

Vickie locked into Gustav Kamerun's hard-working mind and connected to the semi-consciousness Mark Norwich retained in the Body of Janus. Through his physical synapses she reached for the perceptions of the incorporeal Spirit forty-seven hundred kilometers away in the regional capital of Nuschgich. She was just in time for Wildflower's entrance.

The establishment they had chosen was a popular one, on a midtown square with a lush green commons in the center. Janet Flowers stepped from the rear seat of a three-wheeled conveyance she had arrogantly commandeered several blocks away, left the driver without so much as a backward glance and strode across the street unmindful of the gaping populace.

Janet pushed through the thick curtain covering the entrance of the pharsch house and stood still, letting her eyes adjust to the traditionally torch-lit room. She was an exact duplicate of the Head of Ertain, dressed in formal maroon and black uniform with his jewel-festooned platinum disk of office centered in the straps crossing his torso.

The big saloon was crowded with late afternoon customers. Many of the patrons turned at the flash of sunlight from the parted curtain. The raucous banter met a sudden death as they recognized the newcomer.

Janet-Head scowled at the list of pharsch brands behind the serving bar, ignoring the stares with arrogant aplomb. After her eyes adjusted to the dim interior she strode forward and motioned to the server to clear a space at the bar. Customers scattered as their supreme leader approached. The server hastily ran a cleaning cloth over the vacated space and stood at rigid attention.

Janet-Head placed her palms down on the bar, planted her feet, and growled in her most commanding Head tone, "Khadditcz, in whole milk, stirred."

A stifled murmur echoed through the quiet room. The server gaped at his sovereign, then bowed and rushed to comply. He opened a cabinet behind him and snatched out a small cannister of the planet's smoothest, richest and most expensive pharsch. He scooped a generous portion of the powder into a hexagonal pitcher, then went to the cooler for a jug of doohickey milk he used for cooking and poured it over the pharsch.

It was the best malted powder ever refined mixed with an organic fluid so fatty it was almost cream. With shaking hands, he used a thin spurtle to blend the hideous concoction, but his best efforts only formed a viscous, grainy soup. He did all he could, then poured it into a wide-mouthed mug. Sweeping his hand in a no-charge gesture, he placed it in front of his Head.

Janet-Head got a whiff from the tall mug and almost gagged. Nevertheless, she slid her six-fingered hand into the handle and turned to the room at large. Leaning back on the bar, she raised the mug toward the crowd and loudly intoned, "To His Supremacy, the Head of Ertain!"

Hearing that from the object of the toast stunned the patrons, but a lifetime of habit drove them to their feet. No one spoke.

The bogus Head growled, stepped away from the bar and angrily swept an arm at them. "*To His Supremacy*, the *Head* of *Ertain!*"

This time the chorus came back in those exact words, in unison and loud enough to rattle the mugs on their pegs behind the bar.

The Head waited a beat, then nodded sharply and tilted the mug to his mouth. Everyone in the bar followed suit, including the servers holding someone else's dregs.

It was all Janet could do to stifle her choking in the silent tavern. Only the quality of the top-rated malt kept her stomach from heaving the mix right back where it came from.

Nonetheless, she drained it, dreading what it would do to her body. While pharsch was not intoxicating to Gaeans, the malted grain was overloaded with saturated fat. The thick milk compounded the issue and assured her of an uncomfortable week to come.

She spun and slammed the mug down on the

counter, glared at the server and sucked in a deep breath as if to scream at him.

Instead, she released a long, loud, gurgling belch.

"Aaaahh!" she finished, blowing a fetid reek of pharsch and heavy milk directly into his face. "That is a very good blend. You must add it to your menu."

The server started to recoil, then thought better of it. "O-of course, Your Supremacy. I'll do it tonight!"

"Good." She turned slowly to survey the crowd, all of whom were still on their feet, empty mugs in hand. No one said a word, no one dared turn away.

She reached behind her and slapped the counter, the six-fingered hand loud as a gunshot. "Set up another for me and everyone else. I'll be right back." She spun away and headed for the lavatory.

The collective sigh sounded like a windstorm as Janet-Head strode through the curtains to the back room. Most of the customers sagged into their seats; more than a few headed for the exit. As the counter server started to build another round of the Head's concoction, whispered conversations started everywhere: Is he buying us a refill? Can we get our own blend? Does he want us to order his blend? How long is he staying? Why don't we just get out of here? ... The floor servers staggered together and shuffled through their order sheets.

The curtain at the entrance rustled, afternoon sunlight streamed in from outside, and into the tavern strode the Head.

Hortensia Gutiérrez, identical to Janet Flowers in

every way, dressed exactly alike, and just as haughty, stared back at the instantly hushed and utterly confused crowd. Every patron knew there was only one way out of the lavatory, yet here was the Head walking in like he had never gone there.

With utter disdain, Tensia tossed her head and stalked to the counter. The server hastily finished stirring the Head's blend, poured it into a fresh mug and pushed it forward.

Tensia looked down at the mug, bent to sniff it, and drew back with a look of disgust. "What is going on here? What is this garbage?"

The server's lemon-yellow face turned a shade of mustard. "It-it's what you ordered, Your Supremacy! Your special blend!" His muscles twitched like snakes.

"Nonsense!" she snarled. "Didn't you see me just walk in? Who ordered this... sewage?" She leaned toward him, slitted eyes glowing. "What is going on here? Are you trying to poison me?"

"N-n-no, of c-course not!" A wet spot appeared on the front of the server's trousers. "It-it was ordered by s-someone who looks just like you!"

"Ridiculous! The is only one Head, and he is me!" She swept the mug off the counter with the back of her hand. The handle broke off as it hit the floor, and the smelly concoction splashed wide. "I would see this fool. And while we wait, set me up something decent!"

"O-of course, Your Supremacy!" W-what would

you like?"

Tensia glared at the pharsch list. "I want Nifutcz, in schodiqç, shaken. Make it quick."

The server stared, aghast. It was the cheapest rot-gut pharsch mixed with the most exotic high-end plant juice on the market. What Tensia-Head wanted was the exact opposite of what Janet-Head ordered. The server staggered to the cabinet for the ingredients.

As he reached for the middle-shelf cannister of Nifutcz, a customer in the rear of the crowd sidled toward the curtain that led to the tavern's office space. He slipped through it unnoticed by everyone but the telepath monitoring the ghosts, then rushed to the telecom unit attached to the wall and frantically called the local law. The telepath passed it on to the ghosts and to the Spirit, where Gus and Vickie caught it and alerted Gayland, waiting in Hanash form.

Tensia spun to the room at large. "Where is this impostor!?" she roared. "I will see him, now!"

The customers shrank back from her fury, fear in every quiver of their brow fur.

"*Where?!?*"

One of the floor servers pointed shakily with an empty mug. "In the lav..."

Tensia-Head glared at him, then spun and marched for the door to the lavatory. As soon as the curtain closed behind her, there was a rush to the exit.

None managed to escape. As soon as the lav curtain stopped moving it was again swept aside, and Janet-Head calmly strolled in. The crowd froze in place.

Janet stepped to the counter and saw the lumpy goo on the floor. She frowned at the server, who was shaking Tensia-Head's blend on reflex alone. "What a mess! What is going on here? Did you do this? Where is my drink?"

The server stumbled forward, almost missed the counter with the shaker and fumbled for a mug. He spilled some of the blend while making the transfer, but by then he was too rattled to care. When the mug was full he dared not lift it. He simply shoved it forward, leaving a wet trail on the counter matching the one on his trousers.

Janet looked down at the mug, bent to sniff it, and drew back with a look of disgust. "What is this garbage?" she growled. "I ordered Khadditcz in whole milk. What is this supposed to be?"

The server's knees buckled and he barely caught himself on the counter. "Yo-your last order, Your Excementzy... He blubbered to a drooling stop.

Janet glared at him, then swept the mug onto the floor to join the previous glop. She stepped back from the mess and turned to the customers, who shrank back like an ebbing tide. "What madness is this? I thought this place was class!"

Then Tensia-Head swept aside the curtain and stomped back in from the lavatory.

Each apparently not noticing the other, the identical Heads simultaneously raised their fists and roared, *"What is going on here?!?"*

CHAPTER 31

Far away in the cavern, Vickie watched and heard the comedy through the Spirit's senses. She felt frustrated that the dim-witted Spirit was not observant enough to properly gauge the crowd's reactions. She tried an application of her telepathic power she had used many times before, to meld with a remote variant mind and project her own intelligence through that mind. But with the Spirit, she found herself thwarted by his lack of intellect and Mentor's forceful control of what little was there. There simply was not enough consciousness left for her to latch onto.

She set up a side conversation with Mentor. <"Gustav, I see that you keep the Body's mental processes dormant while you direct the Spirit.">

<"Ja. When they are both fully awake, the Body tends to dominate and pretty much grounds the Spirit. The result is Janus as a struggling bipolar ego. For the Spirit to roam free, the half-mind that anchors him to the Body must be entranced.">

<"Hm. I don't like it. It's a waste of resources. Pull the Spirit back.">

Gustav's thoughts conveyed his surprise.

<"*Right now? We're in the middle of an operation!*"> Terry, listening in, wordlessly expressed her own astonishment.

Vickie strengthened her response with a ring of command. <"*Right now. I'm not satisfied with what I'm seeing and it's past time it was addressed.*"> She saw Gustav's protest forming and sternly overrode it. <"*Now, Corpsman! And clean up your thoughts – don't you dare upset him!*">

Kamerun obeyed, suppressing his annoyance. He directed his thoughts into the Body and aroused the consciousness there, which automatically reached out to the Spirit and drew him back.

Mark Norwich awakened on his cot and shot a puzzled look at Mentor. "Hey, Gus. What am I doing back here?"

Vickie overrode Kamerun's answer. <"*Mark, I need you to let us in for a quick therapy session. I think I have a way for you never to have to split your intellect again.*">

Mark sat up, eyes wide. <"*Really? How?*">

Vickie sent a calming wave of empathy with her reply. <"*Right now, you're separating your conscious mind to allow the Spirit to roam. That means the Spirit is never in command of more than half your faculties, with the Body retaining the rest.*">

Mark nodded ruefully. <"*Yeah, it's frustrating.*">

<"*Well, if you let me do it, I believe I can divert the split to an unconscious level, so you can retain your full consciousness with the Spirit while the Body*

is comatose."> She saw the fear rising in his mind. <"*Yes, when I say comatose, I mean exactly that – you'll be helpless. You'll be giving up motor control and be completely dependent on Mentor to protect you and keep your body alive. And you won't come out of it until he cancels it himself. Every instinct we've got rebels against it. But think of the advantages of having a fully intelligent Spirit roaming free.*">

Gustav broke in, <"*But with no consciousness in the Body, I'll have no link to the Spirit. He could be galaxies away and I wouldn't have a clue where he is or what he's doing.*">

<"*I'm not leaving you out, Mentor,*"> Vickie thought. <"*In fact, you're crucial to the process. I can show you the doorways to Janus's unconscious mind. That's the place where dreams live when we sleep, but it's also where our minds make leaps of logic, and where ideas form to be grasped by the conscious mind. Connecting to it is a much more subliminal process than normal telepathy, but your familiarity with each other is such that we can make it work. It will take full trust and cooperation between the two of you, of course.*">

In their quiet nook in the cavern, Gustav and Mark met each other's eyes. In rapport, they replied, <"*We have that.*">

<"*I know you do. So, if you're willing, I need you both relaxed so I can work my magic. It won't take long to establish the links. Chloe, please remain on tap to monitor vitals.*">

<*"Of course, Alpha."*> Kirkland picked up on the precision of the operation and was solidly professional.

Janus lay down on the cot and shifted over to make room, and Mentor joined him. Side by side, they broadened their rapport to include Lady Alpha, and she set to work.

IN THE TAVERN, the comedy continued.

"What is going on here?!?"

Janet-Head spun on her heels and discovered Tensia-Head behind her. Their simultaneous roars had frozen the crowd, giving the two Heads center stage. Timed by their monitoring telepath, the two Heads roared through a perfectly synchronized duet.

"Who are you?"

"I am the Head of Ertain!"

"Nonsense! There is only one Head, and he is me!"

"How dare you question me?"

"There can be only one Head!"

"And he is me!"

"What are you doing in my uniform?"

"What are you doing with my face?"

"What is going on here?"

Almost on cue, a squad of six uniformed lawmen pushed through the curtain from the street. Two of them each grabbed half the curtain and held it to either side. The late afternoon sun, low in the sky behind them, flooded the tavern with light. The other four cops saw two Heads where there should be none and came to attention in parallel lines facing each other, inadvertently framing the exit.

Both Heads raised their left hands to shield their eyes and snarled in unison, "Right. Outside!" The two of them marched shoulder to shoulder between the cops and out the door.

By now the word had gotten out that the Head was in the neighborhood and quite a crowd had gathered in the street and in the grassy commons, clustered around the patrons who had escaped to tell the tale. They parted swiftly as the two Heads marched in lockstep across the street and onto the grass. Silent now, they stayed identical until they approached the center of the commons. Then, by deliberate accident, Tensia tripped.

Janet reached out to catch her. "Watch out, you charlatan! You'll make me look foolish!"

Tensia pushed her away. "Back away, you forgery! No one lays hands on the Head of Ertain!"

"I am the Head of Ertain, and I can touch anyone I wish!" Janet pushed back.

And it was on. The shoves became more violent, the shouts more raucous. The crowd backed off, leaving the two antagonists wrestling in the center of a dense circle of spectators. No one dared intervene, or even speak. The only sounds in the commons came from the two untouchable Heads.

Until the screeching of tires and the crackle of an abused suspension caused the spectators to scatter. Over the curb and into the commons came another three-wheeled vehicle. It swerved into the center near the Heads, scattering the crowd, and ground to a halt in a shower of dirt and grass. The rear door opened, and out stormed ... another Head.

Medina Hussein. *"What is going on here?!?"*

CHAPTER 32

Steele pulled a mug of coffee from the dumb-waiter-sized telebooth on the wall of his office, grateful to be back in the Ertain system with a full crew in the galley. Most Corpsmen had multiple jobs, and their best barista had stayed with Vickie on Ertain to service the computer hardware. She was now back at the coffee bar and Jander was back to his proper caffeine fix.

He returned to his desk and speedball-scrolled the ship's log on his center monitor, highly conscious of Vickie's full-length sprawl on the couch to his left as he checked the integration of her reports with his.

The *Angel* had made the round trip in a little over five weeks and had brought back a tale of rousing success. While they were gone Vickie and her team had made the Twin Planets downright miserable. The parallel log entries presented an epic saga of accomplishments.

The Ertainians' passive strategy on Æzant had actually handed the Corps a bigger victory than a fleet action would have. They had lost three cruisers: two had collided in the troposphere, killing their Sabarian pilots, and the third had been damaged by gunfire and had never started. One telepath had taken a laser through the mesh on his back during the fighting but had nonetheless managed to get his ship off the ground.

The cost of "Shoplift" to the Æzants had been fewer than two thousand police and hostages killed, with very limited material damage beyond what the Ertainians had already caused.

The budding Æzant space force was richer by two hundred thirteen warships, plus the one damaged, to partly compensate them for the terrible beating they had taken before the *Angel* arrived. Steele had left behind several mechanical educators of Squn manufacture along with most of the Sabarians, each proudly sporting an omega-shaped sapphire collar pin commemorating their service to the Corps.

A call to the delighted Spart informed the Confederation of the location of Æzant and the story of its rescue. Spart promised an armed expedition of first contact specialists at the first opportunity. There was little chance the planet would be threatened again.

Steele had tried to apologize to the women for getting two of them killed, but they had literally shouted him down. Their sisters had died free and fighting, and the Corps had already saved them all from a far more gristly fate, so shut up about it. He let it go.

A few Sabarians who knew too much, including that sharp lieutenant, had been kept on board to undergo Alpha's surreptitious brainwashing. They

were joined on Deck Twenty-Three by the thirty surviving members of En'tal's crew, pulled out to keep
the Ertainians from retaliating against them for
the loss of Seventh Fleet. The rescued Ygnians and
Dwatans, packed and wired into the wardroom on
the deck below sick bay, had remained in such thorough isolation that they had no idea the *Angel* had
even moved.

Vickie had the remarkable talent of reading his
mind even though no one could. "I'm glad to get rid
of all that excess baggage. I never realized we had so
many secrets to keep." She stretched and sat up.

"Well, you must admit it was an interesting
change."

"Especially for Pavel," she agreed. "He likes the
misplaced type."

"Oh? I was beginning to wonder if he liked any
type."

"You bet. Why do you think he spent so much time
on interviews? He has a very carefully researched
profile on every member of the Palace guard – a third
of whom are already dead."

He waved airily. "Don't tell him that. He refuses
to admit the possibility of any weakness."

"If love was a weakness, we'd never have gotten off
Gaea." Her languid hazel eyes told him five dangerous weeks' worth of more; then, typically for her, she
changed the subject. "You haven't read my report."

"Sure I have – didn't you see me flick the screen
a while back? You did your average magnificent job.

I'm not going to give you strokes for the expected."

"All right, nerd." She made a magician's gesture and his monitor went dark. "Quiz time. Start talking."

"Do you want direct quotes, or can I use more colorful and appropriate verbiage? Those reports read like a Dali novel."

"I admit using Angela to consolidate the reports wasn't the best idea. She seems to be struggling with the abstract, like she has two minds all of a sudden. How do you explain a ghost to a computer?"

"Which leads to the Lievan raid. After Chelsea and her ghosts kicked down a few town walls and let the lizards in, there was discord throughout the fleets. The mercenaries wanted to pick up their loose marbles and go home. Happy?"

"Reasonably. Next?"

"Well, let's see. Terry and the Transmutators are a popular band, turning Heads... "

"Oh, please!"

"...out of every accidental death they can find. Plus the other Phase Two pranks and sabotage, such as having a fleet cruiser open up on its squadron mates and similar irritations. But the most surprising development is the rash of assassinations carried on by the Ertainians themselves."

He paused to savor his coffee. "A number of military and political leaders have gotten into their aircars and turned the ignition; the cars went up and a considerable variety of spare parts came down.

The instant screwdriver is a compound similar to C-4, which implies some measure of military training and possibly some sort of organization. Though I think the notion of a freedom movement is a bit far-fetched."

"I tend to agree. Ertainian society has been regimented for generations, and there have been no instances of organized opposition in the past unless it's during a transition. And even your humiliating dialogue with the Head had little effect on general thinking. I'd assume one or two ambitious types are taking advantage of the confusion."

Jander stared unfocused as he thought about it. "Probably so, but we can't discount the possibility. We'll get Pavel on it, and if there is such an underground we'll have to quash it."

"Really? I don't follow you – I would have thought that was what you wanted." She lifted herself off the couch and moved to sit in a chair in front of his desk.

"No, I only want to sow uncertainty, not rebellion. Our plan calls for the Head to retain his position after being thoroughly beaten. To trade one master for another would mean having to bludgeon another Head. A change of Heads at this juncture could infuse the Ertainians with a new will to resist, and we'd have to start all over again."

Vickie uncrossed and recrossed her legs, a distracting maneuver she reserved for debates. "Suppose we get the new Head to surrender unconditionally?"

"He would be setting a precedent, Legs. We

might end up having to deal with an endless succession of dictators. Keeping the present leadership intact will project a sense of continuity through the Confederation occupation and leave the Ertainians better resigned to their fate. Nothing breeds discontent like a victor who dictates the loser's form of government – look what happened in Germany after the Treaty of Versailles."

She grinned. "You passed the test. That's what I think, exactly."

"That's what I thought you thought." He let his eyes linger for a while, then added, "But all this is probably academic. I agree with your verdict of abrupt retirement."

"My, you do have a way with words. And speaking of other Heads, what do you think of our little dramas down below?"

He chuckled and shook his head. "Between you and our three doppelgangers they don't stand a chance. Psychological warfare with the woman's touch – the end of the universe as we know it."

She recrossed her legs and treated him to a shoulder stretch. "So, continue, sir."

"Let me pull a few off the top. Wildflower strode into a corner pharsch house and ordered Khadditcz for everyone, then proceeded – or pretended – to get orbital along with everyone else. The patrons were forced to keep pace and associate on a friendly basis with their number one big cheese – kind of like finding J. Edgar at a pot party."

She laughed with him and moved gracefully to sit on the edge of the desk. "It was precious. And when she started doing her little ghost tricks it was even better. She would dematerialize the plate and spill shaginzh all over the place, or reach through a tabletop and pull out a toothpick – sleight of hand stuff. She had them, well, haunted."

"And I can imagine the reaction when she left – through the ceiling."

"And she skipped on the bill. There was a full-scale riot."

Jander reached out and absently caressed her thigh. "And the real Head's reaction?"

She playfully slapped at his hand, then grabbed it in both of hers. "Well, there were other incidents, of course. I could give you a dozen examples, such as having the Head give orders that amounted to legal sabotage. All of which led to the Faceoff." She grinned down at him.

Jander took the cue. "Two Heads meet in a pharsch house and fall into an argument over which one is real. The police are called out, but since laying hands on the Head is a capital offense they can't do a thing – and a call to the Palace is intercepted by Gayland in Hanash form and he tells them that the Head is indeed in that city. So, everybody stands around helpless while the debate rages."

Vickie gleefully took up the tale. "Then they take it outside and make it physical, and then a third Head shows up. The words get hotter and hotter, until they're pushing and shoving each other and providing a tremendous show – with a thousand citizens looking on, plus news feeds, everything. It degenerates into a brawl with all three of them rolling in the grass, until they all turn transparent and fly like banshees over and through the crowd screaming. 'What is going on here!' I got to watch most of it, and it was the funniest thing I've ever seen. All three of those girls deserve the highest commendation."

"They'll get it, sweets – along with the telepath who lifted his ship off Æzant with a laser hole through his lung. Achievement in accordance with the highest traditions of the Corps, or something like that. We should commend brains as readily as courage, perhaps even more readily. Denny's flight to Arcadia, Richard's conception of the pathport team, Cielo's action in the Palace, Whitney and Soames and Wize, and for Pete's sake, Dragonfly's defense of Arcadia – hell, we have more heroes than we know what to do with."

"We'll dream up something worthwhile for all of them when this is over." She knew that he would never admit that he was the one most deserving of honors. It never occurred to her that he might be thinking the same about her.

Alpha's therapy on the Mentor/Janus team had produced astonishing results. With the Body rendered comatose, the Spirit commanded nearly all of Janus's intellect. Even better, having the Body in Kamerun's conservatorship allowed Mentor to project his telepathy through the link. The team now not only had eyes and ears but also mind-reading ability to undiscovered distances. The magnitude of that breakthrough left Steele in awe of his amazing wife.

None of which affected her demeanor in the least. "But you almost hit it, Jander. Lieutenant Galen – Niskili, or Niki to her friends – told me it was the biggest thrill of her life when you said, 'Good hunting, Corpsmen', and you included her. The very fact of being associated with the Omega Corps creates a will to excel greater than any possible honor."

"Virtue is its own reward, huh? Maybe you're right. If you can fly or read minds or literally make your own breakfast, what more could you want?"

"Lunch," she responded, and laughed at the workings of her own mind.

"Suits me. Listen, have you tried doohickey shoulder roast? Medium rare, drenched with Nokilonian mushroom sauce...."

CHAPTER 33

With the return of the *Angel*, Phase Three went into full swing. Medium-sized hit-and-run operations were the order of the day, in the air, on the ground, and even in the oceans. The object, as always, was to create maximum confusion consistent with minimum damage. Orion's goal was unconditional surrender with a minimal body count. The fact that they were outnumbered fourteen million to one was not enough in his mind to warrant a high death rate, especially among civilians. Anything mechanical, however, was fair game – and Ertainian nerves were prime targets.

It was discovered that Banshees made excellent submarines, and the Ertainians were forced to spend much-needed effort and expense arming naval ships to protect their merchant marine; even so, sea commerce was virtually paralyzed.

On the ground, gunslingers strode the streets with bland unconcern, shooting to wound anyone who raised a hand against them, did some window-shopping and disappeared. Destructive ghosts were everywhere, blasting equipment and spreading terror in the most unlikely places. And there was an indescribably humiliating touch: two dozen armed and shielded ORVs roared over a hill and down onto a spacefield covered with scores of cruisers under maintenance, setting repairs back for months.

Fully visible Banshees strafed military posts without opposition, running with weakened collision shields to allow the wind to swirl past their retro cones. The shriek of the disturbed air caused terror every time. Sprites used the same configuration while carrying out reconnaissance missions openly and uncontested.

And as a final straw, the *Angel* herself cut through the atmosphere and circled the planet at a clearly visible altitude, ignoring the warships that dove awkwardly around her, then vanished from over the capitol.

The Third and Fourth Fleets were recalled from the useless cordon outside the system and woven into a net around the Twin Planets. The larger harassing operations ceased at the sight of the heavier opposition, and the Head and his people sighed with relief.

Orion smiled complacently.

"VICKIE, WOULD YOU PLEASE call Vice Admiral Ganazan and ask her to mobilize her force? She needs to move to an advanced base so she can reach Ertain on short notice."

Vickie stopped her hairbrush and raised expressive eyebrows. "You want me to call her?"

"Don't you think you can handle her?" He stretched on their gelbed and yawned expansively. More often than not he had been that street-striding gunslinger; at other times he had provided the shooter's impenetrable defensive screen.

"Hell yes, I can handle her! I'm just wondering whether she'll take my direction as readily as yours."

"That's what I want to establish. The Omega Corps may be galactic odd-jobbers, but we're the equal of any force in space. As I am the equal of Nil Spart or the Director, I want my subordinates to be treated as the equal of any high officers. Vanessa, for instance, should be able to stroll into any security office in the Confederation and come out with whatever information she needs. If we're going to do this colossal job of ours, I want the most cooperation the Feds will give us."

"Mmmm... especially since this is likely to be our last big action for some time to come. People will think twice about starting wars with us around. So, the Corps will disburse, and every one of us has to be able to do a job without having to go through channels – meaning you." Not even Alpha could keep up with her husband's long-range planning, but once given a hint her own remarkable mind could fill in the blanks. "I take it we're winding up for the big pitch."

"Bottom of the eighth. We'll have to get word to the Confederation prisoners. With everyone as jumpy as popcorn the guards are getting trigger-happy. One wrong look could net someone a laser in the head a few short days before rescue."

He yawned again, then sobered and stared blankly at the overhead. After a moment's reflection, he said, "What does the Omega Corps consist of?"

Vickie paused while shrugging into a sleek blue cashmere sweater. "Pardon?"

He turned his head to gaze in her direction. "What do we have for personnel?"

Her chin popped through, and a telekinetic thought flared her hair out after it. "Well, sir, we've got the best Gaea has to offer. The finest brains, the strongest wills, the most versatile and skilled people in the world."

"Humph."

She turned her full attention to him. "What are you getting at?"

He shrugged. "Okay, what do we lack?"

She stared at him, then wandered over to a chair and lowered herself into it. Jander locked his hands behind his neck and gazed at her expectantly.

She sat back, hazel eyes hooded in concentration. She knew this was a test, a challenge to her intellect, her station, her profession. It was not her husband talking to her now; it was her commander.

It was not long before she spoke. "We've got the best scientists, technicians, engineers, experts and specialists in all trades and disciplines. What we don't have is... discipline. No... soldiers." She looked at him, face expressionless.

He nodded, his countenance just as deadpan. "Zach Whitney was a criminologist. Freddie Soames was a design programmer. They died as pilot and gunner of a Banshee, jobs that call for a 'top gun' and a shootist.

"We're top-heavy, hon. We need soldiers – fighter pilots, commandos, people trained to the max as disciplined warriors before we even recruit them. Dani Phillips was magnificent in her organization of the defense of Arcadia, but she's a dance teacher with no military experience. Her success came not only from her native talent but from the support she got from Cobb and Badami, warriors both, to provide the tactical knowhow she doesn't possess."

She nodded. "I see your point. We have superiority in arms, but it's clear our equipment is worlds better than our operatives."

"Uh-huh. We came out here with the best of our best, not realizing that the so-called civilized beings in the galaxy can be just as nasty as we Gaeans have been at our worst. The Head isn't much worse than Hitler or Amin. He just comes from a society that has embraced the lifestyle for a lot longer. We need to be capable of meeting them on even ground."

She smiled crookedly. "You're right, of course. We need badasses – you can't expect a biologist to become a SEAL just because she's a genius transmutator. We'll have to break the six hundred-member cap on the Corps, but I can't see another way to do it."

"Yup. We need pioneers for Arcadia, too, tough folks with wilderness skills and adaptability. That means we go on a recruiting trip when we get home."

Her eyebrows flickered. "So... we have a vacation coming up?"

He smiled soberly. "A world tour, you bet. As soon as this mess is over and we get Arcadia better protected, we'll go home and start looking around." He yawned again. "And time off does sound pretty good."

She rose and went back to the mirror for a few finishing touches. "Sounds great to me, too. I think we all need a breather at this point."

"Roger that. And I want to go over some ideas Arden's design group has about better and stronger fighting ships. Arcadia's too vulnerable."

He gazed at her with unabashed appreciation. "How can you work so hard and look so good?"

She chuckled in her lilting way. "It's a secret known to women only. Spend half your time on your profession, half on your family and half on yourself. That way the more you work, the better you look." She smoothed an eyebrow and swayed over to kiss him. "You can get a few hours' sleep before the fly-over. Then while you work, I can sleep."

"That's the most depressing thing I've heard all day." He collared her with a forcefield and drew her close. "Let's wind this up and take that vacation, shall we?"

She snuggled full-length against him and tickled his neck with her nose. "With pleasure, sir." A few more wriggles and a peck, then she bounced to her feet. "Sleep well, darling."

He responded with a loud groan.

GENERAL SLICHEN STOOD at attention with a dazed look on his face. The general, virtually unemployed since the destruction of the Elite Guard, had recently taken over as the Head's aide after Hanash marched away glassy-eyed and literally went off the wall. Slichen was still adjusting to his position as sounding board; he had heard things that from any other mouth would have been considered high treason.

The Head pondered the latest outrages in silence, then looked up. "Any word from the Seventh Fleet?"

"None, Your Supremacy." Slichen hesitated, being unused to offering information, then went on, "The rest of the Æzant crew disappeared last night."

"Verdict?"

"That Orion was behind the disappearance of the captain, in order to get information on the Æzant system. He silenced the Seventh somehow, and when we began to worry he took the other Æzants to keep us from interrogating them. It is known that the Æzants alone could not have stood against us."

"So, in your opinion the Seventh is lost." It was a statement, not a question, and Slichen maintained a tight-lipped silence. "Very well," the Head sighed. "Send a recall to them just in case. Anything else?"

"It appears that our new cordon is working. In the

past few weeks there are no heavy assaults in any quarter, although we must still cope with skirmishes and pranks. The arming of the wet fleet has recently been completed."

"Now that we no longer need it. I was remiss in not ordering the Third and Fourth in earlier." He saw the general clamp his teeth together and smiled tightly. "I hope you understand, Slichen, that anything I say in private does not leave this room."

"Of course, Your Supremacy," the general said hastily. No wonder Hanash had gone insane.

"Of course, Your Supremacy," another voice mocked. The Head wrinkled his brow. Did I say that? The he saw the look of sheer terror on Slichen's face as the general went for his gun. The Head shouted with alarm and dove for cover as the first shot went over his head.

"Slichen! What is going – " He stopped cold. Directly behind the chair he had occupied only a moment before stood a transparent figure that was his exact double. He stared, frozen by the biggest shock he had ever experienced, as the whimpering general pumped shot after shot through the apparition with absolutely no effect.

"Tsk. Pointless. A waste of bullets. Tsk." The ghost answered every shot with a verbal one of her own. When the storm of lead ceased, she said, "You'd better reload. You never know when you'll need a loaded sidearm."

It's not right, the Head thought. No one should

enter the presence of the Head alone with a loaded gun. Was Slichen.... What the hell am I thinking? "Who are you? What are you doing here?"

"Who do I look like?" Medina Hussein treated him to his own hard sneer. "Who has a better right to be in this office?" She paused as another nine bullets pounded into the wall behind her. "Tsk."

Slichen moaned pitifully and clawed at the door; it did not budge. He spun and propped himself against it, fumbling for more bullets.

"Stop it, Slichen, for Cxuzeik's sake," Medina growled testily. "I'm not planning to hurt you. If I were, you'd already be dead."

She stepped away from the wall and glided to the Head's chair, and became the first person, or whatever, to sit in the presence of a standing Head. She propped her non-existent feet on the corner of the desk and eyed the Head expectantly. "Aren't you going to take out the garbage?" She poked a lazy thumb in the direction of the slavering general.

Rattled as he was, the arrogance remained. "How dare you speak to me like that? This is my office!"

"Oh, really? How do you plan to take it back?"

The Head stared at her, then stumbled to the door and steadied himself against it. "Slichen!" he rapped in a broken voice. "Come to attention!"

The general ignored him, staring white-eyed and still fumbling with the pistol. The head supported himself over and tore the gun from his hands, then slapped him repeatedly with it. "Stop it, Slichen, for

Cxu – " He snapped his mouth shut, suddenly aware that he was using the same words his double had used.

Medina giggled, though in the Head's voice it sounded far more sinister. "Forget it, Heddy-baby. He's a lost cause – and you're not so with it, yourself. That's called the blind leading the blind, I believe."

The Head pistol-whipped the general again, then pulled his face up to meet his eyes. Slichen screamed at the sight and rolled into a ball. The Head gave up in disgust and turned the weapon to the desk. "What do you…."

His voice trailed off. Save for the whimpering madman at his feet, he was alone.

The *ANGEL* MADE HER APPEARANCE halfway between the planets and bulleted into the thick atmosphere of Liev. Hundreds of warships broke formation and sped after her, watching in impotent fury as she braked to a halt and serenely blasted the pudding out of the primary Lievan spaceport with pulse spheres empty of nuclear force. Then she resumed her leisurely tour around the planet, vanishing over the long horizon with the swarm far behind.

By the time the Ertainians rallied to the other side of the planet their quarry was no longer in sight, and could have set down literally anywhere in the unexplored jungles. The fleets spread out to search. While they were thus employed the *Angel* sneaked away invisible and reappeared four million kilometers away, high in the skies of Ertain.

She skipped lightly over the planet, ignoring the small force left to guard it, and popped away at anything of strategic value. When the fleets returned to harass her, she shot her way through their sloppy lines and vanished again.

Half the force was ordered to return to cover Liev, so the *Angel* reappeared over Ertain and blasted two fortress-armed, Lievan-manned space stations full of holes. While she was so occupied three of her Banshee fighters dropped into the seas and sank several of the ships that had been armed to stop them, then redocked with the *Angel* fully visible. Steele promptly directed his ship back to Liev at twice the speed of her pursuers, where they looked around peacefully and again disappeared. The Ertainian fleets were reduced by several score and thoroughly scattered around the Twin Planets.

The Head, thoroughly scattered himself and still frazzled by the ghost (and, it must be admitted, the accompanying mental twisting of poor Slichen by Lady Alpha), took the only course he had remaining. He sent out a general call to the First, Sixth and Ninth Fleets, ordering them to return from their scouting missions to protect the home planet.

SCORES OF PARSECS AWAY, Vice Admiral Mati Ganazan lifted her force from the Confederation's base on the Leosan perimeter planet of Xszëkphrzzh. By the time she completed the journey and deployed her fleet, every Ertainian vessel would be bottled up in the home system.

CHAPTER 34

"To the Head of Ertain, greetings. This is Lord Orion."

The Head snapped erect and glared at the intercom with unbridled hatred. "I am listening, tomcat. Have we gotten too strong for you, that you now wish to negotiate?"

Steele chuckled gently. "You needn't strive for appearances. This is a private conversation, between you and me."

The Head inhaled deeply through clenched teeth. "What do you want, tomcat?"

The intercom chuckled again. "You'll have to choose a stronger curse than that. Some of my best friends are Sforans."

"What? Sforans!" The Head leaped to his feet, chair flying, his face contorted by loathing. "We destroyed them centuries ago!"

"Five thousand, three hundred some-odd of your years ago a small force of primitive Ertainian cruisers attacked and decimated a helpless and unassuming species of feline equivalence – the first of a long list of atrocities you are guilty of. As yet the Sforans have not been advised of your identity or galactic position.

Otherwise, you might already be dead, along with your entire race. Not only have they recovered from your treacherous blow, they have surpassed you in many ways. At least they were smart enough not to oppose me."

He chuckled again. "Truth to tell, you and the Sforans are a lot alike. I'd love to witness a dialogue between you and the Sforan Sovereign."

The Head was speechless with revulsion. He could only sputter incoherently at these blasphemous assertions.

Steele went on calmly, "Of course, such a dialogue is inevitable. Once you surrender to me, I could personally facilitate the meeting..."

"*Never!*" the Head exploded. "Never would I treat with... cats! Or any detestable beast of a being that would! And never would I take one step back before an insufferably gutless ape that would torment my people with contemptible tricks! Tricks that cannot possibly lead to anything even close to a victory! The Way of Power is with me alone, and I will never surrender it! *Never!*"

Steele waited until he ran down, then sighed. "Well, if you feel so strongly about it..." He waited until the Head again ran out of breath, then resumed, "I'm afraid I'll have to continue my little campaign. I'll call back later in case you want to reconsider." The intercom clicked to silence.

The Head screamed his defiance into the dead speaker.

THE *ANGEL* APPEARED FAR AWAY from Ertain, between the fourth and fifth planets of the system. Still fuming, the Head hysterically ordered half his combined fleet after her. With the grinning Nwoye Lam at the helm, the *Angel* dodged around for half a day, keeping out of reach of the larger groups and snapping up a few stragglers here and there.

Meanwhile, the four baffled Banshees, each crewed with military veterans, sneaked around the home world knocking out some of the close-packed warships and damaging dozens. The trigger-happy Ertainians added to the confusion by blasting away at nothing, coming nowhere near the agile fighters. At the end of the twelve-hour period the *Angel* vanished, and the fleets dashed back to surround the Twin Planets.

Steele gave them time to settle in, then directed a lightning foray into the crowded space, tearing completely through the cordon and sending a solid beam of carefully directed force into a corner of the Palace. The beam pierced concrete, steel and bedrock to a depth of three hundred meters, creating a meter-wide well that pierced the aquifer beneath the city. The pressurized groundwater surged upward and flooded an office wing before bursting through a gate in the palace wall and finding a swift channel through the streets. Miles of devastation later the flood cascaded into the city's central river, carrying tons of debris with it. Few on the ground were hurt, but the effect on both infrastructure and morale was colossal.

Liev was the next target; it was as if the *Angel* had jumped straight from Ertain to her giant neighbor. Again, the fleet was unprepared; the Palace attack had brought half the ships in the system around the smaller planet. The *Angel* again had her way with the Lievan spaceport, then they were off into the vast ocean. The fleets, unable to follow because the nucleonic drive would fail in water, set the ocean to boiling in an effort to flush the invader. Naturally, she was long gone – and within the atmosphere of Ertain.

They would never know how close they came to getting her then. The sensors recorded that a massive concentration of nucleonic energy overloaded the energy screens, broke through the defensive shields in four places and melted several of the delicate tablicy disks just as she teleported clear. After that narrow escape Steele decided to call a short recess to repair the damage and let both sides catch their breath.

Meanwhile Vice Admiral Ganazan maneuvered her fleet into a net just outside sensor range of the system. She and Vickie had a long, sisterly chat, and the admiral chortled with glee at the *Angel*'s tactics. With one ship, four Banshees and two hundred sixty men and women, they had over fifteen hundred capital ships, eight fortress space stations and more than four billion people hopping around like fleas on a griddle. Within a few days they would all be asleep at their posts, waiting, waiting for the better mouse-trap to snap again.

THE HEAD TRUDGED INTO his office and closed the door more softly than he normally did. For a moment he just stood there, savoring the silence so different from the bedlam of the communications center.

With Hanash dead and Slichen broken, he was forced to get his own updates, rubbing shoulders with people previously so far beneath him as to be unnoticeable. The fear and desperation of the common folk had seeped into his own psyche and left him exhausted.

He moved around his desk and sank into his chair with a sigh. For a moment he laid his head back and closed his eyes, letting the waves of fatigue wash over him.

"Getting tired, guy?"

He jerked awake up and glared at his computer monitor. It displayed a dark, shapeless silhouette of a broad-shouldered hominin on a gray background. No features were visible, but the voice was Orion's.

The Head opened his mouth to reply, then closed to with an audible clack. He would not be baited again

"Well, then, tell you what," Steele continued conversationally, "All you have to do is send a message to the fleets, order them to ground and discharge their crews." The silhouette swept its arms upward.

"Bing, all over."

Again the Head made to speak, again he stopped himself by main force.

"Or, if you so choose, you can watch your fleets destroyed piecemeal, watch your ships obliterated one by one. You have the option between honorable submission to the inevitable, or childish and stupid resistance. Surrender, while you still have anything to give up."

"Never," he whispered hoarsely, then, committed, he spoke more strongly. "Never will I surrender to you, monster. There is no honor in surrender, there is only humiliation. And I will not surrender to one who has treated with... cats." His voice rose, and with it his flagging defiance. "Anyone who could so defile himself is obviously so deficient in honor that any surrender would be pointless. You would merely enslave us and bring us down to the level of... felines. I will never surrender to you!"

"You're going to have to — Who else is around? In this neighborhood, only the Confederation rivals me in power, and they certainly have no incentive to help you. I'm it, son — or, as I say, you can sit there and watch your forces whittled away until you couldn't take on a mouse, much less a cat. When are you going to see reason?"

"Reason?" He rose to his feet and planted his hands on the desk, glaring down at the monitor. "Reason! What reason is there in humiliation? As long as there is one Ertainian living, the Way of Power is with us.

We cannot be defeated by such as you!"

"Are you still on that? That's almost as ridiculous as your insane hatred of cats. By the way, do you know I have a lower-order feline as a pet?"

The Head looked aghast, then took the opportunity to get in a shot of his own. "Now I know you're a liar as well as a tomcat."

"Oh, really? Look behind you."

The Head jerked away from his desk and turned. There stood his double, solid this time, with a purring multicolored feline cradled lovingly in "his" arms. The bona fide Head shrieked in the sight and threw himself across the room with his eyes jammed tightly shut. He sobbed and sank to his knees, huddling with his arms wrapped around his head and quaking in very real, very intense and debilitating terror.

And yet, like a child with a deliciously horrifying nightmare, he could not resist the impulse to look again. The other Head was gone with the cat – but on his desk was a tiny collar. "Oh, no!" he sobbed again.

"Oh, yes," Steele assured him. "Is your cowering before a playful little pet an indication of your Way of Power?"

The Head recovered slowly, gasping, struggling to control his instinctive terror. He cursed, even more volubly than before.

Steele let him finish, then coolly said, "I assume you're still determined to oppose me. Very well, then. I'll call back in a few hours. I'm sure you'll keep yourself busy until then." The monitor went dark.

The Head sat on the floor for a long time, drawing great gulps of air into his lungs, glancing sideways at the collar and muttering feeble curses under his breath. The collar stayed there as if laughing at him, snickering at his weakness, the embodiment of the humiliating reactions of his paranoid race.

He did not know how long he cowered there, staring at that collar and muttering to himself. He came to his senses with a start, then scrambled to his feet and staggered back to his desk. He snatched up a huge pile of papers and crashed it down to cover the collar, then slammed the intercom and started shouting orders, putting the fleet and every person in the system on the highest possible alert.

Steele had already retired to get six hours of sound sleep.

JUST AS THE HEAD DECIDED to get some much needed rest, the *Angel* reappeared. She came into being halfway between the twin planets, two million kilometers away from either cordoning force and well out of reach of both. There she waited – and waited.

There is nothing more demoralizing to a force than seeing its enemy in plain sight and being unable to do a thing about it. The Head glared blearily at his monitor in open frustration; Orion could be planning literally anything and he could not oppose him. To do so would be to relax the cordon somewhere – and the greater stealth and mobility of the *Angel* would exploit such an opening instantly. The Head had a terrible respect for his opposite number; he knew he was outmatched even with his fifteen hundred ships against one. He had to wait – and wait.

And wait. For three screaming hours, not a ship moved. Then the *Angel* vanished.

The Head sent a squadron of light, fast VTOL fighters to the spot the *Angel* had vacated. There was nothing there, they reported – and suddenly blew apart. When the blinding flash subsided there was the *Angel*, in the same place they had searched. And there was nothing the Head or his fleet could do about it.

For another two hours, they waited.

Orion set his ship in motion at last, curving out and toward the capitol city at the almost crawling speed of one gravity per second. The weary and over-anxious admirals edged their ships to intercept his line of flight, forgetting their orders to stand firm in their furious desire to come to grips. The Head spotted the movement and angrily ordered them back. They sped to comply.

When their movements were at their height the *Angel* grabbed for her maximum speed and bored inward toward the capitol. The startled admirals again overreacted and rushed to intercept. The invader abruptly changed her line of flight, curled over the horizon, blasted through the thinned cordon and dropped gently into the ocean.

The Head had to scream to prevent his fleet from

boiling the sea as they had done on Liev. The delicate tidal balance the giant neighbor held over Ertain could have been upset, and the resulting tsunami could have inundated millions of people. They had to wait – and wait.

Five hours later the *Angel* leaped out of the jungles of Liev, burst through the defenses from the inside, and once again took her position between the planets. The frustrated ships that pursued her were driven back with heavy losses. The stalemate resumed.

"READY TO TALK, HEAD?"

The Head spun and glared at the silhouette. He had to put out a hand to steady himself as his exhausted body refused to obey his foggy mind.

"This isn't doing either one of us any good," Steele continued. "Why don't you call a halt?"

"Never," he said almost by instinct, then he shook the cobwebs from his brain. "You have my answer, tomcat. Even if you destroy us utterly, we will never surrender to you."

"There's no 'even if' about it. My power is as much greater than yours as yours was above the Sforans thousands of – "

"Do *not* mention your damned Sforans to me!" the Head rasped. "It is your very –"

"Silence, fool, and listen to me!" The silhouette leaned forward to nearly fill the monitor.

Even as frayed as he was, the Head was stunned by words no Head had ever heard addressed to him. He jerked to his full height, but any retort was stillborn as Orion went on in tense urgency.

"I said we are as much stronger than you as you were of the Sforans, and you know it is true! And like the Sforans you have no allies, no friends to turn to. And just like the Sforans you will be utterly destroyed and hurled back thousands of years if you do not surrender. All your numbers are wasted on me, and if you continue to defy me you will find yourself on the same level as those ancient Sforans! The damage will be greater than after the Great War, and the result will be even more devastating. You *know* this is true!"

"Yes, it is true!" The Head raged hysterically. "But you leave me no choice! I cannot surrender to you, and I will not! Yes, we have no friends or allies – we have only ourselves, and our Way of Power. We will be destroyed before we are beaten!"

"You must surrender! Save your people!"

"I cannot! I must not!" he cried, crazed and nearly incoherent with exhaustion and despair.

Steele was silent for long seconds. When he spoke, his voice was softer, every word carefully chosen.

"I pity you, Head, how I pity you! But I cannot let you go. You say I leave you no choice but to resist. Very well, I accept that. But by your decision you in turn leave me no choice. I must continue this conflict, and I must neutralize the power of Ertain.

"However strong you believe yourself to be, there is always someone stronger. Anyone who turns his strength against the weaker for his own profit does not deserve to keep it; anyone who uses his superiority so that the innocent come to harm must and should be deprived of it.

"But the strong who use their strength for the protection of the weak can not only invariably defeat one such as you, but can be considered the equal of any powerful force in existence. If you and I were exactly equal, with the same technology and numbers, it is I who would win.

"Why? Because of the way of power. You believe the way of power is domination; you could not be more wrong. It is justice, pure and simple; it is faith in the belief that one is fighting for a worthy cause.

"If I were besieging you for my own benefit you can be certain that the Confederation would be willing to help you. But since I am fighting to defend the innocent that your greed would harm, you cannot turn to them for strength. That would be contrary to their way of power. That leaves you alone, alone with your petty dreams of conquest and your inevitable defeat.

"I am a fair man, regardless of what you think of me. I will give you six hours of thought. When next I call, you may either surrender to me or face the inevitable destruction. The choice is yours."

The monitor clicked off.

The Head stood where he was, swaying tiredly on

leaden legs, staring at the floor with misted eyes. He had nothing to say, and only painful, empty thoughts to think. When he moved it was like a man in a dream, and he swerved dazedly to the desk and sank exhausted into his chair. The monitor mocked him with its silence, the physical platform of his power topped with the herald of his weakness. He lowered his head to shaking hands and sobbed soundlessly.

Orion was right, damn him; he knew Orion was right. His position was hopeless, his future worse. But he had no choice, no choice! The very instincts that made him the most powerful Ertainian absolutely forbade his surrender to Orion. Defeat itself was horrible, impossible to contemplate; defeat at the hands of a cat-loving... the words failed him; the emotion of cursing was lost to him as were all the others. Even that most useless and pitiful of reliefs was denied him. He, the most powerful of his power-filled race, could not even gather the energy to curse his fate.

And his very position as supreme ruler ordained that he had no one to turn to. The suicide of Hanash and the breakdown of Slichen meant he had no confidants, no sounding boards... no allies. Orion was right about that, too, He, Ertain, was alone; he had no friends, no allies, no chance...

The thought came to him slowly, through the fog of exhaustion and despair. I was a long time before he saw it and recognized it for what it was.

There was a chance, after all. Orion by his own

admission had given him a way out. He grasped at the idea like a man in a desert would clutch at a canteen, even if there were only the merest drop of moisture within.

He rose slowly, supporting himself on aching arms, then tottered erect. He had to move his body before his feet followed; his bowed head led the way for his body. His very thoughts, humiliating and degrading as they were, led the way for his entire being. And he was the Head of Ertain; his was the power supreme. Where he led, his people followed, without question, without hope.

He pulled the door open and plodded past the secretary, sound asleep with his furred forehead pressed into his desk. Through the outer doors, past the sentry who swayed blearily to attention, as exhausted as he was because the Palace Guard was so decimated. Down the corridor with dragging steps, into the lift that seemed to move so fast, out again into another corridor to the courtyard, across the cold stone under the leaden skies. In the near distance he could hear the gurgling growl of the water flowing from the deep well Orion had drilled through his Palace, proof of how utterly defenseless he truly was.

He felt a few drops of rain from the pitiless skies as he pushed open the door to the communications studio, needing all his strength to press his body through.

The score of operators turned to him, falling silent before the backdrop of the combined fleet's admirals repeating their pleas for orders. A hologram with the Twin Planets at its center displayed their deployment in a corner of the room. The Head stared at the hundreds of blips, automatically calculating what he could do to make the cordon tighter. It would make no difference, he knew, but the part of him that made him the Head of Ertain refused to give up the hope.

"Out," he said thickly, "all of you."

The operators stared at him, at his haggard face and shaking body and unkempt fur, and obeyed without question. As they all did, as they could not help but do. He was the Head of Ertain, his was the power supreme.

He weaved across the room and sagged into the chair before the general orders console, flipped the switch that would bring it to life. He opened the call book and squinted with glazed eyes to find the frequency he needed, set the controls carefully, then dragged the microphone toward his dried lips. But now that the moment had come, he paused. Head down, eyes squeezed tightly shut, his mind formed what for his pragmatic race was almost a prayer.

Forgive me, my people, I have no choice. But at least with this action I am not giving in to Orion. We are still strong; the Way of Power is with us. I will prove to that cat lover that I am still in command of Ertain's destiny. In our own way, we have won!

He straightened his back and opened the microphone. He paused again to compose himself, to instill his voice with the calm and courage of the Head of

Ertain. If he had to do this, he would do it with power.

He filled his lungs, then spoke as naturally as he could.

"To any planet, ship or entity of the Stellar Confederation, greetings. This is the Head of Ertain, and I am in need of assistance..."

ABOUT THE AUTHOR

Keith Huntsman moved from Maine to Texas as a teenager and never left. After the University of  Texas and a stint in hotel management, he took a temporary job in government civil service for food money while trying to make it as an author. The temp job became permanent and he's been there ever since, rising from the mailroom to project management and legislative analysis. But *The Omega Corps* was always there, waiting forty years to mature with him and find its way to print.

An inveterate reader, Keith lives in Austin with two spoiled cats and an enormous media library touching every subject.